Sixteen by Twelve

This short story anthology presents the work of twelve Canadian writers. As a writer deeply committed to his work, and to the short story form, John Metcalf was ideally qualified to make the selection. Each writer was asked to contribute a commentary explaining the how and why of his writing and commenting specifically on the stories chosen.

Sixteen by Twelve

Short Stories by Canadian Writers

Edited by John Metcalf

Ryerson Educational Division

McGraw-Hill Company of Canada Limited

Toronto/Montreal/New York/Sydney/Mexico/Panama/Düsseldorf/
Singapore/Rio De Janeiro/Kuala Lumpur/New Delhi

Printed and bound in Canada

27 28 29 W 02 01 00

Acknowledgments

For permission to reprint copyrighted material, grateful acknowledgment is made to the following publishers and authors:

George Bowering for "Time and Again". Originally appeared in *Quarry*, vol. 15, no. 2. Morley Callaghan for an excerpt from his acceptance speech on receiving the Royal Bank Award. Morley Callaghan and the Macmillan Company of Canada Limited for "A Sick Call" and "All the Years of Her Life" from *Morley Callaghan's Stories*. Clarke, Irwin and Company Limited for "The Estuary", by John Metcalf, from *New Canadian Writing 1969*. © 1969 by Clarke, Irwin and Company Limited. Reprinted by permission. Also for "The Girl Who Went to Mexico", by Alden Nowlan, from *Miracle at Indian River*. © 1968 by Clarke, Irwin and Company Limited. Reprinted by permission. Shirley Faessler for "A Basket of Apples". Originally appeared in *The Atlantic*, January 1969. Hugh Garner for "The Yellow Sweater" from *The Yellow Sweater and Other Stories*. Copyright Hugh Garner, 1952, 1970. Hugh Hood for "Getting to Williamstown". Originally appeared in *The Tamarack Review*, Winter 1965. McClelland and Stewart Ltd. for "The Tomorrow-Tamer" from *The Tomorrow-Tamer* by Margaret Laurence, for "A Bird in the House" from *A Bird in the House* by Margaret Laurence, and for "Bambinger" from *The Street* by Mordecai Richler. Reprinted by permission of The Canadian Publishers, McClelland and Stewart Limited, Toronto. John Metcalf for "A Bag of Cherries". Copyright 1970 by John Metcalf. Oberon Press for One Evening" by David Helwig from *The Streets of Summer*. Mordecai Richler for "The Uncertain World". Originally appeared in *Canadian Literature*, no. 41. The Ryerson Press for "Boys and Girls" and "An Ounce of Cure" from *Dance of the Happy Shades* by Alice Munro. Ray Smith for "Colours". Originally appeared in *Prism International*, Autumn 1968. PHOTO CREDITS: p. 7, Toronto Star Syndicate; p. 23, Harold Brillinger; p. 37, Robert Ragsdale; p. 89, Canada Wide Feature Service.

Contents

Introduction

It might take a writer five years to put together a collection of stories. A good collection might have a first printing in Canada of 3,000 copies. The book costs, say, five dollars. The writer receives a royalty of ten percent. There are roughly 20 million people in Canada. It is probable that the 3,000 copies will take five years to sell.

Over five years, the writer will earn $1,500.

The American writer and critic, Granville Hicks, wrote:

"A serious novel is by definition the work of a man who has learned to pay attention to what goes on in him and about him. And it not only brings to you and involves you in some small segment of the world that has been really looked at; it also, in a mysterious fashion, increases your own capacity for experience. The more completely you yield yourself to a novel–or any other work of art–as an experience, the less likely it is that your own experiences will be wasted on you."

If something of what Hicks says becomes true for you, if any of our work moves you, moves in you, help us by buying our books. You will be buying for us the time necessary to keep on writing, the time to write more; you will be letting us know that our transmissions are being received, that our "small segments of the world" have become yours.

Pester librarians–people often possessed of a deep hatred for books and writers. Importune parents and rich relatives. Create disturbances in book stores when they tell you that Mrs. Richler hasn't published recently; that the House of Anansi doesn't exist or has stopped publishing; that they don't have Margaret Laurence's *The Fire-Dwellers* but they might have a copy of her *Sons and Lovers*.

And when they say, "Oh, we don't stock that kind of thing", reply loudly, WHY NOT?

John Metcalf
March 1970
Montreal

Morley Callaghan

Morley Callaghan was born in Toronto in 1903. He attended the University of Toronto and Osgoode Hall Law School and articled briefly as a lawyer prior to becoming a full time writer. While working part time for the *Toronto Star* he met Ernest Hemingway, to whose work Callaghan's fiction has often been compared. Later in Paris he made the acquaintance of James Joyce and F. Scott Fitzgerald.

Callaghan wrote and published prolifically during the late 1920's and throughout the following decade; for some years following the outbreak of World War Two, however, he suffered what he has referred to as a "period of spiritual dryness." In 1948 he began the novel *The Loved and the Lost* which was published in 1951 and won the Governor-General's Award.

Since that time he has continued to publish novels and short stories and worked in both CBC radio and television. He is married, has two sons, and lives in Toronto.

All the Years of Her Life

They were closing the drugstore, and Alfred Higgins, who had just taken off his white jacket, was putting on his coat and getting ready to go home. The little gray-haired man, Sam Carr, who owned the drugstore, was bending down behind the cash register, and when Alfred Higgins passed him, he looked up and said softly, "Just a moment, Alfred. One moment before you go."

The soft, confident, quiet way in which Sam Carr spoke made Alfred start to button his coat nervously. He felt sure his face was white. Sam Carr usually said, "Good night," brusquely, without looking up. In the six months he had been working in the drugstore Alfred had never heard his employer speak softly like that. His heart began to beat so loud it was hard for him to get his breath. "What is it, Mr. Carr?" he asked.

"Maybe you'd be good enough to take a few things out of your pocket and leave them here before you go," Sam Carr said.

"What things? What are you talking about?"

"You've got a compact and a lipstick and at least two tubes of toothpaste in your pockets, Alfred."

"What do you mean? Do you think I'm crazy?" Alfred blustered. His face got red and he knew he looked fierce with indignation. But Sam Carr, standing by the door with his blue eyes shining brightly behind his glasses and his lips moving underneath his gray moustache, only nodded his head a few times, and then Alfred grew very frightened and he didn't know what to say. Slowly he raised his hand and dipped it into his pocket, and with his eyes never meeting Sam Carr's eyes, he took out a blue compact and two tubes of toothpaste and a lipstick, and he laid them one by one on the counter.

"Petty thieving, eh, Alfred?" Sam Carr said. "And maybe you'd be good enough to tell me how long this has been going on."

"This is the first time I ever took anything."

"So now you think you'll tell me a lie, eh? What kind of a sap do I look like, huh? I don't know what goes on in my own store, eh? I tell you you've been doing this pretty steady," Sam Carr said as he went over and stood behind the cash register.

Ever since Alfred had left school he had been getting into trouble wherever he worked. He lived at home with his mother and his father, who was a printer. His two older brothers were married and his sister had got married last year, and it would have been all right for his parents now if Alfred had only been able to keep a job.

While Sam Carr smiled and stroked the side of his face very delicately with the tips of his fingers, Alfred began to feel that familiar terror growing in him that had been in him every time he had got into such trouble.

"I liked you," Sam Carr was saying. "I liked you and would have trusted you, and now look what I got to do." While Alfred watched with his alert, frightened blue eyes, Sam Carr drummed with his fingers on the counter. "I don't like to call a cop in point-blank," he was saying as he looked very worried. "You're a fool, and maybe I should call your father and tell him you're a fool. Maybe I should let them know I'm going to have you locked up."

"My father's not at home. He's a printer. He works nights," Alfred said.

"Who's at home?"

"My mother, I guess."

"Then we'll see what she says." Sam Carr went to the phone and dialed the number. Alfred was not so much ashamed, but there was that deep fright growing in him, and he blurted out arrogantly, like a strong, full-grown man, "Just a minute. You don't need to draw anybody else in. You don't need to tell her." He wanted to sound like a swaggering, big guy who could look after himself, yet the old, childish hope was in him, the longing that someone at home would come and help him. "Yeah, that's right, he's in trouble," Mr. Carr was saying. "Yeah, your boy works for me. You'd better come down in a hurry." And when he was finished Mr. Carr went over to the door and looked out at the street and watched the people passing in the late summer night. "I'll keep my eye out for a cop," was all he said.

Alfred knew how his mother would come rushing in; she would rush in with her eyes blazing, or maybe she would be crying, and she would push him away when he tried to talk to her, and make him feel her dreadful contempt; yet he longed that she might come before Mr. Carr saw the cop on the beat passing the door.

While they waited – and it seemed a long time – they did not speak, and when at last they heard someone tapping on the closed door, Mr. Carr, turning the latch, said crisply, "Come in, Mrs. Higgins." He looked hard-faced and stern.

Mrs. Higgins must have been going to bed when he telephoned, for her hair was tucked in loosely under her hat, and her hand at her throat held her light coat tight across her chest so her dress would not show. She came in, large and plump, with a little smile on her friendly face. Most of the store lights had been turned out and at first she did not see Alfred, who was standing in the shadow at the end of the counter. Yet as soon as she saw him she did not look as Alfred thought she would look: she smiled, her blue eyes never wavered, and with a calmness and dignity that made them forget that her clothes seemed to have been thrown on her, she put out her hand to Mr. Carr and said politely, "I'm Mrs. Higgins. I'm Alfred's mother."

Mr. Carr was a bit embarrassed by her lack of terror and her simplicity, and he hardly knew what to say to her, so she asked, "Is Alfred in trouble?"

"He is. He's been taking things from the store. I caught him red-handed. Little things like compacts and toothpaste and lipsticks. Stuff he can sell easily," the proprietor said.

As she listened Mrs. Higgins looked at Alfred sometimes and nodded her head sadly, and when Sam Carr had finished she said gravely, "Is it so, Alfred?"

"Yes."

"Why have you been doing it?"

"I been spending money, I guess."

"On what?"

"Going around with the guys, I guess," Alfred said.

Mrs. Higgins put out her hand and touched Sam Carr's arm with an understanding gentleness, and speaking as though afraid of disturbing him, she said, "If you would only listen to me before doing anything." Her simple earnestness made her shy; her humility made her falter and look away, but in a moment she was smiling gravely again, and she said with a kind of patient dignity, "What did you intend to do, Mr. Carr?"

"I was going to get a cop. That's what I ought to do."

"Yes, I suppose so. It's not for me to say, because he's my son. Yet I sometimes think a little good advice is the best thing for a boy when he's at a certain period in his life," she said.

Alfred couldn't understand his mother's quiet composure, for if they had been at home and someone had suggested that he was going to be arrested, he knew she would be in a rage and would cry out against him. Yet now she was standing there with that gentle, pleading smile on her face, saying, "I wonder if you don't think it would be better just to let him come home with me. He looks a big fellow, doesn't he? It takes some of them a long time to get any sense," and they both stared at Alfred, who shifted away with a bit of light shining for a moment on his thin face and the tiny pimples over his cheekbone.

But even while he was turning away uneasily Alfred was realizing that Mr. Carr had become aware that his mother was really a fine woman; he knew that Sam Carr was puzzled by his mother, as if he had expected her to come in and plead with him tearfully, and instead he was being made to feel a bit ashamed by her vast tolerance. While there was only the sound of the mother's soft, assured voice in the store, Mr. Carr began to nod his head encouragingly at her. Without being alarmed, while being just large and still and simple and hopeful, she was becoming dominant there in the dimly lit store. "Of course, I don't want to be harsh," Mr. Carr was saying, "I'll tell you what I'll do. I'll just fire him and let it go at that. How's that?" and he got up and shook hands with Mrs. Higgins, bowing low to her in deep respect.

There was such warmth and gratitude in the way she said, "I'll never forget your kindness," that Mr. Carr began to feel warm and genial himself.

"Sorry we had to meet this way," he said. "But I'm glad I got in touch with you. Just wanted to do the right thing, that's all," he said.

"It's better to meet like this than never, isn't it?" she said. Suddenly they clasped hands as if they liked each other, as if they had known each other a long time. "Good night, sir," she said.

"Good night, Mrs. Higgins. I'm truly sorry," he said.

The mother and son walked along the street together, and the mother was taking a long, firm stride as she looked ahead with her stern face full of worry. Alfred was afraid to speak to her, he was afraid of the silence that was between them, so he only looked ahead too, for the excitement and relief was still pretty strong in him; but in a little while, going along like that in silence made him terribly aware of the strength and the sternness in her; he began to wonder what she was thinking of as she stared ahead so grimly; she seemed to have forgotten that he walked beside her; so when they were passing under the Sixth Avenue elevated and the rumble of the train seemed to break the silence, he said in his old, bluster-way, "Thank God it turned out like that. I certainly won't get in a jam like that again."

"Be quiet. Don't speak to me. You've disgraced me again and again," she said bitterly.

"That's the last time. That's all I'm saying."

"Have the decency to be quiet," she snapped. They kept on their way, looking straight ahead.

When they were at home and his mother took off her coat, Alfred saw that she was really only half-dressed, and she made him feel afraid again when she said, without even looking at him, "You're a bad lot. God forgive you. It's one thing after another and always has been. Why do you stand there stupidly? Go to bed, why don't you?" When he was going, she

11

said, "I'm going to make myself a cup of tea. Mind, now, not a word about tonight to your father."

While Alfred was undressing in his bedroom, he heard his mother moving around the kitchen. She filled the kettle and put it on the stove. She moved a chair. And as he listened there was no shame in him, just wonder and a kind of admiration of her strength and repose. He could still see Sam Carr nodding his head encouragingly to her; he could hear her talking simply and earnestly, and as he sat on his bed he felt a pride in her strength. "She certainly was smooth," he thought. "Gee, I'd like to tell her she sounded swell."

And at last he got up and went along to the kitchen, and when he was at the door he saw his mother pouring herself a cup of tea. He watched and he didn't move. Her face, as she sat there, was a frightened, broken face utterly unlike the face of the woman who had been so assured a little while ago in the drugstore. When she reached out and lifted the kettle to pour hot water in her cup, her hand trembled and the water splashed on the stove. Leaning back in the chair, she sighed and lifted the cup to her lips, and her lips were groping loosely as if they would never reach the cup. She swallowed the hot tea eagerly, and then she straightened up in relief, though her hand holding the cup still trembled. She looked very old.

It seemed to Alfred that this was the way it had been every time he had been in trouble before, that this trembling had really been in her as she hurried out half-dressed to the drugstore. He understood why she had sat alone in the kitchen the night his young sister had kept repeating doggedly that she was getting married. Now he felt all that his mother had been thinking of as they walked along the street together a little while ago. He watched his mother, and he never spoke, but at that moment his youth seemed to be over; he knew all the years of her life by the way her hand trembled as she raised the cup to her lips. It seemed to him that this was the first time he had ever looked upon his mother.

A Sick Call

Sometimes Father Macdowell mumbled out loud and took a deep wheezy breath as he walked up and down the room and read his office. He was a huge old priest, white-headed except for a shiny baby-pink bald spot on the top of his head, and he was a bit deaf in one ear. His florid face had many fine red interlacing vein lines. For hours he had been hearing confessions and he was tired, for he always had to hear more confessions than any other priest at the cathedral; young girls who were in trouble, and wild but at times repentant young men, always wanted to tell their confessions to Father Macdowell, because nothing seemed to shock or excite him, or make him really angry, and he was even tender with those who thought they were most guilty.

While he was mumbling and reading and trying to keep his glasses on his nose, the house girl knocked on the door and said, "There's a young lady here to see, father. I think it's about a sick call."

"Did she ask for me especially?" he said in a deep but slightly cracked voice.

"Indeed she did, father. She wanted Father Macdowell and nobody else."

So he went out to the waiting-room, where a girl about thirty years of age, with fine brown eyes, fine cheek-bones, and rather square shoulders, was sitting daubing her eyes with a handkerchief. She was wearing a dark coat with a gray wolf collar. "Good evening, father," she said. "My sister is sick. I wanted you to come and see her. We think she's dying."

"Be easy, child; what's the matter with her? Speak louder. I can hardly hear you."

"My sister's had pneumonia. The doctor's coming back to see her in an hour. I wanted you to anoint her, father."

"I see, I see. But she's not lost yet. I'll not give her extreme unction now. That may not be necessary. I'll go with you and hear her confession."

"Father, I ought to let you know, maybe. Her husband won't want to let you see her. He's not a Catholic, and my sister hasn't been to church in a long time."

"Oh, don't mind that. He'll let me see her," Father Macdowell said, and he left the room to put on his hat and coat.

When he returned, the girl explained that her name was Jane Stanhope, and her sister lived only a few blocks away. "We'll walk and you tell me about your sister," he said. He put his black hat square on the top of his head, and pieces of white hair stuck out awkwardly at the sides. They went to the avenue together.

The night was mild and clear. Miss Stanhope began to walk slowly, because Father Macdowell's rolling gait didn't get him along the street very quickly. He walked as if his feet hurt him, though he wore a pair of large, soft, specially constructed shapeless shoes. "Now, my child, you go ahead and tell me about your sister," he said, breathing with difficulty, yet giving the impression that nothing could have happened to the sister which would make him feel indignant.

13

There wasn't much to say, Miss Stanhope replied. Her sister had married John Williams two years ago, and he was a good, hard-working fellow, only he was very bigoted and hated all church people. "My family wouldn't have anything to do with Elsa after she married him, though I kept going to see her," she said. She was talking in a loud voice to Father Macdowell so that he could hear her.

"Is she happy with her husband?"

"She's been very happy, father. I must say that."

"Where is he now?"

"He was sitting beside her bed. I ran out because I thought he was going to cry. He said if I brought a priest near the place he'd break the priest's head."

"My goodness. Never mind, though. Does your sister want to see me?"

"She asked me to go and get a priest, but she doesn't want John to know she did it."

Turning into a side street, they stopped at the first apartment house, and the old priest followed Miss Stanhope up the stairs. His breath came with great difficulty. "Oh dear, I'm not getting any younger, not one day younger. It's a caution how a man's legs go back on him," he said. As Miss Stanhope rapped on the door, she looked pleadingly at the old priest, trying to ask him not to be offended at anything that might happen, but he was smiling and looking huge in the narrow hallway. He wiped his head with his handkerchief.

The door was opened by a young man in a white shirt with no collar, with a head of thick, black, wavy hair. At first he looked dazed, then his eyes got bright with excitement when he saw the priest, as though he were glad to see someone he could destroy with pent-up energy. "What do you mean, Jane?" he said. "I told you not to bring a priest around here. My wife doesn't want to see a priest."

"What's that you're saying, young man?"

"No one wants you here."

"Speak up. Don't be afraid. I'm a bit hard of hearing," Father Macdowell smiled rosily. John Williams was confused by the unexpected deafness in the priest, but he stood there, blocking the door with sullen resolution as if waiting for the priest to try to launch a curse at him.

"Speak to him, father," Miss Stanhope said, but the priest didn't seem to hear her; he was still smiling as he pushed past the young man, saying, "I'll go in and sit down, if you don't mind, son. I'm here on God's errand, but I don't mind saying I'm all out of breath from climbing those stairs."

John was dreadfully uneasy to see he had been brushed aside, and he

14

followed the priest into the apartment and said loudly, "I don't want you here."

Father Macdowell said, "Eh, eh?" Then he smiled sadly. "Don't be angry with me, son," he said. "I'm too old to try and be fierce and threatening." Looking around, he said, "Where's your wife?" and he started to walk along the hall, looking for the bedroom.

John followed him and took hold of his arm. "There's no sense in your wasting your time talking to my wife, do you hear?" he said angrily.

Miss Stanhope called out suddenly, "Don't be rude, John."

"It's he that's being rude. You mind your business," John said.

"For the love of God let me sit down a moment with her, anyway. I'm tired," the priest said.

"What do you want to say to her? Say it to me, why don't you?"

Then they both heard someone moan softly in the adjoining room, as if the sick woman had heard them. Father Macdowell, forgetting that the young man had hold of his arm, said, "I'll go in and see her for a moment, if you don't mind," and he began to open the door.

"You're not going to be alone with her, that's all," John said, following him into the bedroom.

Lying on the bed was a white-faced, fair girl, whose skin was so delicate that her cheek-bones stood out sharply. She was feverish, but her eyes rolled toward the door, and she watched them coming in. Father Macdowell took off his coat, and as he mumbled to himself he looked around the room, at the mauve-silk bed-light and the light wall-paper with the tiny birds in flight. It looked like a little girl's room. "Good evening, father," Mrs. Williams whispered. She looked scared. She didn't glance at her husband. The notion of dying had made her afraid. She loved her husband and wanted to die loving him, but she was afraid, and she looked up at the priest.

"You're going to get well, child," Father Macdowell said, smiling and patting her hand gently.

John, who was standing stiffly by the door, suddenly moved around the big priest, and he bent down over the bed and took his wife's hand and began to caress her forehead.

"Now, if you don't mind, my son, I'll hear your wife's confession," the priest said.

"No, you won't," John said abruptly. "Her people didn't want her and they left us together, and they're not going to separate us now. She's satisfied with me." He kept looking down at her face as if he could not bear to turn away.

Father Macdowell nodded his head up and down and sighed. "Poor boy," he said. "God bless you." Then he looked at Mrs. Williams, who had closed her eyes, and he saw a faint tear on her cheek. "Be sensible, my boy," he said. "You'll have to let me hear your wife's confession. Leave us alone a while."

"I'm going to stay right here," John said, and he sat down on the end of the bed. He was working himself up and staring savagely at the priest. All of a sudden he noticed the tears on his wife's cheeks, and he muttered as though bewildered, "What's the matter, Elsa? What's the matter, darling? Are we bothering you? Just open your eyes and we'll get out of this room and leave you alone till the doctor comes." Then he turned and said to the priest, "I'm not going to leave you here with her, can't you see that? Why don't you go?"

"I could revile you, my son. I could threaten you; but I ask you, for the peace of your wife's soul, leave us alone." Father Macdowell spoke with patient tenderness. He looked very big and solid and immovable as he stood by the bed. "I liked your face as soon as I saw you," he said to John. "You're a good fellow."

John still held his wife's wrist, but he rubbed one hand through his thick hair and said angrily, "You don't get the point, sir. My wife and I were always left alone, and we merely want to be left alone now. Nothing is going to separate us. She's been content with me. I'm sorry, sir; you'll have to speak to her with me here, or you'll have to go."

"No; you'll have to go for a while," the priest said patiently.

Then Mrs. Williams moved her head on the pillow and said jerkily, "Pray for me, father."

So the old priest knelt down by the bed, and with a sweet unruffled expression on his florid face he began to pray. At times his breath came with a whistling noise as though a rumbling were inside him, and at other times he sighed and was full of sorrow. He was praying that young Mrs. Williams might get better, and while he prayed he knew that her husband was more afraid of losing her to the Church than losing her to death.

All the time Father Macdowell was on his knees, with his heavy prayer book in his two hands, John kept staring at him. John couldn't understand the old priest's patience and tolerance. He wanted to quarrel with him, but he kept on watching the light from overhead shining on the one baby-pink bald spot on the smooth, white head, and at last he burst out, "You don't understand, sir! We've been very happy together. Neither you nor her people came near her when she was in good health, so why should you bother her now? I don't want anything to separate us now; neither does she. She came with me. You see you'd be separating us, don't you?" He was trying to talk like a reasonable man who had no prejudices.

16

Father Macdowell got up clumsily. His knees hurt him, for the floor was hard. He said to Mrs. Williams in quite a loud voice, "Did you really intend to give up everything for this young fellow?" and he bent down close to her so he could hear.

"Yes, father," she whispered.

"In Heaven's name, child, you couldn't have known what you were doing."

"We loved each other, father. We've been very happy."

"All right. Supposing you were. What now? What about all eternity, child?"

"Oh, father, I'm very sick and I'm afraid." She looked up to try to show him how scared she was, and how much she wanted him to give her peace.

He sighed and seemed distressed, and at last he said to John, "Were you married in the church?"

"No, we weren't. Look here, we're talking pretty loud and it upsets her."

"Ah, it's a crime that I'm hard of hearing, I know. Never mind, I'll go." Picking up his coat, he put it over his arm; then he sighed as if he were very tired, and he said, "I wonder if you'd just fetch me a glass of water. I'd thank you for it."

John hesitated, glancing at the tired old priest, who looked so pink and white and almost cherubic in his utter lack of guile.

"What's the matter?" Father Macdowell said.

John was ashamed of himself for appearing so sullen, so he said hastily, "Nothing's the matter. Just for a moment. I won't be a moment." He hurried out of the room.

The old priest looked down at the floor and shook his head; and then, sighing and feeling uneasy, he bent over Mrs. Williams, with his good ear down to her, and he said, "I'll just ask you a few questions in a hurry, my child. You answer them quickly and I'll give you absolution." He made the sign of the cross over her and asked if she repented for having strayed from the Church, and if she had often been angry, and whether she had always been faithful, and if she had ever lied or stolen – all so casually and quickly as if it hadn't occurred to him that such a young woman could have serious sins. In the same breath he muttered, "Say a good act of contrition to yourself and that will be all, my dear." He had hardly taken a minute.

When John returned to the room with the glass of water in his hand, he saw the old priest making the sign of the cross. Father Macdowell went on praying without even looking up at John. When he had finished, he turned and said, "Oh, there you are. Thanks for the water. I needed it. Well, my boy, I'm sorry if I worried you."

John hardly said anything. He looked at his wife, who had closed her eyes, and he sat down on the end of the bed. He was too disappointed to speak.

Father Macdowell, who was expecting trouble, said "Don't be harsh, lad."

"I'm not harsh," he said mildly, looking up at the priest. "But you weren't quite fair. And it's as though she turned away from me at the last moment. I didn't think she needed you."

"God bless you, bless the both of you. She'll get better," Father Macdowell said. But he felt ill at ease as he put on his coat, and he couldn't look directly at John.

Going along the hall, he spoke to Miss Stanhope, who wanted to apologize for her brother-in-law's attitude. "I'm sorry if it was unpleasant for you, father," she said.

"It wasn't unpleasant," he said. "I was glad to meet John. He's a fine fellow. It's a great pity he isn't a Catholic. I don't know as I played fair with him."

As he went down the stairs, puffing and sighing, he pondered the question of whether he had played fair with the young man. But by the time he reached the street he was rejoicing amiably to think he had so successfully ministered to one who had strayed from the faith and had called out to him at the last moment. Walking along with the rolling motion as if his feet hurt him, he muttered, "Of course they were happy as they were . . . in a worldly way. I wonder if I did come between them?"

He shuffled along, feeling very tired, but he couldn't help thinking, "What beauty there was to his staunch love for her!" Then he added quickly, "But it was just a pagan beauty, of course."

As he began to wonder about the nature of this beauty, for some reason he felt inexpressibly sad.

Some of the stories were very easy to write, and some were hard, and I used to wonder why this was so. Years later I thought I had figured out why. When a story came easily for me it seemed to mean that I had suddenly found a structure, or an incident that drew out of me an emotion or a view of things that I had been nursing for a long time. Not that the incident or the person in the story I came upon made me think, "I've often brooded over this kind of a relationship." No. There would be no awareness at all of the long-nurtured emotion. That's why the form of the story would come easily. The story would come along, I would be sure I was exploring something that was new for me.

These two stories were written with astonishing ease – almost as if I were remembering something. A writer is very lucky when someone tells him a little story that is half complete. What has been given to him in this way seems to set his imagination off, and almost at once he finds himself completing the story in his mind. The story about the old priest was told to me as a kind of joke. I forget who told it to me. Whoever told it, as I recall, was amused that an old priest in his parish had managed to administer the last rites of the church to a sick young wife in spite of her husband's fierce resentment. About a week after hearing the story, I remember, I got to thinking about what might have gone on in the mind of the old priest after he left the couple. I seemed to know at once. This was the thing I must have been thinking of for a long time before I heard the first part of the story. I used to work on a little typewriter I could carry under my arm. I sat down at the kitchen table, wrote the story in about two and a half hours and knew it was right. I doubt that I ever changed a word.

The story "All The Years of Her Life" came out of a scene that had been very real to me. I saw a middle-aged woman who had just saved her son from some trouble with the law. Her simple effortless dignity, which was all she had to protect her son, had been overwhelming. It had actually embarrassed the man who had proposed to prosecute her son. Of course the mother afterwards was really rattled. The son at first didn't understand her strange magic. His wonder was in his face. I knew about this story for a long time before I wrote it. Then one day I seemed to know what went on in the boy's heart as he watched his mother at home, having a cup of tea after the battle, and he tried to understand the years of her life – his own mother, his own life with her.

I started to write this story late one afternoon. I had finished it by dinner time. I knew that the whole success or failure of the story had to come in the last paragraph. So I kept the story around for about a week, repeating it aloud, and knew I didn't want to change any of it.

There was no plotting or planning of these stories. They had to come out like poems; there had to be a total poignant impact, and first, of course, this impact had to be in me.

MORLEY CALLAGHAN

An excerpt from Morley Callaghan's speech of acceptance on receiving the Royal Bank Award, June 15, 1970

A country may have great corporations, but it it has no literature it is a country that has no soul. It is a shop keeper's society. The new nationalists, it seems to me, are concerned only with who is minding the store.

Yet I hear of busy men, saying in the newspapers, "I have no time for novels." Or if they are critics of a certain sophistication they say, "The story form is exhausted. Narrative is dead. It's a technological age. What we want is information. Useful information."

A long time ago Jesus of Nazareth told stories, baffling parables that go on haunting men. But I'm sure there was some business-like Pharisee in the listening crowd who muttered, "Why doesn't he give us the facts? Why the mystery? Why doesn't he give us some real information?"

Information! Instead of the knowledge, the intuitions of imagination. It is the bedeviling fantasy of our time. We are stuffed with information. It pours in on us from a thousand machines until life has no meaning at all.

Well, I like to think that the Bay of Pigs operation was the end product of a deluge of unconsidered, undigested, confusing information – handled without imagination. It gets worse, too. I understand that the avenues of information to the great intelligence agencies are so heavy, that the directors never really know what is going on from one day to another. What a wild, fascinating and mystery period to live in.

But it is a time of comedy, too. Parents, grown men, stuffed with facts about life, ask their kids, "What is the matter with our lives? Teach us how to live." And they wonder why the kids look down on them. A time when there are no great new temples, no gods and no tombs, because there is no sense of eternity.

Just information. Just technology. Outer space and inner despair. Yet it is the artist in words, or in paint or sculpture or in music who has a sense of form; in the glory of form is a sense of eternity. In short, it is the artist alone in this wild babble of information who tries to give some meaning to life.

Yes, I firmly believe that the young, more and more, will be driven out of dreadful necessity to the story teller, the mythmaker; for now there is a world we are all in that now belongs to him alone. It is the private world, the domain of secret private relationships, the dead of night in a man's heart that drives us all to alcohol or drugs or suicide.

Technology may triumphantly take a man to the moon, but the man takes all his despairing questions and his secret loneliness with him, no matter how far away he flies. Since all art has to do with the relationship of things, the great writer deals with man's relationship in his lonely inner world.

Unlike the psychoanalyst, he gives it form and meaning; he places it against eternity; he takes you with him into this world that is really your own, though you hide from it. He lifts you out of it in contemplation.

Loneliness! I don't mean the kind of romantic loneliness that has been fascinating students in the work of the German writer, Herman Hesse, *Steppenwolf*. Yes, the lone wolf exulting in his loneliness loping across the steppes. No, that's not it. That was nineteenth century German romanticism.

I mean the desperate real loneliness we suffer in our relationship with other people. A few weeks ago the beautiful, rich and successful young actress, Inger Stevens, committed suicide. Her friends said she felt lonely. The long loneliness of the inner world. The domain left now to the imaginative writer, whispering to the reader about it in this private world.

BIBLIOGRAPHY

Strange Fugitive. New York: Scribners, and Grosset and Dunlap, 1928. [Novel]

A Native Argosy. Toronto: Macmillan, 1929. [Stories]

It's Never Over. Toronto: Macmillan, 1930. [Novel]

No Man's Meat. Paris: Black Manikin Press, 1931. (Limited edition). [Stories]

A Broken Journey. Toronto: Macmillan, 1932. [Novel]

Such Is My Beloved. Toronto: Macmillan, 1934. [Novel]

They Shall Inherit the Earth, Toronto: Macmillan, 1935. [Novel]

Now That April's Here and Other Stories. Toronto: Macmillan, 1936.

More Joy in Heaven. Toronto: Macmillan, 1937. [Novel]

Luke Baldwin's Vow. Toronto: Winston, 1948. [Juvenile Novel]

The Varsity Story. Toronto: Macmillan, 1948. [Novel]

The Loved and the Lost. Toronto: Macmillan, 1951. [Novel]

Morley Callaghan's Stories. Toronto: Macmillan, 1959.

The Many Colored Coat. Toronto: Macmillan, 1960 [Novel]

A Passion in Rome. Toronto: Macmillan, 1961. [Novel]

That Summer in Paris. Toronto: Macmillan, 1963. [Autobiography]

WORKS PUBLISHED IN PAPERBACK

Such Is My Beloved. (*New Canadian Library* Series.) Toronto: McClelland and Stewart, 1957.

More Joy in Heaven. (*New Canadian Library* Series.) Toronto: McClelland and Stewart, 1960.

The Loved and the Lost. (*New American Library* Series.) New York: Signet, 1952.

Morley Callaghan's Stories. (*Laurentian Library* Series.) Toronto: Macmillan, 1967.

A Passion in Rome. New York: Dell, 1962.

That Summer in Paris. New York, Dell, 1964.

Hugh Garner

Hugh Garner was born in England on February 22, 1913, and came to Canada at the age of six. His mother, who had been deserted by his father, settled in the Anglo-Saxon slums and later on in the working class districts of East Toronto, which have since been the locale of many of Garner's novels and short stories.

Garner dropped out of Grade 10 on his sixteenth birthday, and began work as a copy boy at the *Toronto Daily Star* the next day. During the following years he worked at innumerable jobs, travelled as a young hobo across the continent several times, and later served in the Abraham Lincoln Battalion in the Spanish Civil War and in the Royal Canadian Navy in World War Two.

Garner settled down to write on New Year's Day, 1946, quit his clerical job the day he sold his first book, and since that time has written prolifically in a variety of forms, from short stories to novels to magazine articles. His work has been widely anthologized and translated. His collection, *Hugh Garner's Best Stories,* won the Governor-General's Award for Fiction in 1963.

Garner is now the unrepentant grandfather of four.

The Yellow Sweater

He stepped on the gas when he reached the edge of town. The big car took hold of the pavement and began to eat up the miles on the straight, almost level, highway. With his elbow stuck through the open window he stared ahead at the shimmering greyness of the road. He felt heavy and pleasantly satiated after his good small-town breakfast, and he shifted his bulk in the seat, at the same time brushing some cigar ash from the front of his salient vest. In another four hours he would be home – a day ahead of himself this trip, but with plenty to show the office for last week's work. He unconsciously patted the wallet resting in the inside pocket of his jacket as he thought of the orders he had taken.

Four thousand units to Slanders . . . his second-best line too . . . four thousand at twelve percent . . . four hundred and eighty dollars! He rolled the sum over in his mind as if tasting it, enjoying its tartness like a kid with a gumdrop.

He drove steadily for nearly an hour, ignorant of the smell of spring in the air, pushing the car ahead with his mind as well as with his foot against the pedal. The success of his trip and the feeling of power it gave him carried him along toward the triumph of his homecoming.

Outside a small village he was forced to slow down for a road repair crew. He punched twice on the horn as he passed them, basking in the stares of the yokels who looked up from their shovels, and smiling at the envy showing on their faces.

A rather down-at-heel young man carrying an army kitbag stepped out from the office of a filling station and gave him the thumb. He pretended not to see the gesture, and pressed down slightly on the gas so that the car began to purr along the free and open road.

It was easy to see that the warm weather was approaching, he thought. The roads were becoming cluttered up once more with hitch-hikers. Why the government didn't clamp down on them was more than he could understand. Why should people pay taxes so that other lazy bums could fritter away their time roaming the country, getting free rides, going God knows where? They were dangerous too. It was only the week before that two of them had beaten up and robbed a man on this very same road. They stood a fat chance of *him* picking them up.

And yet they always thumbed him, or almost always. When they didn't he felt cheated, as a person does when he makes up his mind not to answer another's greeting, only to have them pass by without noticing him.

He glanced at his face in the rear-view mirror. It was a typical middle-aged businessman's face, plump and well-barbered, the shiny skin stretched taut across the cheeks. It was a face that was familiar to him not only from his possession of it, but because it was also the face of most of his friends. What was it the speaker at that service club luncheon had called it? "The physiognomy of success."

As he turned a bend in the road he saw the girl about a quarter of a mile ahead. She was not on the pavement, but was walking slowly along the shoulder of the highway, bent over with the weight of the bag she was carrying. He slowed down, expecting her to turn and thumb him, but she plodded on as though impervious to his approach. He sized her up as he drew near. She was young by the look of her back . . . stocking seams straight . . . heels muddy but not rundown. As he passed he stared at her face. She was a good-looking kid, probably eighteen or nineteen.

It was the first time in years that he had slowed down for a hiker. His reasons evaded him, and whether it was the feel of the morning, the fact of his going home, or the girl's apparent independence, he could not tell. Perhaps it was a combination of all three, plus the boredom of a long drive. It might be fun to pick her up, to cross-examine her while she was trapped in the seat beside him.

Easing the big car to a stop about fifty yards in front of her he looked back through the mirror. She kept glancing at the car, but her pace had not changed, and she came on as though she had expected him to stop. For a moment he was tempted to drive on again, angered by her indifference. She was not a regular hitch-hiker or she would have waited at the edge of town instead of setting out to walk while carrying such a heavy bag. But there was something about her that compelled him to wait – something which aroused in him an almost forgotten sense of adventure, an eagerness not experienced for years.

She opened the right rear door, saying at the same time, "Thank you very much, sir," in a frightened little voice.

"Put your bag in the back. That's it, on the floor," he ordered, turning towards her with his hand along the back of the seat. "Come and sit up here."

She did as he commanded, sitting very stiff and straight against the door. She was small, almost fragile, with long dark hair that waved where it touched upon the collar of her light-coloured topcoat. Despite the warmth of the morning the coat was buttoned, and she held it to her in a way that suggested modesty or fear.

"Are you going very far?" he asked, looking straight ahead through the windshield, trying not to let the question sound too friendly.

"To the city," she answered, with the politeness and eagerness of the recipient of a favour.

"For a job?"

"Well, not exactly – " she began. Then she said, "Yes, for a job."

As they passed the next group of farm buildings she stared hard at them, her head turning with her eyes until they were too far back to be seen.

Something about her reminded him of his eldest daughter, but he shrugged off the comparison. It was silly of him to compare the two, one a hitch-hiking farm skivvy and the other one soon to come home from finishing school. In his mind's eye he could see the photograph of his daughter Shirley that hung on the wall of the living room. It had been taken with a colour camera during the Easter vacation, and in it Shirley was wearing a bright yellow sweater.

"Do you live around here?" he asked, switching his thoughts back to the present.

"I was living about a mile down the road from where you picked me up."

"Sick of the farm?" he asked.

"No." She shook her head slowly, seriously.

"Have you anywhere to go in the city?"

"I'll get a job somewhere."

He turned then and got his first good look at her face. She was pretty, he saw, with the country girl's good complexion, her features small and even. "You're young to be leaving home like this," he said.

"That wasn't my home," she murmured. "I was living with my Aunt Bernice and her husband."

He noticed that she did not call the man her uncle.

"You sound as though you don't like the man your aunt is married to?"

"I hate him!" she whispered vehemently.

To change the subject he said, "You've chosen a nice day to leave, anyhow."

"Yes."

He felt a slight tingling along his spine. It was the same feeling he had experienced once when sitting in the darkened interior of a movie house beside a strange yet, somehow, intimate young woman. The feeling that if he wished he had only to let his hand fall along her leg . . .

"You're not very talkative," he said, more friendly now.

She turned quickly and faced him. "I'm sorry. I was thinking about – about a lot of things."

"It's too nice a morning to think of much," he said. "Tell me more about your reasons for leaving home."

"I wanted to get away, that's all."

He stared at her again, letting his eyes follow the contours of her body. "Don't tell me you're in trouble?" he asked.

She lowered her eyes to her hands. They were engaged in twisting the clasp on a cheap black handbag. "I'm not in trouble like that," she said slowly, although the tone of her voice belied her words.

He waited for her to continue. There was a sense of power in being able to question her like this without fear of having to answer any questions himself. He said, "There can't be much else wrong. Was it boy trouble?"

"Yes, that's it," she answered hastily.

"Where's the boy? Is he back there or in the city?"

"Back there," she answered.

He was aware of her nearness, of her young body beside him on the seat. "You're too pretty to worry about one boy," he said, trying to bridge the gap between them with unfamiliar flattery.

She did not answer him, but smiled nervously in homage to his remark.

They drove on through the morning, and by skillful questioning he got her to tell him more about her life. She had been born near the spot where he had picked her up, she said. She was an orphan, eighteen years old, who for the past three years had been living on her aunt's farm. On his part he told her a little about his job, but not too much. He spoke in generalities, yet let her see how important he was in his field.

They stopped for lunch at a drive-in restaurant outside a small town. While they were eating he noticed that some of the other customers were staring at them. It angered him until he realized that they probably thought she was his mistress. This flattered him and he tried to imagine that it was true. During the meal he became animated, and he laughed loudly at his *risqué* little jokes.

She ate sparingly, politely, not knowing what to do with her hands between courses. She smiled at the things he said, even at the remarks that were obviously beyond her.

After they had finished their lunch he said to her jovially, "Here, we've been travelling together for two hours and we don't even know each other's names yet."

"Mine's Marie. Marie Edwards."

"You can call me Tom," he said expansively.

When he drew out his wallet to pay the checks he was careful to cover the initials G.G.M. with the palm of his hand.

As they headed down the highway once again, Marie seemed to have lost some of her timidity and she talked and laughed with him as though he were an old friend. Once he stole a glance at her through the corner of his eye. She was staring ahead as if trying to unveil the future that was being overtaken by the onrushing car.

"A penny for your thoughts, Marie," he said.

"I was just thinking how nice it would be to keep going like this forever."

"Why?" he asked, her words revealing an unsuspected facet to her personality.

"I dunno," she answered, rubbing the palm of her hand along the upholstery of the seat in a gesture that was wholly feminine. "It seems so – safe here, somehow." She smiled as though apologizing for thinking such things. "It seems as if nothing bad could ever catch up to me again."

He gave her a quick glance before staring ahead at the road once more.

The afternoon was beautiful, the warm dampness of the fields bearing aloft the smell of uncovered earth and budding plants. The sun-warmed pavement sang like muted violins beneath the spinning tires of the car. The clear air echoed the sound of life and growth and the urgency of spring.

As the miles clicked off, and they were brought closer to their inevitable parting, an idea took shape in his mind and grew with every passing minute. Why bother hurrying home, he asked himself. After all he hadn't notified his wife to expect him, and he wasn't due back until tomorrow.

He wondered how the girl would react if he should suggest postponing the rest of the trip overnight. He would make it worth her while. There was a tourist camp on the shore of a small lake about twenty miles north of the highway. No one would be the wiser, he told himself. They were both fancy free.

The idea excited him, yet he found himself too timid to suggest it. He tried to imagine how he must appear to the girl. The picture he conjured up was a mature figure, inclined to stoutness, much older than she was in years but not in spirit. Many men his age had formed liaisons with young women. In fact it was the accepted thing among some of the other salesmen he knew.

But there remained the voicing of the question. She appeared so guileless, so – innocent of his intentions. And yet it was hard to tell; she wasn't as innocent as she let on.

She interrupted his train of thought. "On an afternoon like this I'd like to paddle my feet in a stream," she said.

"I'm afraid the water would be pretty cold."

"Yes, it would be cold, but it'd be nice too. When we were kids we used to go paddling in the creek behind the schoolhouse. The water was strong with the spring freshet, and it would tug at our ankles and send a warm ticklish feeling up to our knees. The smooth pebbles on the bottom would make us twist our feet, and we'd try to grab them with our toes . . . I guess I must sound crazy," she finished.

No longer hesitant he said, "I'm going to turn the car into one of these side roads, Marie. On a long trip I usually like to park for a while under some trees. It makes a little break in the journey."

She nodded her head happily. "That would be nice," she said.

He turned the car off the highway and they travelled north along the road that curved gently between wide stretches of steaming fields. The speed of the car was seemingly increased by the drumming of gravel against the inside of the fenders.

It was time to bring the conversation back to a more personal footing, so he asked. "What happened between you and your boy-friend, Marie?" He had to raise his voice above the noise of the hurtling stones.

"Nothing much," she answered, hesitating as if making up the answer. "We had a fight, that's all."

"Serious?"

"I guess so."

"What happened? Did he try to get a little gay maybe?"

She had dropped her head, and he could see the colour rising along her neck and into the hair behind her ears.

"Does that embarrass you?" he asked, taking his hand from the wheel and placing it along the collar of her coat.

She tensed herself at his touch and tried to draw away, but he grasped her shoulder and pulled her against him. He could feel the fragility of her beneath his hand and the trembling of her skin beneath the cloth of her coat. The odour of her hair and of some cheap scent filled his nostrils.

She cried, "Don't, please!" and broke away from the grip of his hand. She inched herself into the far corner of the seat again.

"You're a little touchy, aren't you?" he asked, trying to cover up his embarrassment at being repulsed so quickly.

"Why did you have to spoil it?"

His frustration kindled a feeling of anger against her. He knew her type all right. Pretending that butter wouldn't melt in her mouth, while all the time she was secretly laughing at him for being the sucker who picked her up, bought her a lunch, and drove her into town. She couldn't fool him; he'd met her type before.

29

He swung the car down a narrow lane, and they flowed along over the rutted wheel tracks beneath a flimsy ceiling of budding trees.

"Where are we going?" she asked, her voice apprehensive now.

"Along here a piece," he answered, trying to keep his anger from showing.

"Where does this road lead?"

"I don't know. Maybe there's a stream you can paddle in."

There was a note of relief in her voice as she said, "Oh! I didn't mean for us – for you to find a stream."

"You don't seem to know *what* you mean, do you?"

She became silent then and seemed to shrink farther into the corner.

The trees got thicker, and soon they found themselves in the middle of a small wood. The branches of the hardwoods were mottled green, their buds flicking like fingers in the breeze. He brought the car to a stop against the side of the road.

The girl watched him, the corners of her mouth trembling with fear. She slid her hand up the door and grabbed the handle. He tried to make his voice matter-of-fact as he said, "Well, here we are."

Her eyes ate into his face like those of a mesmerized rabbit watching a snake.

He opened a glove compartment and pulled out a package of cigarettes. He offered the package to her, but she shook her head.

"Let's get going," she pleaded.

"What, already? Maybe we should make a day of it."

She did not speak, but the question stood in her eyes. He leaned back against the seat, puffing on his cigarette. "There's a tourist camp on a lake a few miles north of here. We could stay there and go on to the city tomorrow."

She stifled a gasp. "I can't. I didn't think – I had no idea when we –"

He pressed his advantage. "Why can't you stay? Nobody'll know. I may be in a position to help you afterwards. You'll need help, you know."

"No. No, I couldn't," she answered. Her eyes filled with tears.

He had not expected her to cry. Perhaps he had been wrong in his estimation of her. He felt suddenly bored with the whole business, and ashamed of the feelings she had ignited in him.

"Please take me back to the highway," she said, pulling a carefully folded handkerchief from her handbag.

"Sure. In a few minutes." He wanted time to think things out; to find some way of saving face.

"You're just like he was," she blurted out, her words distorted by her handkerchief. "You're all the same."

Her outburst frightened him. "Marie," he said, reaching over to her. He wanted to quiet her, to show her that his actions had been the result of an old man's foolish impulse.

As soon as his hand touched her shoulder she gave a short cry and twisted the door handle. "No. No, please!" she cried.

"Marie, come here!" he shouted, trying to stop her. He grabbed her by the shoulder, but she tore herself from his grasp and fell through the door.

She jumped up from the road and staggered back through the grass into the belt of trees. Her stockings and the bottom of her coat were brown with mud.

"Don't follow me!" she yelled.

"I'm not going to follow you. Come back here and I'll drive you back to the city."

"No you don't! You're the same as he was!" she cried. "I know your tricks!"

He looked about him at the deserted stretch of trees, wondering if anybody could be listening. It would place him in a terrible position to be found with her like this. Pleading with her he said, "Come on, Marie. I've got to go."

She began to laugh hysterically, her voice reverberating through the trees.

"Marie, come on," he coaxed. "I won't hurt you."

"No! Leave me alone. Please leave me alone!"

His pleas only seemed to make things worse. "I'm going," he said hurriedly, pulling the car door shut.

"Just leave me alone!" she cried. Then she began sobbing, "Bernice! Bernice!"

What dark fears had been released by his actions of the afternoon he did not know, but they frightened and horrified him. He turned the car around in the narrow lane and let it idle for a moment as he waited, hoping she would change her mind. She pressed herself deeper into the trees, wailing at the top of her voice.

From behind him came a racking noise from down the road, and he looked back and saw a tractor coming around a bend. A man was driving it and there was another one riding behind. He put the car in gear and stepped on the gas.

Before the car reached the first turn beneath the trees he looked back. The girl was standing in the middle of the road beside the tractor and she was pointing his way and talking to the men. He wondered if they had his license number, and what sort of a story she was telling them.

He had almost reached the highway again before he remembered her suitcase standing on the floor behind the front seat. His possession of it seemed to tie him to the girl; to make him partner to her terror. He pulled the car to a quick stop, leaned over the back of the seat and picked the suitcase up from the floor. Opening the door he tossed it lightly to the side of the road with a feeling a relief. The frail clasp on the cheap bag opened as it hit the ground and its contents spilled into the ditch. There was a framed photograph, some letters and papers held together with an elastic band, a comb and brush, and some clothing, including a girl's yellow sweater.

"I'm no thief," he said, pushing the car into motion again, trying to escape from the sight of the opened bag. He wasn't to blame for the things that had happened to her. It wasn't his fault that her stupid little life was spilled there in the ditch.

"I've done nothing wrong," he said, as if pleading his case with himself. But there was a feeling of obscene guilt beating his brain like a reiteration. Something of hers seemed to attach itself to his memory. Then suddenly he knew what it was – the sweater, the damned yellow sweater. His hands trembled around the wheel as he sent the car hurtling towards the safe anonymity of the city.

He tried to recapture his feelings of the morning, but when he looked at himself in the mirror all he saw was the staring face of a fat frightened old man.

I write short stories for two reasons. First, because they are the shortest way in both time and effort for me to reveal as much as I can of the human condition, and secondly because the short story is a tremendous technical challenge to any writer. To repeat something I have been quoted as saying many times, the classic short story is the most difficult literary art form, yet is the most satisfying accomplishment to the prose writer.

Most amateur writers – and by this I mean writers who have not yet become professionals – choose the short story as a means of honing their budding talents and as an apprenticeship training school in writing. They do this generally for the reasons I gave in the first paragraph: the short story takes less time and, generally, less effort to write. This is most important to the beginning writer, for he is impatient for publication and recognition. Actually he should try a loosely-structured novel first.

The short story writer becomes aware almost immediately of the difficult technical feat of writing the classic short story. Unlike the novel, non-fiction article or essay, the classic short story has inflexible rules, and if they are broken the story, no matter how competent the writing, becomes what Norman Mailer has called merely "writing words."

The short story must have a beginning, a middle and an end. It must start at the beginning and not before it, and must end immediately when its theme is resolved. The short story must be told from the point of view of only one person, usually the protagonist or the narrator, whether or not the latter is himself part of the story. *Only the narrator's thoughts may be described. The thoughts of all the other characters must be inferred by the narrator, or implied by the words or actions of the other people in the story.* This rule cannot be broken by the writer.

The short story is not a chapter or an incident from a novel, a "literary" mood piece, an anecdote, a piece of descriptive writing, or a vignette. It is a literary art form complete and conclusive in itself. The short story describes the efforts or the results of one or more characters who resolve, overcome, accept, or deny a facet of life with which they are faced at a particular time or times, and in one place or several.

The short story may involve man against nature, man against his environment, man against man, man against fate, or man against himself.

The short story may be as short as the writer's intent or skill allows it to be, or it may be as long as a novella. It may cover only a brief moment in human time, or a period stretching over months or years.

The short story is usually written in the first or third person, and the writer must decide upon one or the other of these before he starts, for he cannot change person during the story's telling. If he decides to write the story in the first person, that is with himself as the "I saw" narrator (and the way most short story writers begin their early stories, and wrongly I think), he can only describe what he himself saw or what is described to him, through dialogue, by others. The easiest way to write a short story is from the third person point of view, that is, "They did this, or said that." This is the best form for the beginning short story writer to use, for it not only keeps his own subjectivity out of his story, but allows him to be an omnipresent and omnipercipient observer, removed from participation in the story and able to view things from the lofty throne of a god.

Perhaps I can best illustrate some of these things, negatively, by telling how "The Yellow Sweater" was written.

In most of my eighty-odd short stories I have generally first hit on a catchy title, then written a story to fit it. I do this because I think eye-catching titles are very important, and act as the come-on to the reader to read the story beneath it. I have not always adhered to this rule — I didn't in this particular story — so that some of my titles are as banal as, well, "The Yellow Sweater." Among what I consider to be some of my best short story titles are: "The Conversion of Willie Heaps", "E Equals MC Squared", "The Sound of Hollyhocks", "Hunky", and "One, Two Three Little Indians". Generally speaking a title is better if it contains none of the articles, such as "a", "the", and so on.

I began writing "The Yellow Sweater" with a vague theme in mind: that of writing about a middle-aged middle-class salesman picking up a young girl hitch-hiker and attempting to seduce her. How the story would resolve itself — how it would turn out — did not occur to me when I began to write it. As the story progressed the sub-themes began to occur to me: the girl's implied pregnancy, her uncle being the possible putative father of her child, the erotic but timid arousing of the salesman, and finally, through the falling open of the young girl's suitcase when it is tossed from the car, of the man's glimpse of her yellow sweater, which is almost identical with that of his own young daughter. This gave me the *denouement,* which is of the man getting a frightening glimpse of himself as an incestuous old man.

Had I wanted to I could have written the story from the girl's point of view, with her as the protagonist, but it would have been a different story. I chose, wisely I think as it turned out, to use the "villain" of the piece as my protagonist, and end up making him the sympathetic, if distasteful character.

I no longer remember the time or place of writing this particular story, but my log book tells me it was sold first to *Chatelaine* magazine in April, 1951, became the title story of my first short story collection, and has been sold and reprinted a half dozen times since. I broke nearly every one of my own short-story-writing rules with this story, which proves, I suppose, that in literature as in anything else rules are made to be broken.

Not all of them however. In the short story *everything* written must be written to have a meaning for the story itself. As Chekhov once said, "If you describe a gun hanging on a wall at the beginning of a story, that gun must go off before the story ends."

To me the necessary ingredients of the classic short story (I use "classic" to differentiate between the real short story and the formula boy-meets-girl-is-turned-down-finally-marries-girl fiction of the slick magazines) are the following:

Theme: what the story is about.

Characterization: the description, through dress, habits, actions and conversation of the individual characters, thereby bringing them to life for the reader.

Dialogue: this is not only an integral part of characterization, but is also used to carry the story along. It can also be used to reveal the past and future of the characters, that is their lives before the story begins and after it comes to an end.

Implication: the writer must imply rather than reveal some things in a short story (as the uncle's seduction of the girl is not stated but only implied in "The Yellow Sweater"). The reader must be allowed to discover for himself some things between the lines of a story, or read them into it on his own.

Plot: the plot of a story is a very minor part of writing, despite alleged teaching manuals. The plot is merely the path the story takes from its opening to its end. I can re-write all of my stories, changing the plot in each, and still have them come out the same at the end.

Denouement: a fancy word which means the ending of the story or the resolution of the problems the character or characters have faced from the beginning. The trick ending, used in the short, short stories of O. Henry, some of De Maupassant, and even some regular short stories, is sometimes necessary, but not always. Sometimes a story rolls on inevitably to a preconceived end, while others startle or delight the reader with a revelatory ending or the changing of the character of the protagonist (like the change in Scrooge in "A Christmas Carol"). Don't make a fetish of looking for a surprise ending in those stories that do not call for one.

And that's about all I know of writing short stories, except to say that their successful writing can be one of the most exciting things that can happen to a writer.

HUGH GARNER

35

BIBLIOGRAPHY

Storm Below. Toronto: William Collins Sons, 1949. [Novel]
Cabbagetown. Toronto: William Collins Sons, 1950. [Novel]
Waste No Tears. News Stand Library, 1950. [Novel]
Present Reckoning. Toronto: William Collins Sons, 1951. [Novel]
The Yellow Sweater. Toronto: William Collins Sons, 1952. [Short Stories]
Silence on the Shore. Toronto: McClelland and Stewart, 1962. [Novel]
Hugh Garner's Best Stories. Toronto: Ryerson Press, 1963.
Author! Author! Toronto: Ryerson Press, 1964. [Humorous Essays]
Men and Women. Toronto: Ryerson Press, 1966. [Short Stories]
Cabbagetown. Toronto: Ryerson Press, 1968. [Reprint]
The Sin Sniper. Toronto: Pocket Books, 1970. [Novel]
A Nice Place to Visit. Toronto: Ryerson Press, 1970. [Novel]

BOOKS PUBLISHED IN PAPERBACK

Storm Below. Toronto: Ryerson Press, 1968.
Silence on the Shore. Toronto: Ryerson Press, 1968.
Hugh Garner's Best Stories. Toronto: Ryerson Press, 1968.
The Sin Sniper. Toronto: Pocket Books, 1970.

Margaret Laurence

Margaret Laurence was born in 1926 in Neepawa, Manitoba. She attended the University of Manitoba. She married in 1947. She accompanied her husband to Somaliland and Ghana, where he had work to do as an engineer. She has two children, a son of fourteen and a daughter of seventeen. For the last seven years she has lived in Buckinghamshire in England. She spent the academic year 1969-70 as Writer-in-Residence at the University of Toronto. She plans to move back permanently to Canada in a few years' time.

The Tomorrow-Tamer

The dust rose like clouds of red locusts around the small stampeding hooves of taggle-furred goats and the frantic wings of chickens with all their feathers awry. Behind them the children darted, their bodies velvety with dust, like a flash and tumble of brown butterflies in the sun.

The young man laughed aloud to see them, and began to lope after them. Past the palms where the tapsters got wine, and the sacred grove that belonged to Owura, god of the river. Past the shrine where Nana Ayensu poured libation to the dead and guardian grandsires. Past the thicket of ghosts, where the graves were, where every leaf and flower had fed on someone's kin, and the wind was the thin whisper-speech of ancestral spirits. Past the deserted huts, clay walls runnelled by rain, where rats and demons dwelt in unholy brotherhood. Past the old men drowsing in doorways, dreaming of women, perhaps, or death. Past the good huts with their brown baked walls strong against any threatening night-thing, the slithering snake carrying in its secret sac the end of life, or red-eyed Sasabonsam, huge and hairy, older than time and always hungry.

The young man stopped where the children stopped, outside Danquah's. The shop was mud and wattle, like the huts, but it bore a painted sign, green and orange. Only Danquah could read it, but he was always telling people what it said. *Hail Mary Chop-Bar & General Merchant.* Danquah had gone to a mission school once, long ago. He was not really of the village, but he had lived here for many years.

Danquah was unloading a case of beer, delivered yesterday by a lorry named *God Helps Those*, which journeyed fortnightly over the bush trail into Owurasu. He placed each bottle in precisely the right place on the shelf, and stood off to admire the effect. He was the only one who could afford to drink bottled beer, except for funerals, maybe, when people made a show, but he liked to see the bright labels in a row and the bottle-tops winking a gilt promise of forgetfulness. Danquah regarded Owurasu as a mudhole. But he had inherited the shop, and as no one in the village had the money to buy it and no one outside had the inclination, he was fixed here for ever.

He turned when the children flocked in. He was annoyed at them, because he happened to have taken his shirt off and was also without the old newspaper which he habitually carried.

The children chuckled surreptitiously, hands over mouths, for the fat on Danquah's chest made him look as though the breasts of a young girl had been stuck incongruously on his scarred and aging body.

"A man cannot even go about his work," Danquah grumbled, "without a whole pack of forest monkeys gibbering in his doorway. Well, what is it?"

The children bubbled their news, like a pot of soup boiling over, fragments cast here and there, a froth of confusion.

Attah the ferryman – away, away downriver (half a mile) – had told them, and he got the word from a clerk who got it from the mouth of a government man. A bridge was going to be built, and it was not to be at Atware, where the ferry was, but – where do you think? At Owurasu! This very place. And it was to be the biggest bridge any man had ever seen – big, really big, and high – look, like this (as high as a five-year-old's arms).

"A bridge, eh?" Danquah looked reflectively at his shelves, stacked with jars of mauve and yellow sweets, bottles of jaundice bitters, a perfume called *Bint el Sudan,* the newly-arranged beer, two small battery torches which the village boys eyed with envy but could not afford. What would the strangers' needs be? From the past, isolated images floated slowly to the surface of his mind, like weed shreds in the sluggish river. Highland Queen whisky. De Reszke cigarettes. Chivers marmalade. He turned to the young man.

"Remember, a year ago, when those men from the coast came here, and walked all around with sticks, and dug holes near the river? Everyone said they were lunatics, but I said something would come of it, didn't I? No one listened to me, of course. Do you think it's true, this news?"

The boy grinned and shrugged. Danquah felt irritated at himself, that he had asked. An elder would not have asked a boy's opinion. In any event, the young man clearly had no opinion.

"How do I know?" the boy said. "I will ask my father, who will ask Nana Ayensu."

"I will ask Nana Ayensu myself," Danquah snapped, resenting the implication that the boy's father had greater access to the chief than he did, although in fact this was the case.

The young man's broad blank face suddenly frowned, as though the news had at last found a response in him, an excitement over an unknown thing.

"Strangers would come here to live?"

"Of course, idiot," Danquah muttered. "Do you think a bridge builds itself?"

Danquah put on his pink rayon shirt and his metal-rimmed spectacles so he could think better. But his face remained impassive. The boy chewed thoughtfully on a twig, hoisted his sagging loincloth, gazed at a shelf piled with patterned tradecloth and long yellow slabs of soap. He watched the sugar ants trailing in amber procession across the termite-riddled counter and down again to the packed-earth floor.

Only the children did not hesitate to show their agitation. Shrilling like cicadas, they swarmed and swirled off and away, bearing their tidings to all the world.

Danquah maintained a surly silence. The young man was not surprised, for the villagers regarded Danquah as a harmless madman. The storekeeper had no kin here, and if he had relatives elsewhere, he never mentioned them. He was not son or father, nephew or uncle. He lived by himself in the back of his shop. He cooked his own meals and sat alone on his step in the evenings, wearing food-smirched trousers and yellow shoes. He drank the costly beer and held aloft his ragged newspaper, bellowing the printed words to the toads that slept always in clusters in the corners, or crying sadly and drunkenly, while the village boys peered and tittered without pity.

The young man walked home, his bare feet making light crescent prints in the dust. He was about seventeen, and his name was Kofi. He was no one in particular, no one you would notice.

Outside the hut, one of his sisters was pounding dried cassava into *kokonte* meal, raising the big wooden pestle and bringing it down with an unvaried rhythm into the mortar. She glanced up.

"I saw Akua today, and she asked me something." Her voice was a teasing singsong.

Kofi pretended to frown. "What is that to me?"

"Don't you want to know?"

He knew she would soon tell him. He yawned and stretched, languidly, then squatted on his heels and closed his eyes, miming sleep. He thought of Akua as she had looked this morning, early, coming back from the river with the water jar on her head, and walking carefully, because the vessel was heavy, but managing also to sway her plump buttocks a little more than was absolutely necessary.

"She wants to know if you are a boy or a man," his sister said.

His thighs itched and he could feel the slow full sweetness of his amiable lust. He jumped to his feet and leapt over the mortar, clumsy-graceful as a young goat. He sang softly, so his mother inside the hut would not hear.

> *Do you ask a question,*
> *Akua, Akua?*
> *In a grove dwells an oracle,*
> *Oh Akua –*
> *Come to the grove when the village sleeps –*

The pestle thudded with his sister's laughter. He leaned close to her. "Don't speak of it, will you?"

She promised, and he sat cross-legged on the ground, and drummed on the earth with his outspread hands, and sang in the cool heat of the late afternoon. Then he remembered the important news, and put on a solemn face, and went in the hut to see his father.

His father was drinking palm wine sorrowfully. The younger children were crawling about like little lizards, and Kofi's mother was pulling out yams and red peppers and groundnuts and pieces of fish from bowls and pots stacked in a corner. She said "Ha – ei – " or "True, true – " to everything the old man said, but she was not really listening – her mind was on the evening meal.

Kofi dutifully went to greet his grandmother. She was brittle and small and fleshless as the empty shell of a tortoise. She rarely spoke, and then only to recite in her tenuous bird voice her genealogy, or to complain of chill. Being blind, she liked to run her fingers over the faces of her grandchildren. Kofi smiled so that she could touch his smile. She murmured to him, but it was the name of one of his dead brothers.

"And when I think of the distance we walked," Kofi's father was saying, "to clear the new patch for the cocoyam, and now it turns out to be no good, and the yams are half the size they should be, and I ask myself why I should be afflicted in this way, because I have no enemies, unless you want to count Donkor, and he went away ten years ago, so it couldn't be him, and if it is a question of libation, who has been more generous than I, always making sure the gods drank before the planting – "

He went on in this vein for some time, and Kofi waited. Finally his father looked up.

"The government men will build a bridge at Owurasu," Kofi said. "So I heard."

His father snorted.

"Nana Ayensu told me this morning. He heard it from Attah, but he did not believe it. Everyone knows the ferryman's tongue has diarrhoea. Garrulity is an affliction of the soul."

"It is not true, then?"

"How could it be true? We have always used the Atware ferry. There will be no bridge."

Kofi got out his adze and machete and went outside to sharpen them. Tomorrow he and his father would begin clearing the fallow patch beside the big baobab tree, for the second planting of cassava. Kofi could clear quickly with his machete, slicing through underbrush and greenfeather ferns. But he took no pride in the fact, for every young man did the same.

He was sorry that there would be no bridge. Who knows what excitement might have come to Owurasu? But he knew nothing of such things. Perhaps it was better this way.

A week later, three white men and a clerk arrived, followed by a lorry full of tents and supplies, several cooks, a mechanic and four carpenters.

"Oh, my lord," groaned Gerald Wain the Contractor's Superintendent, climbing out of the Land-Rover and stretching his travel-stiffened limbs, "is this the place? Eighteen months – it doesn't bear thinking about."

The silence in the village broke into turbulence. The women who had been filling the water vessels at the river began to squeal and shriek. They giggled and wailed, not knowing which was called for. They milled together, clambered up the clay bank, hitched up their long cloths and surged down the path that led back to the village, leaving the unfilled vessels behind.

The young men were returning from the farms, running all together, shouting hoarsely. The men of Owurasu, the fathers and elders, had gathered outside the chief's dwelling and were waiting for Nana Ayensu to appear.

At the *Hail Mary,* Danquah found two fly-specked pink paper roses and set them in an empty jam jar on his counter. He whipped out an assortment of bottles – gin, a powerful red liquid known as Steel wine, the beer with their gleaming tops, and several sweet purple Doko-Doko which the villagers could afford only when the cocoa crop was sold. Then he opened wide his door. In the centre of the village, under the sacred fire tree, Nana Ayensu and the elders met the new arrivals. The leader of the white men was not young, and he had a skin red as fresh-bled meat. Red was the favoured colour of witches and priests of witchcraft, as everyone knew, so many remarks were passed, especially when some of the children, creeping close, claimed to have seen through the sweat-drenched shirt a chest and belly hairy as the Sasabonsam's. The other two white men were young and pale. They smoked many cigarettes and threw them away still burning, and the children scrambled for them.

Badu, the clerk-interpreter, was an African, but to the people of Owurasu he was just as strange as the white men, and even less to be trusted, for he was a coast man. He wore white clothes and pointed shoes and a hat like an infant umbrella. The fact that he could speak their language did not make the villagers any less suspicious.

"The stranger is like a child," Nana Ayensu said, "but the voice of an enemy is like the tail of a scorpion – it carries a sting."

The clerk, a small man, slight and nervous as a duiker, sidled up to weighty Opoku, the chief's spokesman, and attempted to look him in the eye. But when the clerk began to speak his eyes flickered away to the gnarled branches of the old tree.

"The wise men from the coast," Badu bawled in a voice larger than himself, "the government men who are greater than any chief – they have said that a bridge is to be built here, an honour for your small village. Workmen will be brought in for the skilled jobs, but we will need local men as well. The bungalows and labourers' quarters will be started at once, so we can use your young men in that work. Our tents will be over there on the hill. Those who want to work can apply to me. They will be paid for what they do. See to it that they are there tomorrow morning early. In this job we waste no time."

The men of Owurasu stood mutely with expressionless faces. As for the women, they felt only shame for the clerk's mother, whoever she might be, that she had taught her son so few manners.

Badu, brushing the dust from his white sleeves, caught their soft deploring voices and looked defiant. These people were bush – they knew nothing of the world of streets and shops. But because they had once thrown their spears all along the coast, they still scorned his people, calling them cowards and eaters of fish-heads. He felt, as well, a dismal sense of embarrassment at the backwardness of rural communities, now painfully exposed to the engineers' eyes. He turned abruptly away and spoke in rapid stuttering English to the Superintendent.

With a swoosh and a rattle, the strangers drove off towards the river, scattering goats and chickens and children from the path, and filling the staring villagers' nostrils with dust. Then – pandemonium. What was happening? What was expected of them? No one knew. Everyone shouted at once. The women and girls fluttered and chattered like parrots startled into flame-winged flight. But the faces of the men were sombre.

Kofi came as close as he dared to the place where Nana Ayensu and the elders stood. Kofi's father was speaking. He was a small and wiry man. He plucked at his yellow and black cloth, twirling one end of it across his shoulder, pulling it down, flinging it back again. His body twitched in anger.

"Can they order us about like slaves? We have men who have not forgotten their grandfathers were warriors –"

Nana Ayensu merely flapped a desolate hand. "Compose yourself, Kobla. Remember that those of our spirit are meant to model their behaviour on that of the river. We are supposed to be calm."

Nana Ayensu was a portly man, well-fleshed. His bearing was dignified, especially when he wore his best *kente* cloth, as he did now, having hastily donned it upon being informed of the strangers' approach. He was, however, sweating a great deal – the little rivers formed under the gold and leather amulets of his headband, and trickled down his forehead and nose.

"Calm," he repeated, like an incantation. "But what do they intend to do with our young men? Will there be the big machines? I saw them once, when I visited my sister in the city. They are very large, and they feed on earth, opening their jaws – thus. Jaws that consume earth could consume a man. If harm comes to our young men, it is upon my head. But he said they would be paid, and Owurasu is not rich –"

Okomfo Ofori was leaning on his thornwood stick, waiting his turn to speak. He was older than the others. The wrinkled skin of his face was hard and cracked, as though he had been sun-dried like an animal hide. He had lived a long time in the forest and on the river. He was the priest of the river, and there was nothing he did not know. Watching him covertly, Kofi felt afraid.

"We do not know whether Owura will suffer his river to be disturbed," Okomfo Ofori said. "If he will not, then I think the fish will die from the river, and the oil palms will wither, and the yams will shrink and dwindle in the planting places, and plague will come, and river-blindness will come, and the snake will inhabit our huts because the people are dead, and the strangler vine will cover our dwelling places. For our life comes from the river, and if the god's hand is turned against us, what will avail the hands of men?"

Kofi, remembering that he had casually, without thought, wished the bridge to come, felt weak with fear. He wanted to hide himself, but who can hide from his own fear and from the eyes of god?

That night, Kofi's father told him they were to go to the sacred grove beside the river. Without a word or question, the boy shook off sleep and followed his father.

The grove was quiet. The only sounds were the clicking of palm boughs and the deep low voice of Owura the river. Others were there – Kofi never knew who – young men and old, his friends and his uncles, all now changed, distorted, grown ghostly and unknown in the grey moonlight.

"Here is wine from our hands," Okomfo Ofori said. "God of the river, come and accept this wine and drink."

The palm wine was poured into the river. It made a faint far-off splash, then the river's voice continued unchanged, like muted drums. The priest lifted up a black earthen vessel, an ordinary pot fashioned from river clay, such as the women use for cooking, but not the same, for this one was consecrated. Into the pot he put fresh river water, and, leaves he had gathered from the thicket of ghosts, and eggs, and the blood

44

and intestines of a fowl whose neck he wrung, and white seeds, and a red bead and a cowrie shell. He stirred the contents, and he stared for a long time, for this was the vessel wherein the god could make himself known to his priest. And no one moved.

Then – and the night was all clarity and all madness – the priest was possessed of his god, Owura the river. Kofi could never afterwards remember exactly what had happened. He remembered a priest writhing like a snake with its back broken, and the clothing trance-torn, and the god's voice low and deep. Finally, dizzied with sleeplessness and fear, he seemed to see the faces and trees blurred into a single tree face, and his mind became as light and empty as an overturned water vessel, everything spilled out, drained, gone.

Back at the hut, Kofi's father told him the outcome. Libation would be poured to the ancestors and to the god of the river, as propitiation for the disturbance of the waters. Also, one young man had been selected to go to the bridge work. In order that the village could discover what the bridgemen would do to the sons of Owurasu, one young man had been chosen to go, as a man will be sent to test the footing around a swamp.

Kofi was to be that young man.

He was put to work clearing a space for the bridgemen's dwellings. He knew his machete and so he worked well despite his apprehension, swinging the blade slowly, bending low from the waist and keeping his legs straight. The heat of the sun poured and filtered down the leaves and bushes, through the fronds and hairy trunks of the oil palms. The knotted grasses and the heavy clots of moss were warm and moist to the feet, and even the ferns, snapping easily under the blade, smelled of heat and damp. Kofi wore only his loincloth, but the sweat ran down his sides and thighs, making his skin glossy. He worked with his eyes half closed. The blade lifted and fell. Towards mid-day, when the river had not risen to drown him, he ventured to sing.

> *We are listening, we are listening.*
> *Vine, do not harm us, for we ask your pardon.*
> *We are listening, River, for the drums.*
> *Thorn, do not tear us, for we ask your pardon.*
> *River, give the word to Crocodile.*
> *The crocodile, he drums in the river.*
> *Send us good word, for we ask your pardon.*

Before he left at nightfall, he took the gourd bottle he had brought with him and sprinkled the palm oil on the ground where his machete had cleared.

"Take this oil," he said to the earth, "and apply it to your sores."

Kofi returned home whole, day after day, and finally Nana Ayensu gave permission for other young men to go, as many as could be spared from the farming and fishing.

Six bungalows, servants' quarters, latrines and a long line of labourers' huts began to take shape. The young men of Owurasu were paid for their work. The village had never seen so much cash money before. The white men rarely showed their faces in the village, and the villagers rarely ventured into the strangers' camp, half a mile upriver. The two settlements were as separate as the river fish from the forest birds. They existed beside one another, but there was no communication between them. Even the village young men, working on the bungalows, had nothing to do with the Europeans, whose orders filtered down to them through Badu or the head carpenter. The bridgemen's cooks came to the village market to buy fruit and eggs, but they paid good prices and although they were haughty they did not bother anyone. The carpenters and drivers came to Danquah's in the evening, but there were not many of them and the villagers soon took them for granted. The village grew calm once more in the prevailing atmosphere of prosperity.

In the *Hail Mary Chop-Bar* the young men of Owurasu began to swagger. Some of them now kept for themselves a portion of the money they earned. Danquah, bustling around his shop, pulled out a box of new shirts and showed them off. They were splendid; they shimmered and shone. Entranced, the young men stared. A bottle of beer, Danquah urged. Would the young men have another bottle of beer while they considered the new shirts? They drank, and pondered, and touched the glittering cloth.

Kofi was looked up to now by the other young men. Some of them called him the chief of the young men. He did not admit it, but he did not deny, either. He stretched to his full height, yawned luxuriously, drank his beer in mighty gulps, laughed a little, felt strength flooding through his muscles, walked a trifle crookedly across the room to Danquah, who, smiling, was holding up a blue shirt imprinted with great golden trees. Kofi reached out and grabbed the shirt.

When he left the *Hail Mary* that night, Kofi found Akua waiting for him in the shadows. He remembered another purchase he had made. He drew it out and handed it to her, a green bottle with a picture of flowers. Akua seized it.

"For me? Scent?"

He nodded. She unstopped it, sniffed, laughed, grasped his arm.

"Oh, it is fine, a wonder. Kofi – when will you build the new hut?"

"Soon," he promised. "Soon."

It was all settled between their two families. He did not know why he hesitated. When the hut was built, and the gifts given and received, his life would move in the known way. He would plant his crops and his children. Some of his crops would be spoiled by worm or weather; some of his children would die. He would grow old, and the young men would respect him. That was the way close to him as his own veins. But now his head was spinning from the beer, and his mouth was bitter as lime rind. He took Akua by the hand and they walked down the empty path together, slowly, in the dark, not speaking.

The next week the big machines came rolling and roaring into Owurasu. Lorries brought gangs of skilled labourers, more Europeans and more cooks. The tractor drivers laughed curses at the gaping villagers and pretended to run them down until they shrieked and fled in humiliation like girls or mice.

Gong-gong beat in Owurasu that night, and the drums did not stop their rumble until dawn. The village was in an uproar. What would the machines do? Who were these men? So many and so alien. Low-born coast men, northern desert men with their tribal marks burned in long gashes onto their cheeks and foreheads, crazy shouting city men with no shame. What would become of the village? No one knew.

Nana Ayensu visited the shrine where the carved and blackened state stools of dead chiefs were kept and where the ancestral spirits resided.

"Grandsires, we greet you. Stand behind us with a good standing. Protect us from the evils we know and from the evils we do not know. We are addressing you, and you will understand."

Danquah sat at the counter of the *Hail Mary* with a hurricane lamp at his elbow. He was laboriously scrawling a letter to his cousin in the city, asking him to arrange for four cases of gin and ten of beer, together with fifty cartons of cigarettes, to be sent on the next mammy-lorry to Owurasu.

Okomfo Ofori scattered sacred *summe* leaves to drive away spirits of evil, and looked again into his consecrated vessel. But this time he could see only the weeping faces of his father and his mother, half a century dead.

When morning came, the big machines began to uproot the coconut palms in the holy grove beside the river. The village boys, who had been clearing the coarse grass from the river bank, one by one laid down their machetes and watched in horrified fascination as the bulldozers assaulted the slender trees. Everyone had thought of the river's being invaded by strangers. But it had never occurred to anyone that Owura's grove would be destroyed.

Kofi watched and listened. Under the noise of the engines he could hear the moaning of Owura's brown waters. Now would come the time of tribulation; the plague and the riverblindness would strike now. The bulldozer rammed another tree, and it toppled, its trunk snapping like a broken spine. Kofi felt as though his own bones were being broken, his own body assaulted, his heart invaded by the massive blade. Then he saw someone approaching from the village.

Okomfo Ofori was the river's priest, and there was nothing he did not know. Except this day, this death. Kofi stared, shocked. The old priest was running like a child, and his face was wet with his tears.

At the work site, the Superintendent listened wearily while the old man struggled to put his anguish into words.

"What's he saying, Badu? If it isn't one damn thing, it's another – what's the trouble now?"

"He says the grove belongs to the gods," Badu explained.

"All right," Wain sighed. "Ask him how much he wants. It's a racket, if you ask me. Will ten pounds do it? It can be entered under Local Labour."

The village boys looked towards Kofi, who stood unmoving, his machete dangling uselessly from his hand.

"What does it mean? What will happen?"

He heard their questioning voices and saw the question in their eyes. Then he turned upon them in a kind of fury.

"Why do you ask me? I know nothing, nothing, nothing!"

He dropped his machete and ran, not knowing where he was going, not seeing the paths he took.

His mother was a woman vast as mountains. Her blue cloth, faded and tinged with a sediment of brown from many washings in river water, tugged and pulled around her heavy breasts and hips. She reached out a hand to the head of her crouched son.

So the grove was lost, and although the pleas were made to gods and grandsires, the village felt lost, too, depleted and vulnerable. But the retribution did not come. Owura did not rise. Nothing happened. Nothing at all.

In the days following, Kofi did not go to the bridge work. He built the new hut, and when the gifts were given and taken, Akua made a groundnut stew and half the villagers were invited to share this first meal. Kofi, drinking palm wine and eating the food as though he could never get enough, was drawn into his new wife's smile and lapped around with laughter.

48

After a week, the young men of Owurasu went back to work for the bridgemen.

The approaches were cleared and the steamy river air was filled with the chunking of the pile-driver and the whirr of the concrete-mixer, as the piers and anchor blocks went in.

To the villagers, the river bank no longer seemed bald without the grove. Kofi could scarcely remember how the palms had looked when they lived there. Gradually he forgot that he had been afraid of the machines. Even the Europeans no longer looked strange. At first he had found it difficult to tell them apart, but now he recognized each.

Akua bought a new cloth and an iron cooking-pot. On one memorable day, Kofi came home from the *Hail Mary* with a pocket torch. It was green and handsome, with silver on its end and silver on the place one touched to make the light come on. Kofi flicked the switch and in the tiny bulb a faint glow appeared. Akua clapped her hands in pleasure.

"Such a thing. It is yours, Kofi?"

"Mine. I paid for it."

The glow trembled, for the battery was almost worn out from the village boys' handling. Kofi turned it off hastily. Danquah had forgotten to tell him and so he did not know that the power could be replaced.

At the bridge, Kofi's work had changed. Now he helped in the pouring of concrete as the blocks were made. He unloaded steel. He carried tools. He was everywhere. Sweat poured from him. His muscles grew tough as liana vines. He talked with the ironworkers, some of whom spoke his tongue. They were brash, easy-laughing, rough-spoken men, men of the city. Their leader was a man by the name of Emmanuel, a man with a mighty chest, hugely strong. Emmanuel wore a green felt hat enlivened with the white and lightly dancing feathers of the egrets that rode the cattle on the grasslands of the coast. He spoke often to Kofi, telling of the places he had been, the things he had seen.

"The money goes, but who cares? That's an ironworker's life – to make money and spend it. Someday I will have a car – you'll see. Ahh – it'll be blue, like the sea, with silver all over it. Buick – Jaguar – you don't know those names. Learn them, hear me? I'm telling them to you. Wait until you see me on the high steel. Then you'll know what an ironworker does. Listen – I'll tell you something – only men like me can be iron-workers, did you know that? Why? Because I know I won't fall. If you think you might fall, then you do. But not me. I'll never fall, I tell you that."

Kofi listened, his mouth open, not understanding what Emmanuel was talking about, but understanding the power of the man, the fearlessness.

More and more Kofi was drawn to the company of the bridgeman in the evenings at the *Hail Mary*. Akua would click her tongue disapprovingly.

"Kofi – why do you go there so much?"

"I am going," he would reply, not looking into her eyes. "It is not for you to say."

He still went each evening to see his father and his mother. His father was morose, despite the money, and had taken to quoting proverbs extensively.

"Man is not a palm-nut that he should be self-centred. At the word of the elder, the young bends the knee. If you live in an evil town, the shame is yours."

He would continue interminably, and Kofi would feel uneasy, not certain why his father was offended, not knowing where his own offence lay. But after he had returned to his own hut and had filled himself with bean soup and *kokonte*, he would feel better and would be off again to the *Hail Mary*.

One evening Kofi's father sent the women and younger children away and began to speak with his son. The old man frowned, trying to weave into some pattern the vast and spreading spider-web of his anxieties.

"The things which are growing from the river – we did not know the bridge would be like this, a defiance. And these madmen who go about our village – how many girls are pregnant by them already? And what will the children be like? Children of no known spirit –"

Kofi said nothing at all. He listened silently, and then he turned and walked out of the hut. It was only when he was halfway to the *Hail Mary* that he realized he had forgotten to greet or say farewell to the grandmother who sat, blind and small, in the darkened hut, repeating in her far-off voice the names of the dead.

At the *Hail Mary*, Kofi went over to Emmanuel, who was drinking beer and talking with Danquah. Danquah no longer complained about the village. These days he said that he had always known something wonderful would happen here; he had prayed and now his prayers had been answered. Emmanuel nodded and laughed, shrugging his shoulders rhythmically to the highlife music bellowed by the gramophone, a recent investment of Danquah's. Kofi put one hand on Emmanuel's arm, touching the crimson sheen of the ironworker's shirt.

"I am one of the bridgemen," he said. "Say it is true."

Emmanuel clapped him on the shoulder.

"Sure," he said. "You are a bridgeman, bush boy. Why not?"

He winked at Danquah, who stifled a guffaw. But Kofi did not notice.

The dry *harmattan* wind came down from the northern deserts and

50

across the forest country, parching the lips and throats of fishermen who cast their moon-shaped nets into the Owura river, and villagers bent double as they worked with their hoes in the patches of yam and cassava, and labourers on the sun-hot metal of the bridge.

More than a year had passed, and the bridge had assumed its shape. The towers were completed, and the main cables sang in the scorching wind.

Kofi, now a mechanic's helper, scurried up and down the catwalks. He wore only a loincloth and he had a rag tied around his forehead as slight insulation against the fiery sun. He had picked up from the mechanics and ironworkers some of the highlife songs, and now as he worked he sang of the silk-clad women of the city.

Badu, immaculate in white shirt and white drill trousers, called to him.

"Hey, you, Kofi!"

Kofi trotted over to him.

"The bridge will be completed soon," Badu said. "Do you want to stay on as a painter? We will not need so many men. But you have worked well. Shall I put your name down?"

"Of course," Kofi said promptly. "Am I not a bridgeman?"

Badu gave him a quizzical glance.

"What will you do when the bridge is finished? What will you do when we leave?"

Kofi looked at him blankly.

"You will be leaving? Emmanuel, he will be leaving?"

"Naturally," Badu said. "Did you think we would stay forever?"

Kofi did not reply. He merely walked away. But Badu, watching him go, felt uneasily that something somewhere was disjointed, but he could not exactly put his finger on it.

To the people of Owurasu, the bridge was now different. It had grown and emerged and was an entity. And so another anxiety arose. Where the elders had once been concerned only over the unseemly disturbance of Owura's waters and grove, now they wondered how the forest and river would feel about the presence of this new being.

The forest was alive, and everywhere spirit acted upon spirit, not axe upon wood, nor herb upon wound, nor man upon steel. But what sort of spirit dwelt in the bridge? They did not know. Was it of beneficent or malicious intent? If a being existed, and you did not know whether it meant you good or ill, nor what it required of you, how could you possibly have peace of mind?

A series of calamities enforced the villagers' apprehension. Two of the pirogues drifted away and were found, rock-battered and waterlogged, some distance downriver. A young child fell prey to the crocodile that dwelt under the river bank. Worst of all, three of the best fishermen, who worked downstream near the rapids where the waterflies flourished, developed river-blindness.

When the council of elders met, Kofi was told to attend. He was not surprised, for he had now been the spokesman of the village youth for some time. Nana Ayensu spoke.

"The bridge is beside us, and we live beside this bridge, but we do not know it. How are we to discover its nature?"

Danquah, who was there by reason of his wealth, flatly stated that the bridge had brought good fortune to the village. Business was brisk; money flowed. He could not see why anyone should be worried.

Kofi's father leapt to his feet, quavering with rage. The bridge might have brought good fortune to Danquah, but it had brought ill fortune to everyone else.

"What of my son, spending all his time in the company of strangers? What of Inkumsah's child, buried in the river mud until his limbs rot soft enough for the crocodile to consume? What of –"

"Kobla, Kobla, be calm," Nana Ayensu soothed. "Remember the river."

"The river itself will not be calm," Kofi's father cried. "You will see – Owura will not suffer this thing to remain."

Okomfo Ofori and Opoku the linguist were nodding their heads. They agreed with Kobla. Kofi looked from face to face, the wise and wizened faces of his father, his uncles, his chief and his priest.

"Something is dwelling in it – something strong as Owura himself."

Silence. All of them were staring at him. Only then did Kofi realize the enormity of his utterance. He was terrified at what he had done. He could not look up. The strength was drained from his body. And yet – the belief swelled and grew and put forth the leaf. The being within the bridge was powerful, perhaps as powerful as Owura, and he, Kofi, was a man of the bridge. He knew then what was meant to happen. The other bridgemen might go, might desert, might falter, but he would not falter. He would tend the bridge as long as he lived. He would be its priest.

When the paint began to appear on the bridge, the people of Owurasu gathered in little groups on the river bank and watched. The men shook their heads and lifted their shoulders questioningly. The women chirped like starlings.

"What's the matter with them?" Gerald Wain asked. "Don't they like the aluminium paint?"

"They like it," Badu replied. "They think it is real silver."

52

"What next?" the Superintendent said. "I hope they don't start chipping it off."

But the villagers were not primarily concerned with monetary value. The bridge was being covered with silver, like the thin-beaten silver leaf on a great queen's chair. Silver was the colour of queen mothers, the moon's daughters, the king-makers. The villagers wondered, and pondered meanings, and watched the bridge grow moon-bright in the kingly sun.

Kofi, who had been shunned at home ever since his insolence, himself brightened and shone with every brushful of paint he splashed and slapped on the metal. He painted like one possessed, as though the task of garbing the bridge lay with him alone.

In the *Hail Mary* he questioned Emmanuel.

"Where will you go, when you go from here?"

"Back to the city. First I'll have a good time. Everything a man does in the city, I'll do it – hear me? Then I'll look around for another job."

Kofi was amazed. "You do not know where you will go?"

"I'll find out," Emmanuel said easily. "What about you, bush boy?"

"I will tend the bridge," Kofi said in a low voice.

Emmanuel's laughter boomed. "Do you think it needs looking after? Do you think it would fall down tomorrow if no one was here?"

That was not what Kofi had meant. But he did not perceive the difference in their outlooks. He heard only one thing – the bridge did not need a priest. Emmanuel must be wrong. But if he were not? Kofi thought once again of the bridgemen, coming together for a while and then separating once more, going away to look for other places, somewhere. The thought could not be borne. He clicked it off like the little light of the green and silver torch.

He could return to his father's farm. That would please Akua and his mother. His father would welcome another pair of hands at the planting. He thought of his machete and adze. They would need a lot of sharpening. He stood up indecisively, looking from the counter to the door and back again. In his pocket the silver shillings clashed softly as he moved. He pulled them out and held them in his hand, staring at the last of the thin bright discs. Then he grasped Emmanuel's arm, clutching it tightly.

"What will I do? What will I do now?"

Emmanuel looked at him in astonishment.

"Why ask me?"

The towers were painted from small platforms run up on pulleys, and the cables were painted from the catwalks. Then the day came for painting the cross-members at the top of the towers. It was not a job which many men would have wanted, for one had to leave the safety of the catwalk and crawl gingerly out onto the steel beam.

Kofi at once volunteered. He swung himself lightly over the catwalk and onto the exposed steel. He straddled the beam, two hundred feet above the river, and began to paint.

On either side of the brown waters lay the forest, green and dense, heavy-hanging, sultry and still at mid-day. The palms rose above the tangle of underbrush and fern, and the great buttressed hardwoods towered above the palms. Through and around it all, the lianas twisted and twined. Poinsettia and jungle lily blood-flecked the greens with their scarlet.

Kofi listened to the steely twanging of the cables. The sound, high and sweet as bees or bells, clear as rain, seemed to grow louder and louder, obscuring the bird-voiced forest, surpassing even the deep-throated roar of Owura the river.

Squinting, Kofi could make out other villages, huts like small calabashes in the sun. Then he saw something else. At a distance a straight red-gold streak pierced like a needle through the forest. It was the new road. He had heard about it but he had not seen it before and had not believed it was really there. Now he saw that it would emerge soon here and would string both village and bridge as a single bead on its giant thread.

Emmanuel would ride along there in a mammy-lorry, shouting his songs. At some other village, some other bridge, Emmanuel would find his brothers waiting for him, and he would greet them and be with them again.

Then Kofi knew what to do. He was no longer the bridge's priest, but now the thought could be borne. He was fearless, fearless as Emmanuel. He knew the work of the bridge. In the far places, men would recognize him as a bridgeman. The power of it went with him and in him. Exultant, he wanted to shout aloud his own name and his praises. There was nothing he could not do. Slowly, deliberately, he pulled himself up until he was standing there on the steel, high above the forest and the river. He was above even the bridge itself. And above him, there was only the sky.

Then he did something that Emmanuel would never have done on the high steel – he looked up. The brightness of the bridge seemed strangely to pale in the sunfire that filled his eyes. For an instant he looked straight into the sun. Then, blinded, he swayed and his foot slipped on the silver paint. He pitched forward, missing the bridge entirely, and arched into the river like a thrown spear.

The bridgeworkers' shouted alarm, as they saw him, was each man's cry of terror for himself, who might have been the one to fall. The pirogues went out, and the men of the village dragged the river. But Kofi's body was not found.

"What could have possessed the idiot?" the Superintendent cried, in anger and anguish, for it was the only fatal accident on the job.

"He did not believe the bridge would hurt him, perhaps," Badu said.

"Did he think it was alive?" Wain said despairingly. "Won't they ever learn?"

But looking up now, and hearing the metallic humming of the cables, it seemed to him that the damn thing almost was alive. He was beginning to have delusions; it was time he went on leave.

As for the people of Owurasu, they were not surprised. They understood perfectly well what had happened. The bridge, clearly, had sacrificed its priest in order to appease the river. The people felt they knew the bridge now. Kofi had been the first to recognize the shrine, but he had been wrong about one thing. The bridge was not as powerful as Owura. The river had been acknowledged as elder. The queenly bridge had paid its homage and was a part of Owurasu at last.

The boy's father quoted, stoically and yet with pride, the proverb – "A priest cannot look upon his god and live." Kofi's mother and his widow mourned him, and were not much consoled by the praises they heard of him. But even they, as they listened, felt a certain awe and wondered if this was indeed the Kofi they had known.

Many tales were woven around his name, but they ended always in the same way, always the same.

"The fish is netted and eaten; the antelope is hunted and fed upon; the python is slain and cast into the cooking-pot. But – oh, my children, my sons – a man consumed by the gods lives forever."

A Bird In The House

The parade would be almost over by now, and I had not gone. My mother had said in a resigned voice, "All right Vanessa, if that's the way you feel," making me suffer twice as many jabs of guilt as I would have done if she had lost her temper. She and Grandmother MacLeod had gone off, my mother pulling the low box-sleigh with Roddie all dolled up in his new red snowsuit, just the sort of little kid anyone would want people to see. I sat on the lowest branch of the birch tree in our yard, not minding the snowy wind, even welcoming its punishment. I went over my reasons for not

55

going, trying to believe they were good and sufficient, but in my heart I felt I was betraying my father. This was the first time I had stayed away from the Remembrance Day parade. I wondered if he would notice that I was not there, standing on the sidewalk at the corner of River and Main while the parade passed, and then following to the Court House grounds where the service was held.

I could see the whole thing in my mind. It was the same every year. The Manawaka Civic Band always led the way. They had never been able to afford full uniforms, but they had peaked navy-blue caps and sky-blue chest ribbons. They were joined on Remembrance Day by the Salvation Army band, whose uniforms seemed too ordinary for a parade, for they were the same ones the bandsmen wore every Saturday night when they played "Nearer My God to Thee" at the foot of River Street. The two bands never managed to practise quite enough together, so they did not keep in time too well. The Salvation Army band invariably played faster, and afterwards my father would say irritably, "They play those marches just like they do hymns, blast them, as though they wouldn't get to heaven if they didn't hustle up." And my mother, who had great respect for the Salvation Army because of the good work they did, would respond chidingly, "Now, now, Ewen –" I vowed I would never say "Now, now" to my husband or children, not that I ever intended having the latter, for I had been put off by my brother Roderick, who was now two years old with wavy hair, and everyone said what a beautiful child. I was twelve, and no one in their right mind would have said what a beautiful child, for I was big-boned like my Grandfather Connor and had straight lanky black hair like a Blackfoot or Cree.

After the bands would come the veterans. Even thinking of them at this distance, in the white and withdrawn quiet of the birch tree, gave me a sense of painful embarrassment. I might not have minded so much if my father had not been among them. How could he go? How could he not see how they all looked? It must have been a long time since they were soldiers, for they had forgotten how to march in step. They were old – that was the thing. My father was bad enough, being almost forty, but he wasn't a patch on Howard Tully from the drugstore, who was completely grey-haired and also fat, or Stewart MacMurchie, who was bald at the back of his head. They looked to me like imposters, plump or spindly caricatures of past warriors. I almost hated them for walking in that limping column down Main. At the Court House, everyone would sing *Lord God of Hosts, be with us yet, lest we forget, lest we forget.* Will Masterson would pick up his old Army bugle and blow the Last Post. Then it would be over and everyone could start gabbling once more and go home.

56

I jumped down from the birch bough and ran to the house, yelling, making as much noise as I could.

I'm a poor lonesome cowboy
An' a long way from home –

I stepped inside the front hall and kicked off my snow boots. I slammed the door behind me, making the dark ruby and emerald glass shake in the small leaded panes. I slid purposely on the hall rug, causing it to bunch and crinkle on the slippery polished oak of the floor. I seized the newel post, round as a head, and spun myself to and fro on the bottom stair.

I ain't got no father
To buy the clothes I wear.
I'm a poor lonesome –

At this moment my shoulders were firmly seized and shaken by a pair of hands, white and delicate and old, but strong as talons.

"Just what do you think you're doing, young lady?" Grandmother MacLeod enquired, in a voice like frost on a windowpane, infinitely cold and clearly etched.

I went limp and in a moment she took her hands away. If you struggled, she would always hold on longer.

"Gee, I never knew you were home yet."

"I would have thought that on a day like this you might have shown a little respect and consideration," Grandmother MacLeod said, "even if you couldn't make the effort to get cleaned up enough to go to the parade."

I realized with surprise that she imagined this to be my reason for not going. I did not try to correct her impression. My real reason would have been even less acceptable.

"I'm sorry," I said quickly.

In some families, *please* is described as the magic word. In our house, however, it was *sorry*.

"This isn't an easy day for any of us," she said.

Her younger son, my Uncle Roderick, had been killed in the Great War. When my father marched, and when the hymn was sung, and when that unbearably lonely tune was sounded by the one bugle and everyone forced themselves to keep absolutely still, it would be that boy of whom she was thinking. I felt the enormity of my own offence.

"Grandmother – I'm sorry."

"So you said."

I could not tell her I had not really said it before at all. I went into the den and found my father there. He was sitting in the leather-cushioned armchair beside the fireplace. He was not doing anything, just sitting and smoking. I stood beside him, wanting to touch the light-brown hairs on his forearm, but thinking he might laugh at me or pull his arm away if I did.

"I'm sorry," I said, meaning it.

"What for, honey?"

"For not going."

"Oh – that. What was the matter?"

I did not want him to know, and yet I had to tell him, make him see.

"They look silly," I blurted. "Marching like that."

For a minute I thought he was going to be angry. It would have been a relief to me if he had been. Instead, he drew his eyes away from mine and fixed them above the mantelpiece where the sword hung, the handsome and evil-looking crescent in its carved bronze sheath that some ancestor had once brought from the Northern Frontier of India.

"Is that the way it looks to you?" he said.

I felt in his voice some hurt, something that was my fault. I wanted to make everything all right between us, to convince him that I understood, even if I did not. I prayed that Grandmother MacLeod would stay put in her room, and that my mother would take a long time in the kitchen, giving Roddie his lunch. I wanted my father to myself, so I could prove to him that I cared more about him than any of the others did. I wanted to speak in some way that would be more poignant and comprehending than anything of which my mother could possibly be capable. But I did not know how.

"You were right there when Uncle Roderick got killed, weren't you?" I began uncertainly.

"Yes."

"How old was he, Dad?"

"Eighteen," my father said.

Unexpectedly, that day came into intense being for me. He had had to watch his own brother die, not in the antiseptic calm of some hospital, but out in the open, the stretches of mud I had seen in his snapshots. He would not have known what to do. He would just have had to stand there and look at it, whatever that might mean. I looked at my father with a kind of horrified awe, and then I began to cry. I had forgotten about impressing him with my perception. Now I needed him to console me for this unwanted glimpse of the pain he had once known.

"Hey, cut it out, honey," he said, embarrassed. "It was bad, but it wasn't all as bad as that part. There were a few other things."

58

"Like what?" I said, not believing him.

"Oh – I don't know," he replied evasively. "Most of us were pretty young, you know, I and the boys I joined up with. None of us had ever been away from Manawaka before. Those of us who came back mostly came back here, or else went no further away from town than Winnipeg. So when we were overseas – that was the only time most of us were ever a long way from home."

"Did you want to be?" I asked, shocked.

"Oh well –" my father said uncomfortably. "It was kind of interesting to see a few other places for a change, that's all."

Grandmother MacLeod was standing in the doorway.

"Beth's called you twice for lunch, Ewen. Are you deaf, you and Vanessa?"

"Sorry," my father and I said simultaneously.

Then we went upstairs to wash our hands.

That winter my mother returned to her old job as nurse in my father's medical practice. She was able to do this only because of Noreen.

"Grandmother MacLeod says we're getting a maid," I said to my father, accusingly, one morning. "We're not, are we?"

"Believe you me, on what I'm going to be paying her," my father growled, "she couldn't be called anything as classy as a maid. Hired girl would be more like it."

"Now, now, Ewen," my mother put in, "it's not as if we were cheating her or anything. You know she wants to live in town, and I can certainly see why, stuck out there on the farm, and her father hardly ever letting her come in. What kind of life is that for a girl?"

"I don't like the idea of your going back to work, Beth," my father said. "I know you're fine now, but you're not exactly the robust type."

"You can't afford to hire a nurse any longer. It's all very well to say the Depression won't last forever – probably it won't, but what else can we do for now?"

"I'm damned if I know," my father admitted. "Beth –"

"Yes?"

They both seemed to have forgotten about me. It was at breakfast, which we always ate in the kitchen, and I sat rigidly on my chair, pretending to ignore and thus snub their withdrawal from me. I glared at the window, but it was so thickly plumed and scrolled with frost that I could not see out. I glanced back to my parents. My father had not replied, and my mother was looking at him in that anxious and half-frowning way she had recently developed.

"What is it, Ewen?" Her voice had the same nervous sharpness it bore sometimes when she would say to me, "For mercy's sake, Vanessa, what is it *now*?" as though whatever was the matter, it was bound to be the last straw.

My father spun his sterling silver serviette ring, engraved with his initials, slowly around on the table.

"I never thought things would turn out like this, did you?"

"Please –" my mother said in a low strained voice, "please, Ewen, let's not start all this again. I can't take it."

"All right," my father said. "Only –"

"The MacLeods used to have money and now they don't," my mother cried. "Well, they're not alone. Do you think all that matters to me, Ewen? What I can't bear is to see you forever reproaching yourself. As if it were your fault."

"I don't think it's the comedown," my father said. "If I were somewhere else, I don't suppose it would matter to me, either, except where you're concerned. But I suppose you'd work too hard wherever you were – it's bred into you. If you haven't got anything to slave away at, you'll sure as hell invent something."

"What do you think I should do, let the house go to wrack and ruin? That would go over well with your mother, wouldn't it?"

"That's just it," my father said. "It's the damned house all the time. I haven't only taken on my father's house, I've taken on everything that goes with it, apparently. Sometimes I really wonder –"

"Well, it's a good thing I've inherited some practicality even if you haven't," my mother said. "I'll say that for the Connors – they aren't given to brooding, thank the Lord. Do you want your egg poached or scrambled?"

"Scrambled," my father said. "All I hope is that this Noreen doesn't get married straightaway, that's all."

"She won't," my mother said. "Who's she going to meet who could afford to marry?"

"I marvel at you, Beth," my father said. "You look as though a puff of wind would blow you away. But underneath, by God, you're all hardwood."

"Don't talk stupidly," my mother said. "All I hope is that she won't object to taking your mother's breakfast up on a tray."

"That's right," my father said angrily. "Rub it in."

"Oh Ewen, I'm sorry!" my mother cried, her face suddenly stricken. "I don't know why I say these things. I didn't mean to."

"I know," my father said. "Here, cut it out, honey. Just for God's sake please don't cry."

"I'm sorry," my mother repeated, blowing her nose.

"We're both sorry," my father said. "Not that that changes anything."

After my father had gone, I got down from my chair and went to my mother.

"I don't want you to go back to the office. I don't want a hired girl here. I'll hate her."

My mother sighed, making me feel that I was placing an intolerable burden on her, and yet making me resent having to feel this weight. She looked tired, as she often did these days. Her tiredness bored me, made me want to attack her for it.

"Catch me getting along with a dumb old hired girl," I threatened.

"Do what you like," my mother said abruptly. "What can I do about it?"

And then, of course, I felt bereft, not knowing which way to turn.

My father need not have worried about Noreen getting married. She was, as it turned out, interested not in boys but in God. My mother was relieved about the boys but alarmed about God.

"It isn't natural," she said, "for a girl of seventeen. Do you think she's all right mentally, Ewen?"

When my parents, along with Grandmother MacLeod, went to the United Church every Sunday, I was made to go to Sunday school in the church basement, where there were small red chairs which humiliatingly resembled kindergarten furniture, and pictures of Jesus wearing a white sheet and surrounded by a whole lot of well-dressed kids whose mothers obviously had not suffered them to come unto Him until every face and ear was properly scrubbed. Our religious observances also included grace at meals, when my father would mumble "For what we are about to receive the Lord make us truly thankful Amen," running the words together as though they were one long word. My mother approved of these rituals, which seemed decent and moderate to her. Noreen's religion, however, was a different matter. Noreen belonged to the Tabernacle of the Risen and Reborn, and she had got up to testify no less than seven times in the past two years, she told us. My mother, who could not imagine anyone's voluntarily making a public spectacle of themselves, was profoundly shocked by this revelation.

61

"Don't worry," my father soothed her. "She's all right. She's just had kind of a dull life, that's all."

My mother shrugged and went on worrying and trying to help Noreen without hurting her feelings, by tactful remarks about the advisability of modulating one's voice when singing hymns, and the fact that there was plenty of hot water so Noreen really didn't need to hesitate about taking a bath. She even bought a razor and a packet of blades and whispered to Noreen that any girl who wore transparent blouses so much would probably like to shave under her arms. None of these suggestions had the slightest effect on Noreen. She did not cease belting out hymns at the top of her voice, she bathed once a fortnight, and the sorrel-coloured hair continued to bloom like a thicket of Indian paintbrush in her armpits.

Grandmother MacLeod refused to speak to Noreen. This caused Noreen a certain amount of bewilderment until she finally hit on the answer.

"Your poor grandma," she said. "She is deaf as a post. These things are sent to try us here on earth, Vanessa. But if she makes it into Heaven, I'll bet you anything she will hear clear as a bell."

Noreen and I talked about Heaven quite a lot, and also Hell. Noreen had an intimate and detailed knowledge of both places. She not only knew what they looked like – she even knew how big they were. Heaven was seventy-seven thousand miles square and it had four gates, each one made out of a different kind of precious jewel. The Pearl Gate, the Topaz Gate, the Amethyst Gate, the Ruby Gate – Noreen would reel them off, all the gates of Heaven. I told Noreen they sounded like poetry, but she was puzzled by my reaction and said I shouldn't talk that way. If you said poetry, it sounded like it was just made up and not really so, Noreen said.

Hell was larger than Heaven, and when I asked why, thinking of it as something of a comedown for God, Noreen said naturally it had to be bigger because there were a darn sight more people there than in Heaven. Hell was one hundred and ninety million miles deep and was in perpetual darkness, like a cave or under the sea. Even the flames (this was the awful thing) *did not give off any light.*

I did not actually believe in Noreen's doctrines, but the images which they conjured up began to inhabit my imagination. Noreen's fund of exotic knowledge was not limited to religion, although in a way it all seemed related. She could do many things which had a spooky tinge to them. Once when she was making a cake, she found we had run out of eggs. She went outside and gathered a bowl of fresh snow and used it instead. The cake rose like a charm, and I stared at Noreen as though she were a sorceress. In fact, I began to think of her as a sorceress, someone not quite of this earth. There was nothing unearthly about her broad shoulders and hips and her forest of dark red hair, but even these features took on a slightly sinister significance to me. I no longer saw her through the eyes or the expressed opinions of my mother and father, as a girl who had quit school at grade eight and whose life on the farm had been endlessly drab. I knew the truth – Noreen's life had not been drab at all, for she dwelt in a world of violent splendours, a world filled with angels whose wings of delicate light bore real feathers, and saints shining like the dawn, and prophets who spoke in ancient tongues, and the ecstatic souls of the saved, as well as denizens of the lower regions – mean-eyed imps and crooked cloven-hoofed monsters and beasts with the bodies of swine and the human heads of murderers, and lovely depraved jezebels torn by dogs through all eternity. The middle layer of Creation, our earth, was equally full of grotesque presences, for Noreen believed strongly in the visitation of ghosts and the communication with spirits. She could prove this with her Ouija board. We would both place our fingers lightly on the indicator, and it would skim across the board and spell out answers to our questions. I did not believe whole-heartedly in the Ouija board, either, but I was cautious about the kind of question I asked, in case the answer turn out unfavourable and I would be unable to forget it.

One day Noreen told me she could also make a table talk. We used the small table in my bedroom, and sure enough, it lifted very slightly under our fingertips and tapped once for *Yes*, twice for *No*. Noreen asked if her Aunt Ruthie would get better from the kidney operation, and the table replied *No*. I withdrew my hands.

"I don't want to do it any more."

"Gee, what's the matter, Vanessa?" Noreen's plain placid face creased in a frown. "We only just begun."

"I have to do my homework."

My heart lurched as I said this. I was certain Noreen would know I was lying, and that she would know not by any ordinary perception, either. But her attention had been caught by something else, and I was thankful, at least until I saw what it was.

My bedroom window was not opened in the coldest weather. The storm window, which was fitted outside as an extra wall against the winter, had three small circular holes in its frame so that some fresh air could seep into the house. The sparrow must have been floundering in the new snow on the roof, for it had crawled in through one of these holes and was now caught between the two layers of glass. I could not bear the panic of the trapped bird, and before I realised what I was doing, I had thrown open the bedroom window. I was not releasing the sparrow into any better a situation, I soon saw, for instead of remaining quiet and allowing us to catch it in order to free it, it began flying blindly around the room, hitting the lampshade, brushing against the walls, its wings seeming to spin faster and faster.

I was petrified. I thought I would pass out if those palpitating wings touched me. There was something in the bird's senseless movements that revolted me. I also thought it was going to damage itself, break one of those thin wing-bones, perhaps, and then it would be lying on the floor, dying, like the pimpled and horribly featherless baby birds we saw sometimes on the sidewalks in the spring when they had fallen out of their nests. I was not any longer worried about the sparrow. I wanted only to avoid the sight of it lying broken on the floor. Viciously, I thought that if Noreen said, *God sees the little sparrow fall*, I would kick her in the shins. She did not, however, say this.

"A bird in the house means a death in the house," Noreen remarked.

Shaken, I pulled my glance away from the whirling wings and looked at Noreen.

"What?"

"That's what I've heard said, anyhow."

The sparrow had exhausted itself. It lay on the floor, spent and trembling. I could not bring myself to touch it. Noreen bent and picked it up. She cradled it with great gentleness between her cupped hands. Then we took it downstairs, and when I had opened the back door, Noreen set the bird free.

"Poor little scrap," she said, and I felt struck to the heart, knowing she had been concerned all along about the sparrow, while I, perfidiously, in the chaos of the moment, had been concerned only about myself.

"Wanna do some with the Ouija board, Vanessa?" Noreen asked.

I shivered a little, perhaps only because of the blast of cold air which had come into the kitchen when the door was opened.

"No thanks, Noreen. Like I said, I got my homework to do. But thanks all the same."

"That's okay," Noreen said in her guileless voice. "Any time."

But whenever she mentioned the Ouija board or the talking table, after that, I always found some excuse not to consult these oracles.

"Do you want to come to church with me this evening, Vanessa?" my father asked.

"How come you're going to the evening service?" I enquired.

"Well, we didn't go this morning. We went snow-shoeing instead, remember? I think your grandmother was a little bit put out about it.

64

She went alone this morning. I guess it wouldn't hurt you and me, to go now."

We walked through the dark, along the white streets, the snow squeaking dryly under our feet. The street lights were placed at long intervals along the sidewalks, and around each pole the circle of flimsy light created glistening points of blue and crystal on the crusted snow. I would have liked to take my father's hand, as I used to do, but I was too old for that now. I walked beside him, taking long steps so he would not have to walk more slowly on my account.

The sermon bored me, and I began leafing through the Hymnary for entertainment. I must have drowsed, for the next thing I knew, my father was prodding me and we were on our feet for the closing hymn.

Near the Cross, near the Cross,
Be my glory ever,
Till my ransomed soul shall find
Rest beyond the river.

I knew the tune well, so I sang loudly for the first verse. But the music to that hymn is sombre, and all at once the words themselves seemed too dreadful to be sung. I stopped singing, my throat knotted. I thought I was going to cry, but I did not know why, except that the song recalled to me my Grandmather Connor, who had been dead only a year now. I wondered why her soul needed to be ransomed. If God did not think she was good enough just as she was, then I did not have much use for His opinion. *Rest beyond the river* – was that what had happened to her? She had believed in Heaven, but I did not think that rest beyond the river was quite what she had in mind. To think of her in Noreen's flashy Heaven, though – that was even worse. Someplace where nobody ever got annoyed or had to be smoothed down and placated, someplace where there were never any family scenes – that would have suited my Grandmother Connor. Maybe she wouldn't have minded a certain amount of rest beyond the river, at that.

When we had the silent prayer, I looked at my father. He sat with his eyes closed. He was frowning deeply, and I could see the pulse in his temple. I wondered then what he believed. I did not have any idea what it might be. When he raised his head, he did not look uplifted or anything like that. He merely looked tired. Then Reverend McKee pronounced the benediction, and we could go home.

"What do you think about all that stuff, Dad?" I asked hesitantly, as we walked.

"What stuff, honey?"

"Oh, Heaven and Hell, and like that."

My father laughed. "Have you been listening to Noreen too much? Well, I don't know. I don't think they're actual places. Maybe they stand for something that happens all the time here, or else doesn't happen. It's kind of hard to explain. I guess I'm not so good at explanations."

Nothing seemed to have been made any clearer to me. I reached out and took his hand, not caring that he might think this a babyish gesture.

"I hate that hymn!"

"Good Lord," my father said in astonishment. "Why, Vanessa?"

But I did not know and so could not tell him.

Many people in Manawaka had flu that winter, so my father and Dr. Cates were kept extremely busy. I had flu myself, and spent a week in bed, vomiting only the first day and after that enjoying poor health, as my mother put it, with Noreen bringing me ginger ale and orange juice, and each evening my father putting a wooden tongue-depressor into my mouth and peering down my throat, then smiling and saying he thought I might live after all.

Then my father got sick himself, and had to stay at home and go to bed. This was such an unusual occurrence that it amused me.

"Doctors shouldn't get sick," I told him.

"You're right," he said. "That was pretty bad management."

"Run along now, dear," my mother said.

That night I woke and heard voices in the upstairs hall. When I went out, I found my mother and Grandmother MacLeod, both in their dressing-gowns. With them was Dr. Cates. I did not go immediately to my mother, as I would have done only a year before. I stood in the doorway of my room, squinting against the sudden light.

"Mother – what is it?"

She turned, and momentarily I saw the look on her face before she erased it and put on a contrived calm.

"It's all right," she said. "Dr. Cates has just come to have a look at Daddy. You go on back to sleep."

The wind was high that night, and I lay and listened to it rattling the storm windows and making the dry and winter-stiffened vines of the Virginia creeper scratch like small persistent claws against the red brick. In the morning, my mother told me that my father had developed pneumonia.

Dr. Cates did not think it would be safe to move my father to the hospital. My mother began sleeping in the spare bedroom, and after she

66

had been there for a few nights, I asked if I could sleep in there too. I thought she would be bound to ask me why, and I did not know what I would say, but she did not ask. She nodded, and in some way her easy agreement upset me.

That night Dr. Cates came again, bringing with him one of the nurses from the hospital. My mother stayed upstairs with them. I sat with Grandmother MacLeod in the living room. That was the last place in the world I wanted to be, but I thought she would be offended if I went off. She sat as straight and rigid as a totem pole, and embroidered away at the needle-point cushion cover she was doing. I perched on the edge of the chesterfield and kept my eyes fixed on *The White Company* by Conan Doyle, and from time to time I turned a page. I had already read it three times before, but luckily Grandmother MacLeod did not know that. At nine o'clock she looked at her gold brooch watch, which she always wore pinned to her dress, and told me to go to bed, so I did that.

I wakened in darkness. At first, it seemed to me that I was in my own bed, and everything was as usual, with my parents in their room, and Roddie curled up in the crib in his room, and Grandmother MacLeod sleeping with her mouth open in her enormous spool bed, surrounded by half a dozen framed photos of Uncle Roderick and only one of my father, and Noreen snoring fitfully in the room next to mine, with the dark flames of her hair spreading out across the pillow, and the pink and silver motto cards from the Tabernacle stuck with adhesive tape onto the wall beside her bed – *Lean on Him, Emmanuel Is My Refuge, Rock of Ages Cleft for Me.*

Then in the total night around me, I heard a sound. It was my mother, and she was crying, not loudly at all, but from somewhere very deep inside her. I sat up in bed. Everything seemed to have stopped, not only time but my own heart and blood as well. Then my mother noticed that I was awake.

I did not ask her, and she did not tell me anything. There was no need. She held me in her arms, or I held her, I am not certain which. And after a while the first mourning stopped, too, as everything does sooner or later, for when the limits of endurance have been reached, then people must sleep.

In the days following my father's death, I stayed close beside my mother, and this was only partly for my own consoling. I also had the feeling that she needed my protection. I did not know from what, nor what I could possibly do, but something held me there. Reverend McKee called, and I sat with my grandmother and my mother in the living room.

My mother told me I did not need to stay unless I wanted to, but I refused to go. What I thought chiefly was that he would speak of the healing power of prayer, and all that, and it would be bound to make my mother cry again. And in fact, it happened in just that way, but when it actually came, I could not protect her from this assault. I could only sit there and pray my own prayer, which was that he would go away quickly.

My mother tried not to cry unless she was alone or with me. I also tried, but neither of us was entirely successful. Grandmother MacLeod, on the other hand, was never seen crying, not even the day of my father's funeral. But that day, when we had returned to the house and she had taken off her black velvet overshoes and her heavy sealskin coat with its black fur that was the softest thing I had ever touched, she stood in the hallway and for the first time she looked unsteady. When I reached out instinctively towards her, she sighed.

"That's right," she said. "You might just take my arm while I go upstairs, Vanessa."

That was the most my Grandmother MacLeod ever gave in, to anyone's sight. I left her in her bedroom, sitting on the straight chair beside her bed and looking at the picture of my father that had been taken when he graduated from medical college. Maybe she was sorry now that she had only the one photograph of him, but whatever she felt, she did not say.

I went down into the kitchen. I had scarcely spoken to Noreen since my father's death. This had not been done on purpose. I simply had not seen her. I had not really seen anyone except my mother. Looking at Noreen now, I suddenly recalled the sparrow. I felt physically sick, remembering the fearful darting and plunging of those wings, and the fact that it was I who had opened the window and let it in. Then an inexplicable fury took hold of me, some terrifying need to hurt, burn, destroy. Absolutely without warning, either to her or to myself, I hit Noreen as hard as I could. When she swung around, appalled, I hit out at her once more, my arms and legs flailing. Her hands snatched at my wrists, and she held me, but still I continued to struggle, fighting blindly, my eyes tightly closed, as though she were a prison all around me and I was battling to get out. Finally, too shocked at myself to go on, I went limp in her grasp and she let me drop to the floor.

"Vanessa! I never done one single solitary thing to you, and here you go hitting and scratching me like that! What in the world has got into you?"

I began to say I was sorry, which was certainly true, but I did not say it. I could not say anything.

"You're not yourself, what with your dad and everything," she excused me. "I been praying every night that your dad is with God, Vanessa. I know he wasn't actually saved in the regular way, but still and all –"

"Shut up," I said.

Something in my voice made her stop talking. I rose from the floor and stood in the kitchen doorway.

"He didn't need to be saved," I went on coldly, distinctly. "And he is not in Heaven, because there is no Heaven. And it doesn't matter, see? *It doesn't matter!*"

Noreen's face looked peculiarly vulnerable now, her high wide cheek-bones and puzzled childish eyes, and the thick russet tangle of her hair. I had not hurt her much before, when I hit her. But I had hurt her now, hurt her in some inexcusable way. Yet I sensed, too, that already she was gaining some satisfaction out of feeling sorrowful about my disbelief.

I went upstairs to my room. Momentarily I felt a sense of calm, almost of acceptance. *Rest beyond the river.* I knew now what that meant. It meant Nothing. It meant only silence, forever.

Then I lay down on my bed and spent the last of my tears, or what seemed then to be the last. Because, despite what I had said to Noreen, it did matter. It mattered, but there was no help for it.

Everything changed after my father's death. The MacLeod house could not be kept up any longer. My mother sold it to a local merchant who subsequently covered the deep red of the brick over with yellow stucco. Something about the house had always made me uneasy – that tower room where Grandmother MacLeod's potted plants drooped in a lethargic and lime-green confusion, those long stairways and hidden places, the attic which I had always imagined to be dwelt in by the spirits of the family dead, that gigantic portrait of the Duke of Wellington at the top of the stairs. It was never an endearing house. And yet when it was no longer ours, and when the Virginia creeper had been torn down and the dark walls turned to a light marigold, I went out of my way to avoid walking past, for it seemed to me that the house had lost the stern dignity that was its very heart.

Noreen went back to the farm. My mother and brother and myself moved into Grandfather Connor's house. Grandmother MacLeod went to live with Aunt Morag in Winnipeg. It was harder for her than for anyone, because so much of her life was bound up with the MacLeod house. She was fond of Aunt Morag, but that hardly counted. Her men were gone, her husband and her sons, and a family whose men are gone is no family at all. The day she left, my mother and I did not know what to say. Grandmother MacLeod looked even smaller than usual in her fur coat and her black velvet toque. She became extremely agitated about trivialities, and fussed about the possibility of the taxi not arriving on time. She had forbidden us to accompany her to the station. About my father, or the house, or anything important, she did not say a word. Then, when the taxi had finally arrived, she turned to my mother.

"Roddie will have Ewen's seal ring, of course, with the MacLeod crest on it," she said. "But there is another seal as well, don't forget, the larger one with the crest and motto. It's meant to be worn on a watch chain. I keep it in my jewel-box. It was Roderick's. Roddie's to have that, too, when I die. Don't let Morag talk you out of it."

During the Second World War, when I was seventeen and in love with an airman who did not love me, and desperately anxious to get away from Manawaka and from my grandfather's house, I happened one day to be going through the old mahogany desk that had belonged to my father. It had a number of small drawers inside, and I accidentally pulled one of these all the way out. Behind it there was another drawer, one I had not known about. Curiously, I opened it. Inside there was a letter written on almost transparent paper in a cramped angular handwriting. It began – *Cher Monsieur Ewen* – That was all I could make out, for the writing was nearly impossible to read and my French was not good. It was dated 1919. With it, there was a picture of a girl, looking absurdly old-fashioned to my eyes, like the faces on long-discarded calendars or chocolate boxes. But beneath the dated quality of the photograph, she seemed neither expensive nor cheap. She looked like what she probably had been – an ordinary middle-class girl, but in another country. She wore her hair in long ringlets, and her mouth was shaped into a sweetly sad posed smile like Mary Pickford's. That was all. There was nothing else in the drawer.

I looked for a long time at the girl, and hoped she had meant some momentary and unexpected freedom. I remembered what he had said to me, after I hadn't gone to the Remembrance Day parade.

"What are you doing, Vanessa?" my mother called from the kitchen.

"Nothing," I replied.

I took the letter and picture outside and burned them. That was all I could do for him. Now that we might have talked together, it was many years too late. Perhaps it would not have been possible anyway. I did not know.

As I watched the smile of the girl turn into scorched paper, I grieved for my father as though he had just died now.

Short stories and novels seem to begin in very different ways in my mind. With a novel, the main characters come first; they grow slowly in the imagination until I feel I know them well; what happens to them arises out of what they *are*. Most short stories I've written seem to be triggered off by some event, either in my own life or something I've observed or read about. The characters in a short story seem just as real to me as the characters in a novel, but I have not seen them, in my mind, in as many situations – they are visualized more in relation to one main situation. Perhaps this points up some of the differences between a novel and a short story. One form is not better than the other. They simply do not serve the same function. I see a novel as a fictional form containing many themes, and when I am writing a novel, I feel rather like a juggler trying to keep a dozen plates spinning up there in the air. In my stories, on the other hand, there tends to be one central theme, although of course it may have ramifications. As with a novel, one hopes to set up echoes in the reader's mind, which will lead them beyond anything on the printed page.

Why does a writer put some things in novel form and others in short story form? Every writer might give a different answer to this question, and my answer probably sounds vague, but the closest I can come to an explanation is that some situations and characters are naturally meant for a novel, and others for a short story, depending upon the variety of themes and the emphasis one wants to give these. Actually, I don't decide by doing a long analysis or even by flipping a coin. It is a decision which seems to be taken partly at a subconscious level, perhaps for reasons related to what I've said about stories and novels.

"The Tomorrow-Tamer" began in my mind when I was living in Ghana, where my husband was an engineer working on a new harbour there. One weekend we went to see a bridge which was being constructed across the Volta River. I learned then that few bridges are ever built without at least one casualty. In the years that followed, both in Africa and in Canada, I learned a good deal about the men who work on the high steel. In a sense, they are a breed apart, in whatever country, and there is a kind of cameraderie among them, perhaps because their work is undeniably dangerous. A man has to be able to come to terms with working at heights, on narrow steel girders, and not everyone can do that. Anyway, that day long ago on the Volta, I talked with a bridgeworker who was a cousin of someone I knew in Accra. He told me he was coming to Accra to see his cousin as soon as the bridge was completed. The next week I heard that he had been killed – he'd fallen from the top of the bridge. I didn't write the story until about five years later. But that was its beginning, something I couldn't put from my mind.

Over the years, that accident on the Volta bridge took on many dimensions. I began to think of what it would be like, for a village in West Africa, to have a bridge flung across their river, a river which was sacred and which had an indwelling spirit. I knew enough by then to know that so-called "primitive" societies are not primitive at all. They are different from ours in concepts, outlooks, beliefs, goals. But they are not less complex, and they are neither better nor worse than our society. When two widely varying cultures meet, however, some kind of clash is inevitable.

In "The Tomorrow-Tamer," the boy Kofi changes radically throughout the story, and yet in some ways he does not really change at all until the end, just before his death. He sees the bridge, all along, as the other villagers see it – in terms of his own deep-rooted concepts. Reality is basically spiritual to the villagers, not material. Each tree has its own spirit, and the river (upon which the villagers depend for their livelihood) has its god, whose protection the village seeks and needs – the need is real, even if psychological rather than physical. The only difference between Kofi and the elders is that Kofi becomes a "bridgeman." He identifies with the bridge. He is on its side, believing it to be good in its essential nature; whereas some of the elders are against it, fearing that it has angered the river god. Kofi wants to become the bridge's priest, although in western terms it does not need a priest. He is growing away from his village, and yet he is doing it in terms of his people's concepts. Only at the end, when he looks up into the sun, and knows that the bridge links his village with other villages – indeed, with the world – does he have some inkling of concepts outside his own. This is in itself a bridge – the realization that people do believe different things, have a different world-view, and that this is all right, as long as we can learn to see others' views. Kofi can't reach that point, because the shock of mental separation from his past is too great. But he has gone part of the way. The Englishman who is directing the operation is unable to conceive that men's minds might work in ways other than his own. That is his limitation and his tragedy – he only senses something out there which he doesn't understand; he can't bear to explore it. Kofi, however, although very briefly, has a vision of a world which includes his own and yet goes far beyond it. He dies because he does not really know the rules of survival in any world except his own. He achieves in death something which he could not have achieved in life – in some way, he does tame tomorrow for his people, although they interpret his death in terms of their own concepts. They feel he was the sacrifice made by the bridge to the river, and they say "a man consumed by the gods lives forever." Kofi is both scapegoat, unintentionally, and messiah, also unintentionally. He himself is the bridge, not between better and worse cultures, but simply between different cultures, between people who do not understand one another, and who, at some point, must try.

"A Bird in the House" is a story which happens to be mainly autobiographical. It sets down, in fictional form, the death of my father. It is one of a series of short stories which I've written, all based on my childhood family and set in a small prairie town similar to the one in which I grew up. These stories, published as a collection under the title of *A Bird in the House*, illustrate some of the things I mentioned previously about short stories. They are all concerned with the same characters, but each story takes a single theme and develops it. In other words, the themes in all these stories are developed one at a time, rather than interwoven, as they would be in a novel. One story may take the central character, Vanessa, from the age of twelve to the age of seventeen, as "A Bird in the House" does, following one theme through all these of her ages – her relationship with her father; the ways in which his death affected her; her gradual understanding of him as a person (different from her concept of him as her father); her final recognition that at last she knows enough about him, and about herself, to talk with him, but this is not possible, for he has been dead for many years.

As well as this theme, the story deals with some of the background which I myself experienced as a child. Vanessa is never bereft, really. She is surrounded by people who care about her, and about whom she cares. But she recognizes, also, that her whole background is one of public rigidity, the kind of strength that Grandmother MacLeod has, which is really both a strength and a weakness. Why do they all find it so necessary to keep on saying "Sorry" to one another? Possibly because they know they are not fulfilling Grandmother MacLeod's concept of the granite-like character which their culture holds up as an ideal. But is Grandmother MacLeod like that, either? How does she feel, in the privacy of her heart, about her two dead sons, and about her own attitudes to them when they were alive? Vanessa can only guess, because Grandmother MacLeod will never be able to say.

Under the surface, they are all very emotional, these people, but they are also afraid of emotion. Noreen, with her religious fantasy escape from her drab world, appals them, for they cannot find any such easy and spectacular way out of the restrictions of their own world.

What does the bird trapped in the house really mean? Perhaps in the end Vanessa sees the bird as being in some way all of them.

MARGARET LAURENCE

BIBLIOGRAPHY

This Side Jordan. Toronto: McClelland and Stewart, 1960. [Novel]

The Prophet's Camel Bell. Toronto: McClelland and Stewart, 1963. [Travel]

The Tomorrow-Tamer. Toronto: McClelland and Stewart, 1963. [Short Stories]

The Stone Angel. Toronto: McClelland and Stewart, 1964. [Novel]

A Jest of God. Toronto: McClelland and Stewart, 1966. [Novel]

Long Drums and Cannons. Toronto: McClelland and Stewart, 1968. [Essays on Nigerian literature]

The Fire-Dwellers. Toronto: McClelland and Stewart, 1969. [Novel]

A Bird in the House. Toronto: McClelland and Stewart, 1970. [Short Stories]

Jason's Quest. Toronto: McClelland and Stewart, 1970. [Children's Book]

BOOKS PUBLISHED IN PAPERBACK

The Stone Angel. (*New Canadian Library* Series.) Toronto: McClelland and Stewart, 1968.

A Jest of God. Toronto: McClelland and Stewart, 1966.

The Tomorrow-Tamer. (*New Canadian Library* Series.) Toronto: McClelland and Stewart, 1970.

Hugh Hood

Hugh Hood was born in Toronto in 1928. He was educated in the parochial and high schools of that city, and at the University of Toronto from which he received the Ph.D. degree in 1955. Mr. Hood married Noreen Mallory, a painter and theatrical costume designer, in 1957, and they have four children. The Hood family lives in Montreal.

Hugh Hood has published three novels, two collections of stories, and a book of sports documentary on the career of Montreal Canadiens' hockey star Jean Beliveau. He has also published about sixty short stories in various Canadian, American and European magazines. He is now preparing a new collection of stories and a fourth novel. Mr. Hood teaches English at the University of Montreal.

Getting to Williamstown

Many a green isle needs must be
In the deep wide sea of misery.

Driving out of Montreal in the old days, it used to take me a couple of hours to get off the island – they do it in forty-five minutes now – and by the time I was up around the Ontario line I would decide to bypass Cornwall – "smelly Cornwall," the kids called it, rightly. How it stank, that town, of sulphur and God knows what else! We got off the highway at Lancaster, jog right a hundred yards, jog left onto County Road 19, and away.

MR. FESSENDEN . . . MR. FESSENDEN?

There was a creek we followed upstream for miles – Raisin Creek, was it? More than a creek – almost a river in places, but shallow. Broad but shallow, like a lot of things, with trees bending over in the summer so that they almost formed an arch over the water. We always meant to stop and wade; we could have done it easily. The children would have loved it but we had to get on. Raisin Creek there, with the little bridges and culverts, and from time to time in the distance to the south a view of the main line, and beyond the glitter of the river. It seemed to be always sunny back then.

The road wound back and forth, not a modern highway, badly engineered on the curves so that you couldn't go over forty miles without braking suddenly at every new curve. I taught the children what the highway signs meant: a cross, a curved line to right or left, railroad tracks, intersections at various angles. We were surrounded by rolling, beautifully cultivated fields with the only interruption a few lines of maples bordering the farms, the road, and the river. The fields were expansive and rich, peaceful – ah, God!

I see it now, projected on my walls as though real. Five miles west of Lancaster, about two-fifteen in the afternoon, we pass a gas-pump and a refreshment stand, abandoned for the last few seasons. The pump has a globe of opaque white glass for a head, with three red stars on it. Underneath there is a transparent glass cylinder with gallonage calibrated from zero to twenty, and below that the pump, with a long handle at the side. As the attendant gives you gas, the level drops in the glass cylinder and the clean brilliant red fluid splashes and foams while the children watch fascinated. I pay him, and stand for a moment as he pumps gas back into his apparatus, until at last the cylinder is that beautiful red clear to the top. No nonsense about premium quality or tetraethyl.

Beside the abandoned gas-pump there's this old refreshment stand. In the late twenties somebody used it to sell pop and ice-cream in the summer, and farm produce around harvest time. The shingled walls were green and the roof red; but now in 1934 the paint has flaked and peeled and I can just barely make out the colours. We made up stories about it; it was a little house or an enchanted castle. In truth the stand and pump sat there in overgrown grass, amid wildflowers, lonely and haunted.

Now we are coming to Williamstown; the trees are growing plentiful and the children need, they say, to stop. Deep, deep in the countryside. They can wet in the ditch at the roadside if they must, for there's no one to see or mind very much. But they hope for ice-cream at the general store, so we don't stop by the side of the road. The trees thicken; bright sunlight glances on the green. I see it on these white walls.

The town lies tranquilly in a tiny valley beside the creek, in an island of green under the sun. We dip down in our Chrysler Airflow – there weren't big enough windows in that car; it was too experimental! Down we sail as the highway narrows and becomes King William Street, steep as we come into the town, swooping towards a dangerously narrow bridge at the foot of the hill. As we descend, the foliage obscures the sun. We pass fields on our left, and on our right I have the sense, through the narrow windows of my Airflow, of a white building standing the width of a field from the edge of town, a building in a field that I have never really seen, but shining, always freshly painted, in the last sun before the shade trees crowd in on King William Street.

Careful turning onto the bridge. Cars cannot pass here, but in twenty years I never had to dispute the passage with anyone, certainly not with a citizen of Williamstown. Once, I recall, I came to the bridge, going west into town, just as a farmer arrived, going east and homewards. He had a Model-T truck with a load of crated chickens; the crank stuck out of the face of the Model-T like a pipe. We smiled at one another and I backed off. When he drove past, he waved and nodded politely. Across the bridge we take a right, passing the few houses this side of the stores. This is where my heart stopped, every trip for fifteen years.

Just this side of the stores stands an old house that's for sale, has been ever since I've been driving through. It's yellow, or would be if the paint were restored; the porch sags somewhat. The windows are comprised of sixteen small leaded panes apiece; some are broken. It is a heavenly place. The backyard opens on fields, as do all the backyards in town, and the house will be maybe a hundred and thirty years old. There is a small lawn in front which someone cares for, perhaps the long-dead realtor whose bald sign penetrates the turf. Going by, I sigh and yearn. But for some reason, we never stopped just there. We proceeded to the general store, grocery store, variety store, butcher shop, what would you call it?

Outside Williamstown the highway is paved, but in front of the cluster of stores, for whatever reason, the street is always dusty with a light haze hanging in the air. BUSTIN'S DRUGS: pharmacist's globes dim in the window. DEVLIN'S HARDWARE: a display of C.C.M. bikes and a cream separator. In the window of the grocery store appear the name of the proprietor and the words SALADA TEA arranged in an arc, in white tin letters appliquéd to the glass in some mysterious way. Here we stop, taking no special care to park in this or that direction.

The kids have used the toilet here so often, at least six times a year, that the proprietor believes he knows us. He gives them extra large scoops of ice-cream, dipping it from a cooler with big round holes in the top, and thick lids like gladiators' shields. Then he sprinkles orange and red and chocolate flakes of candy on top of the double-dips; this costs a nickel. He has a glittering and lethal meat slicer with which he cuts boiled ham and pork for picnic lunches, and a superb coffee grinder, and the place smells of spice and coffee. The showcases are bound in a beautiful walnut. I can't smell that smell. I can think of it but I can't recreate it. Later, perhaps.

"That's quite a car, Mister."

"Yes, that's what they call streamlining. It came in this year."

Into the dark hot car, then, and down King William Street westwards past the District Catholic School, just where the sidewalks end. It's three o'clock and we'll have to make time if we're going to be in Maitland for dinner. The highway straightens and we get up to fifty, going straight west away from heaven.

TIME FOR MR. FESSENDEN'S INJECTIONS.

But you couldn't get in and you couldn't get out, in those days. It took half a day to get to Williamstown and another three hours to Maitland, in all a seven-hour drive; a hundred and thirty miles, what with lunch in the car, stops for the toilet, occasional car-sickness. I dreamed of commuting, for it can't have been more than sixty-five miles from the city.

"I could go in by the day."

"No you couldn't, Henry, you'd be exhausted. Now, no, don't begin to explain to me; there can't be any question of driving in and out of Montreal every day. Think of it! Your heart would never stand it."

78

"But I'm a young man, Irma, and there's nothing wrong with my heart. I've just had my checkup and I'm fine, just fine. And only think of the peace in the winter, alone, a couple of feet of snow. Black dark and little lights in the parlour windows; there's a school, a good one I'm sure, and later on we could send them into Lancaster on a bus, or they could come with me."

"And you seriously propose to bury me in that place with the children? Who would they play with?"

"I imagine there are children living there; there must be five hundred people in the place."

"And what about me? What would I do for amusement, with the car gone all day? I'd go mad in a place like that."

"It might be good for you, Irma."

"What are you insinuating?"

"Oh, nothing, nothing. I love you, Irma."

She would have a lightning switch of mood.

"I don't know how you put up with me, Henry, I'm such a mess."

"Well, we all have faults, dear."

"Yes, but think, Henry. No movies, no friends, no theatre."

"We don't go to the theatre."

"But we might sometime, and we CAN if we're desperate. No concerts, no public transit."

"You don't need streetcars in a town that size; you can walk to church and the store. And I want to live there. It wouldn't be like this."

"There's nothing wrong with this. You're doing splendidly. You have all your friends in the office and inside of two years you'll be a trust officer. You'd have to get up at five to drive into Montreal, and you wouldn't get home till nine, which exactly reverses your present hours. It would kill you."

"I could make better time than that."

"We don't have enough money to fix up that ruin."

"Now that's not fair. You've never been inside it."

"Have you?"

"No. I've never been there but with you, driving through on the way to your mother's."

"Henry, you have no idea what it costs to fix up a place in the country. That house looks good to you, seeing it for the first time from the outside; but it'll be full of dry rot and structural faults; there's no plumbing."

"How do you know?"

"There's a little house in the backyard."

"I didn't notice."

"No, you wouldn't! I'm the one who'd have to nurse the children through typhoid."

"I'll bet there isn't any more typhoid, per capita, in Williamstown than here."

"We'll wait till they're a little older before we run the risk!"

She always closed a discussion by tabling the children's needs; we moved from the condition of my health to the children's needs and back. They were the poles of her dialectic. And about most points in the argument, she had fact and reason on her side. I *did* have friends in the office and almost nowhere else, and I *did* become a trust officer in charge of important portfolios, and I didn't have to go to war on account of the family and my public responsibilities as a trust officer. In Montreal, the public responsibilities of a financial officer are taken to be great and pressing.

"Mother, how can my friends come to an upstairs duplex? It was all right when I was small; I didn't understand. But look at the difference between us and the Lewises. It makes me so ashamed. Why can't we have a house like everybody else?"

"Sssshhh! Mustn't disturb your father, Frances. He's lying down before dinner."

"He's always having his rest. What does he have to lie down for?"

"It's better, dear, when a man is middle-aged, for him to conserve his energy. Come into the dining-room." Their steps recede.

"I want to have a skating party with coffee after."

"Aren't some of the children young for coffee?"

"Oh, mother!"

"We can call it a coffee party anyway and no harm done. What sort of house do you think we should have, dear?"

"Mother, I want to live in the Town of Mount Royal!"

"So do I, dear!"

Oh thickening trees, oh shady sunlight, leaded panes and quiet dusty street!

There are no trees in the Town of Mount Royal; this is a fact. Here and there one finds a stunted shrub or two; but when they laid out the developments during, and just after, the war, they bulldozed down all the trees – a bad mistake which nobody seems to regret. Without noticing it, the citizens live on an arid plain where the grass yellows in May. If the land were clear prairie they would see this; but amidst the ranch houses, the desert effect is half-obliterated. That you can't sit in your own backyard in July because of the glare seems to be taken for granted by all but me.

80

It takes me an hour and a half to drive two miles to work, because of a bottleneck at a level crossing. In wintertime it takes much longer.

"Everybody else has a television aerial."

"Some people put them up without a set," says Bunker.

"Oh, your father would never do that, would you, darling?"

"What is it, darling?"

"Frances and Bunker think we should have television."

"Everybody on the street has it but us."

"Then I'll order one today. I hadn't noticed. Are there good programs?"

"I believe it depends on your aerial, dear."

"Ah, like the radio. I'll see about it this afternoon."

At this, the children – and wonderfully they aren't children any more – are silently pleased, as they should be. I've never denied them anything. Irma hugs me, and they observe us indulgently, gratified.

YES, COMATOSE. A TERMINAL CASE, I'M AFRAID.

Terminal, that's what they said when Irma went and the house was empty, Frances married and living in Toronto, and Bunker in Maitland. He's a real grandmother's boy, that one, looking after the store and the farm properties, and seeing about Irma's flowers now and then, something I couldn't do myself from Montreal.

"That's quite a car, Mister."

"Yes, that's a French car, a Citroën. Most comfortable car on the road. You ought to try it sometime."

I can go back and forth to Maitland in under three hours now, with 401 connected to the Metropolitan Highway and only one traffic light between the Town of Mount Royal and Toronto. I don't have to have a fast car; the Citroën isn't what you'd call a fast car. I just average a comfortable sixty miles an hour and I'm there in no time. Why, Bunker might just as well have been living with me, we've seen so much of each other, and he's been in to see me . . . to see me here.

401 follows the river pretty much, about half a mile inland. You pick it up at the Ontario border; you don't go into Lancaster, and naturally you don't go anywhere near Williamstown. I haven't been through Williamstown since before Irma died, I don't believe. Maybe I'll go, one of these days. But I've been going out on 401, and for a while it's pretty country down by the locks and the islands; every few minutes you can see the sunlight on the water. But soon, northwest of Cornwall, the geography changes; you can't see the river and the land is swamp. Scrub timber, marsh, cattails, and the occasional concession road running north into

the scrub. There are probably plenty of flies in there; but I've never stopped to see. Coming back down at night, it's black as a yard up a stove-pipe along 401; there isn't the traffic to justify a superhighway through there, but it had to go in because of Montreal and Toronto. There are only two gas stations between the border and Maitland, and the province has to subsidize them, and the food is bad, especially the coffee.

Going along in my Citroën between the railroad tracks and the river, I can always tell when we're passing Williamstown because I can see the steeple of some church peeking up out of a clump of trees a few miles to my right, a rectangular white tower with a pointed lead steeple on top; the town must be five or six miles off the highway and one of the county roads connects. One of these days I'll take the ramp, turn off north in my Citroën and astonish the grocer, though the children won't be with me.

"You'd be better off to come and live in Maitland, Dad, where you'd be near Mother."

"Well, but Bunker, she's dead. I mean, I can't see that it matters where I am, relative to where she is."

"Haven't you got any feelings on the subject? After all, the DeVebers have been established in Maitland for almost a hundred and fifty years. Grandmother used to tell me, and she showed me pictures."

"I'm not a DeVeber. And I'm a Town of Mount Royal man, if there is such a thing."

"You don't like it in the Town, do you Dad? Think what that big house is costing to keep up, now we're all out of it. And maybe you'd enjoy helping me with the business; there's talk of a shopping plaza out by the 401 cloverleaf and I'm considering putting a store in there. Naturally there would have to be additional capital."

"DeVeber capital, I hope."

"Oh now, Dad, it would be a good investment. You could put in what you get for the house without liquidating any of your other holdings; that might be enough. What do you suppose the house is worth?"

HOW DOES HE SEEM TODAY, NURSE?

Bunker has been in to see me right along; he drives down afternoons and has his supper in the city. Then he goes back after nine o'clock. He's attentive all right and it's cheerful to have somebody here, although I can't work up the strength to discuss the house with him. Perhaps we'll sell. I never liked it, and it looks as if I may be here some time. No use having it standing empty and a tax charge. But I don't feel up to talking now. It wouldn't be good for me. I mean, I'm not well.

"Bunker, if you've brought me all this way on a false alarm, I'll kill you. You think you're the only one in the world with business to look after. Thursday night is Debbie's school play, and I haven't finished her costume. Tomorrow night Butler has tickets for the O'Keefe Centre, and you drag me to Montreal on a wild goose chase. Look at him, he's as comfortable as he could possibly be. They're doing everything they can for him, not that there's much they can do, in his condition."

"He'll hear you!"

"No, he won't. They've got him sedated. They have to because it's very painful at the end if they don't. I don't suppose he's felt a thing for days, poor Dad, but at least he isn't in any pain."

"It's wonderful what they can do with drugs, these days."

"Sometimes they don't help, though. When I had Debbie, they had me doped right up and it still hurt like mad. I screamed my head off. But with this, it seems to work."

"He's quiet enough, all right, poor old man. He was never the same, you know, after he lost Mother. He went right downhill, just as if he'd lost part of himself, and it isn't as if he were that old, either."

"He's sixty-five, isn't he?"

"Sixty-six. He quit the Trust on his sixty-fifth birthday."

"I remember. I guess they'll look after . . . uh . . . things, won't they?"

"Yes, they're the executors, with me."

"With you?"

"If we're going to discuss this, let's whisper, Frances."

"Why you, Mister Smartie? Why not me? I'm older."

"I'm a man."

"I don't see it makes much difference. Anyway you're not that much of a man."

"Frances!"

"Ah, I'm sorry, Bunker, I'll take that back. Who named the executors?"

"Dad."

"Why did he leave me off?"

"I have no idea; he probably thought it didn't matter. When you're making a will, you likely think all will be harmony and concord afterwards."

"Just you try any tricks, Bunker Fessenden, and I'll harmony and concord you!"

"There'll be no tricks; the whole testament is as plain as day. The office wrote it up for us, and as far as succession duties go, it's a masterpiece. We get everything and the government gets nothing."

"Nothing?"

"Practically. The minimum, and you can't do any better than that. The estate is divided equally between us. That's fair, isn't it?"

"I'm older. And I have Debbie."

"But you've got a husband to look after you."

"Hah!"

"Butler supports you, in spite of everything. Nobody supports me, and I've been thinking of getting married."

"You?"

"Yes, me. That's a big house, you know, and with grandma gone, I'm all alone."

Alone in a big house. Our house was the first California-redwood ranch in the Town of Mount Royal, with the refrigerator hung on the kitchen wall – too high to reach comfortably but very stylish. There's much glass, too much. When I wander through the house alone nights, with all the lights on, I'm always exposing myself accidentally to the curious stares of passers-by. It's a house where you have to be careful how you quit bathroom or bedroom; there's always somebody looking at you, surprisedly, from out on the sidewalk. The recreation room gives on the main street; it's the shape of a small bowling alley, with a tiled floor that gives your steps a curious dead ring. Walking back and forth in there at night, with a vast expanse of plate glass on one side of me, and the television and bar on the other, I'm unutterably solitary, like some aquatic creature in a tank, going purposelessly round and round. Now and then I throw darts at the wall. It must look very strange from outside, the brightness, the solitude, the aimless activity. It's a good thing we had that window in the recreation room, because that's how they found me.

Banging on the window, *rap, rap, rap,* reverberations in the sash.

Feet upstairs, then coming down.

Indistinct shapes beside me.

"You were right, Mary, it's Mr. Fessenden, and he's sick."

"Should we get mixed up in this?"

"We can't leave him here."

"We can call the police and wait till they come."

"I'll call them."

"Don't touch anything, and be sure to get a release."

Feet going away and then, later, being carried gently.

"What's his trouble?"

"*Sais pas.* Some kind of a deep coma."

"No fractures, no haemorrhaging? Careful how we handle him; it might be anything."

84

"What do you think?"

"Heart or malignancy."

"Yes."

"The tests will show."

"Yes."

"Off we go."

What is this, this heavenly feeling of being carried, this lightness never felt before? Lie back and float into the white room and the level bed, and afterwards the pictures flashed on the walls and now and then a voice or voices. Being carried . . . ah, ah!

Bunker lives in a stone house; they'll never *find* him when it comes time; he'd better get married, start the whole thing off again in Maitland; but I won't come to the wedding. I'm going to take the ramp when I see that white rectangle, that leaden tower, in the sun above the trees five miles to the north. I see the sun on the walls now, and now coming through the walls. The trees bend over as we glide along beside the river; the walls open and fade and give on the country road and the rich cornfields, a line of trees in the distance and coming closer, lustrous in the sun.

LOOK AFTER THE FESSENDEN BUSINESS, ORDERLY!

Being carried along at the top of the hill and we swoop downwards as trees thicken, a green island, around us, and *here* at the edge of town I see the white building gleaming in the sun under the soft sheen of the tower, one narrow field from town. Being carried gently in by men in white to the porch of the white building in the bright sun. Blaze of glory on leaves moving in the windows as these six bear me kindly up the aisle.

AUTHOR'S COMMENTARY

I: WHY WRITE AT ALL?

People need stories and can't survive without them. If you denied a young child all stories, all of his capacity to make up fantasies about his experience, you'd produce a seriously disturbed, emotionally stunted person by the time the child was seven years old. Nothing is more essential to our lives than stories – the only things of equal importance are food, shelter, human love and some kind of religious activity.

A man comes home from the office at six o'clock and his wife asks him, "How did it go today, dear?" So he starts off, "I really gave it to the boss good this afternoon! Did I ever tell him? I told him if he didn't like the way I'm doing things he could find himself another bookkeeper."

He may in fact have said nothing to his boss. Quite likely he just happened to have a particularly hard time that afternoon. The tale he tells (which isn't really a lie; it's a fantasy) acts out his feelings and helps him get rid of some of his fatigue, anger and resentment.

A young man falls in love for the first time, and tells himself that SHE is all nobleness, all goodness; there is nothing in the world worthy of her! He knows from experience that nobody is perfect, that the best of people have faults, get tired or angry. But he tells himself a story – often quite deliberately – and deepens his emotional life by this imaginative experience.

Human beings never see each other as raw facts; we know one another by the stories we make up: my girl is perfection, my dad has all the money in the world, my son will grow up to be Prime Minister, my wife doesn't understand me. We simply cannot know each other, or anything in the world, without putting it into a narrative. We even do this in our dreams, and may be doing it unconsciously all the time.

The man who makes art out of stories, the tale-teller, is satisfying one of the oldest human needs by giving public expression to his habit of fantasy. He illustrates for his listeners the human ability to organize experience and interpret it by arranging events in formal patterns. Narrative doesn't have to be written down in a book. Books are just one of the ways of preserving and re-telling stories. There was a time when there were no books; there may be such a time in the future, though this doesn't seem likely. Books or no books, people will go on telling stories and listening to them, on the radio or tape-recordings or long-playing records, in television plays and movies – these are all types of narration – for as long as language exists.

The story-teller's art is as rooted in nature as the arts of building and cooking and the rituals of courtship and the choice of a partner for life. Stories are the sweat produced by a man's effort to control and understand the world.

II: WRITING "GETTING TO WILLIAMSTOWN"

This is one of a group of three stories which I wrote in the spring of 1964 as a deliberately related trio. The others are "The Tolstoy Pitch" which appeared in the literary magazine *The Fiddlehead*, #79, March-April 1969, and "A Solitary Ewe" which was in the all-Canadian issue of the American literary magazine *The Literary Review* in 1965. I may reprint these stories in a collection sometime, and then people will be able to read them as a set which belongs together. Each of the three uses a theme which I have found it important to write about. "The Tolstoy Pitch" is about the life of an artist and its problems; "A Solitary Ewe" is about passionate human love. And "Getting to Williamstown" is about death, and the way a man's entire life may prepare him for the manner of his death, and the life after death. These themes are interrelated, because human art and human love are our models of immortality. The life of the dying man in "Getting to Williamstown" doesn't end with his death. He is more alive than he has ever been as "these six bear me up the aisle." He has come into a place of comfort, sunshine and life.

Perhaps because of its commitment to the religious idea of human immortality, "Getting to Williamstown" has been the most popular of the trio. It has been widely reprinted in collections of stories, most notably in the anthology *The Best American Short Stories, 1966*.

The technical possibilities of the short-story form are very great. I used three quite different narrative techniques in these stories. "The Tolstoy Pitch" is almost all spoken dialogue. "A Solitary Ewe" has relatively little dialogue and is more a "narrated" story. And the methods of "Getting to Williamstown" are mainly scenic, that is, symbolic and evocative, where a particular scene or place is made to represent a fundamental human wish and a final human state.

HUGH HOOD

BIBLIOGRAPHY

Flying a Red Kite. Toronto: The Ryerson Press, 1962. [Stories]

White Figure, White Ground. Toronto: The Ryerson Press, 1964. [Novel]

Around the Mountain: Scenes from Montreal Life. Toronto: Peter Martin Associates Limited, 1967. [Stories]

The Camera Always Lies. Toronto: Longmans, Canada, Ltd., 1967. [Novel]

Strength Down Centre: Toronto: Prentice-Hall, Canada, Ltd., 1970. [Sports Documentary]

A Game of Touch. Toronto: Longmans, Canada, Ltd., 1970. [Novel]

BOOKS PUBLISHED IN PAPERBACK

Flying a Red Kite. Toronto: Ryerson Press, 1967.

Mordecai Richler

Mordecai Richler was born in Montreal in 1931. He attended Sir
George Williams University and later worked as a news editor for
the CBC in Montreal. Fifteen years ago he moved to London where
he still lives. He is married and has five children.

In 1961 he was a Guggenheim Fellow; in 1967 he was awarded
a Canada Council Senior Fellowship; in 1968 he won the *Paris
Review* Humour Prize; in 1969 the Governor-General's Award.
During the academic year 1968-9 he returned to Canada as
writer-in-residence at Sir George Williams University.

Mordecai Richler is also well known as a script writer, having
scripted such films as *Life at the Top* and *No Love for Johnny*.

Bambinger

We needed money. But we could not, like the Isenbergs next door, put a "Room To Let" sign in the window. We had standards to maintain.

"Taking in a refugee, a single man," my mother argued, "would help to fight human suffering. It might also mean a husband for Cousin Bessie, poor thing."

So in November, 1942, a phone call was made to the proper agency, and we got our first roomer, a refugee, without advertising. Herr Bambinger was a slight, stooping man with a shiny bald head and almost no chin. He wore thick glasses with steel frames and, even though he rolled his own cigarettes, he used a tortoise-shell cigarette holder.

"I guess," my mother said, "you're thinking of settling down. You'll be looking for a wife."

"You bet your bottom dollar he is," my father said.

On Friday Cousin Bessie was produced at dinner and on Saturday my parents cornered Herr Bambinger.

"Beauty," my mother said, "is only skin deep."

"Ach, so."

"What a man wants in a wife is somebody steady," my father said, offering Herr Bambinger a shot of apricot brandy. "Somebody with a little something in the bank."

Herr Bambinger didn't, like the other refugees, drink black coffee endlessly at the Old Vienna and pontificate about what a dull, uncultured country Canada was. Bambinger spent most of his evenings smoking in the dark in his room, the back bedroom. He wrote a prodigious number of letters, always filling the rice paper pages from top to bottom with the smallest, tightest handwriting I had ever seen. The letters went to the International Red Cross and refugee organizations and camps all over the world, but nothing ever came for him unless it was his own letters returned or copies of the *Aufbau*. Bambinger took a considerable interest in me. He convinced my mother that comic books were a bad influence. Superman, he said, was a glorification of fascism, and the Batman and Robin had a thinly – "very thinly," he said – disguised homosexual relationship. "I don't advise," he'd say to my mother, "that the boy should go without a scarf in such coldness." A couple of days later it was, "The boy shouldn't keep the elbows on the table when he eats." Or, another time, as he switched off the radio abruptly, "A boy can't do his studies and listen to the wireless at the same time."

90

My parents believed that Herr Bambinger had my welfare at heart and when I protested against his intrusions they disciplined me. One Saturday afternoon my mother forced me to go out for a walk with Herr Bambinger.

"Why should I miss the ball game, but?" I asked.

"The poor man has a wife and child of your age and he doesn't know where they are or if they're still alive."

Bambinger – vengefully, I thought – led me to the art museum on Sherbrooke Street. "It is never too early," he said, lighting a cigarette, "for one to learn appreciation of the arts."

"How's about a cig for me?"

"Nicotine is bad for growing boys."

"If you're too cheap to butt me just say so."

"You are not only stupid. You are very impudent. If you were my boy it would not be so. I'd teach you respect."

"Well, I'm not your boy, see."

When Bambinger and I finally did tangle it was over coffee. Coffee, if you remember, was rationed during the war, and at the age of twelve a boy became entitled to a share. There were coupons for it provided in this book. I had waited impatiently for my twelfth birthday and the day after it I demanded a cup. My mother smiled a little. But Bambinger shot her a warning glance and regarded me reproachfully across the table.

"You know you're not allowed to drink coffee," my mother said. "You're still a child."

My sister grinned and took a long sip from her cup.

"As far as the legally elected government of Canada is concerned I am, as of yesterday, allowed to drink coffee."

"The government is full of anti-semites," my father pronounced compulsively.

But I could see that my mother's resolve was weakening.

"One cup," I pleaded. "Would it break your heart?"

"Your mother's right. Coffee is bad for a growing boy."

Staying up late, according to Bambinger, would also stunt my growth. As did evenings spent at the Park Bowling Academy.

"This is family business, so keep your big nose out of it."

"Apologize to Mr. Bambinger immediately."

"Either I get my legal ration or I destroy my coupons."

"You will do no such thing. Now apologize to Mr. Bambinger."

Bambinger smiled mockingly at me, waiting.

"Well, the hell with you," I shouted, turning on Bambinger. "Why'd you run away from Hitler, you chicken? Couldn't you have stayed behind and fought in the underground? Wouldn't that have been better than running out on your wife and kid to save your own skin?"

My mother slapped me.

"Okay," I said, bolting. "I'm leaving home."

Outside, it was raining. Fists jammed into my windbreaker pockets, hastily packed kitbag bouncing against my back, I jogged to the Park Bowling Academy, where Hershey was spotting pins. "Hey," I said, "how'd you like to run away from home with me?"

Hershey wiped the sweat from his forehead, pondering my proposition. "Cancha wait until Monday? We're having *latkas* for dinner tomorrow."

Walking back to St. Urbain with Hershey, I told him about my troubles with Bambinger. It began to rain harder and we sheltered under a winding outside staircase. "Hey, would you do me a favour?" I asked.

"No."

"*Thanks.*"

"What do you want me to do?"

I asked him to ring my doorbell and tell my mother I had fainted or something. "Say you found me lying in the gutter."

"You're chicken. I knew it. You're not running away from home."

Hershey gave me a shove and I scooped up my kitbag to slug him. He began to run. It was almost ten-thirty, the rain had turned to snow.

"You've come back," my mother said, seemingly overjoyed.

"Only for tonight."

"Come," she said, taking me by the hand. "We've just had the most wonderful news."

Bambinger was actually dancing round the dining room table with my sister. He wore a paper hat and had let his glasses slip down to the tip of his nose. "Well," he said, "well, well, the prodigal returns. I told you not to worry."

Bambinger smiled and pinched my cheek, he pinched it very hard before I managed to break free.

"They were going to send out the police to look for you."

"Mrs. Bambinger and Julius are safe," my mother said, clapping her hands.

"They're coming here from Australia," my father said. "By ship. There was a telegram."

"I'm soaked. I'll be lucky if I didn't catch pneumonia."

"Yeah. Just look at him," my father said. "You'd think he'd been out swimming. And what did he prove? Nothing."

"I'll tell you what," Bambinger said, "you may still be too young for coffee but a little brandy won't hurt you."

Everybody laughed. Thrusting past Bambinger, I fled to the bedroom. My mother followed me inside. "Why are you crying?"

"I'm not crying – I'm soaked."

The dining room vibrated with laughter.

"Go back to your party. Enjoy yourself."

"I want you to apologize to Mr. Bambinger."

I didn't say a word.

"You will be allowed one cup of coffee a week."

"Was that his idea?"

My mother looked at me, astonished.

"Alright. I'm going. I'll apologize to him."

I went to Bambinger's room with him. "Well," he said with an ironical smile, "speak up. I won't bite you."

"My mother says to tell you I'm sorry."

"Ach, so."

"You're always picking on me."

"Am I?"

"Maybe they don't understand. I do, but."

Bambinger rolled a cigarette, deliberately slow, and let me stand there for a while before he said, "Your grammar is atrocious."

"This is my room and my bed."

"Ach, so."

"It shoulda been anyway. I was promised. Only they made me stay with my sister and rented it to you instead."

"I think your parents need the money."

"I apologized. Can I go now?"

"You can go."

The next morning Bambinger and I couldn't look at each other and a week went by without his once admonishing, correcting, or trying to touch me. A thick letter came from Australia and Bambinger showed us photographs of a small unsmiling boy in a foreign-type suit that was obviously too tight for him. His wife had stringy grey hair, a squint, and what appeared to be a gold tooth. Bambinger read passages from his letter aloud to my parents. His family, I learned, would not be arriving in Canada for six weeks, the boat trip alone taking a month.

Bambinger now applied himself entirely to work and frugality. He gave up smoking even hand-rolled cigarettes and put in overtime at the factory whenever it was available. On weekends Bambinger searched for bargains. One day he came home with a suit from a fire-sale for his boy and on another he purchased an ancient washing machine and set to repairing it himself. He picked up a table and chairs at an auction and bought a reconditioned vacuum cleaner at a bazaar. All these, and other articles, he stored in the shed; and all this time he ignored me.

One day I surprised Bambinger with a collection of nearly-new comic books – "For your kid," I said, fleeing – and the next morning I found them on top of the garbage pail in the shed. "Julius will not read such trash," he said.

"They cost me a nickel each, but."

"The thought was nice. But you wasted your money."

On Saturday afternoon, only a week before Mrs. Bambinger and Julius should have arrived, my father came into the kitchen carrying the newspaper. He whispered something to my mother.

"Yes, that's the name of the ship. Oh, my God."

Bambinger staggered in from the shed, supporting a table with three legs.

"Brace yourself," my father said.

Bambinger seized the newspaper and read the story at the bottom of page one.

"You can never tell," my mother said. "They could be in a lifeboat. That happens all the time, you know."

"Where there's life, there's hope."

Bambinger went into his room and stayed there for three days and when he came out again it was only to tell us he was moving. The morning of his departure he summoned me to his room. "You can have your bed back again," he said.

I just stood there.

"You've been deprived of a lot. You've suffered a good deal. Haven't you? *Little bastard.*"

"I didn't sink the ship," I said, frightened.

Bambinger laughed. "Ach so," he said.

"Why you moving?"

"I'm going to Toronto."

That was a lie. Two weeks later I saw Bambinger walking toward me on St. Catherine Street. He was wearing a new suit, a fedora with a wide brim, and glasses with thick shell frames. The girl with him was taller than he was. At first I intended to ask him if he was ever going to come round for the stuff in the shed but I crossed to the other side of the street before he spotted me.

94

The Uncertain World

Frequently, I feel I've lost something somewhere. Spontaneity maybe, or honest appetite. Now I'm harnessed to this ritual of being a writer, shaking out the morning mail for cheque-size envelopes – scanning the newspapers – breakfast – then downstairs to work. To try to work. This morning I'm breaking off on a novel I'm still attempting to finish after five years, shirking it by making a start on this piece.

If I get stuck, I can switch to a book review, already overdue.

If it turns out an especially sour, unyielding morning, I can return, in my mind's eye, to Paris, the innocent days, or recite a lecture to myself that begins: Your father had to be out at six every morning, driving to the junk yard in the sub-zero dark, through Montreal blizzards. You work at home, never at your desk before nine.

And then, if I'm not even up to a book review (*What do you mean, not up to it? It pays more for a day's work than your father ever earned, hustling scrap, in a week*), I can stroll downtown. St. Catherine Street. Montreal's Main Stem, as the doyen of our gossip columnists has it. A time-consuming walk while I wait, as the columnist recently put it, the Last Big Deadline In The Sky.

Pretending to browse for books by lesser novelists, I can surreptitiously check out the shops on stacks of the paperback edition of *Cocksure*.

Or I can take in a movie maybe.

Ego dividends. Possibly, I can pick a movie that I had been asked to write myself, but declined. Whatever the movie, it is quite likely I will know the director or the script writer, maybe even one of the stars.

Gee whiz.

Say the star, delicious, twinkly-eyed heroine, wronged in her cinema time by all the cads ever contracted to J. Arthur Rank, who turned to me between takes one afternoon on a restaurant location in Bradford, indicating the crowd assembled since seven A.M., rehearsed – spun into action – shushed – spun into action and shushed again and again – only so that she, the camera tracking after, might sweep through them, making a poignant exit: turned to me, her smile entrancing, and said, "Aren't they marvellous?"

"What?"

"The faces he chose."

The director, she meant. "Oh."

"Are they real people," she then inquired softly, "or only extras?"

So there you have it. In London and New York, I skitter on the periphery of festooned circles, know plenty of inside stories. Bombshells. How Jack Ruby came to die of cancer. What best-selling novel was really stitched together by a cunning editor. Yes, yes, I'll own up to it. I am, after eighteen years as a writer, not utterly unconnected or unknown, as witness the entry in the indispensable *Oxford Companion to Canadian Literature*.

Richler, Mordecai (1931—) Born in Montreal, he was educated at Sir George Williams College and spent two years abroad. Returning to Canada in 1952, he joined the staff of the Canadian Broadcasting Corporation. He now lives in England, where he writes film scripts, novels, and short stories.

The key to Richler's novels is – talent. Hard work. Canada Council grants. Favourable winds.

After eighteen years and six novels there is nothing I cherish so much as the first and most vulnerable book, *The Acrobats*, published in 1954, not only because it marked the first time my name appeared in a Canadian newspaper, a prescient Toronto columnist writing from London, "You've not heard of Mordecai Richler yet, but look out, she's a name to watch for"; but also because it was the one book I could write as a totally private act, with the deep, inner assurance that nobody would be such a damn fool as to publish it. That any editor would boot it back to me, a condescending rejection note enclosed, enabling me to quit Paris for Montreal, an honourable failure, and get down to the serious business of looking for a job. A real job.

Don't blame me, but André Deutsch. To my astonishment (and I say this without false modesty), the novel was published in England and the U.S., and translated into five languages. Now, when somebody asked me what I did, I could reply, without seeming fraudulent to myself, that I was indeed a writer. If I still tended to doubt it in the early hours of the morning, then *The Acrobats*, in shop windows here and there, was the proof I needed. My novel on display side by side with real ones. There is no publication as agonizing or charged with elation as the first.

Gradually, you assume that what you write will be published. After the first book, composing a novel is no longer self-indulgent, a conceit. It becomes, among other things, a living. Though to this day reviews can still sting or delight, it's sales, man – sales, that's the stuff – that buys you the time to get on with the next. Mind you, there are a number of critics whose esteem I prize, whose opprobrium can sear, but, for the most part, I, in common with other writers, have learned to read reviews like a market report. This one will help move the book, that one not.

Writing a book, as George Orwell has observed, is a horrible, exhausting struggle. "One would never undertake such a thing if one were not driven by some demon whom one can neither resist nor understand." Something else. Each novel is a failure, or there would be no compulsion to begin afresh. Critics don't help. Speaking as somebody who fills that office on occasion, I must say that the critic's essential relationship is with the reader, not the writer. It is his duty to celebrate good books, eviscerate bad ones, lying ones.

When I first published, in 1954, it was commonly assumed that to commit a film script was to sell out (Daniel Fuchs, Christopher Isherwood, Irwin Shaw), and that the good and dedicated life was in academe. Now, the inverse seems to be the Canadian case. The creative young yearn to be in films, journeymen retire to the universities. *Seems to be the case*, because, happily, there are exceptions.

All of us tend to romanticize the world we nearly chose. In my case, academe, where, like all good spellers on tenure, I would own a Ph.D. Instead of having to bring home the meat, I would only be obliged to stamp it, rejecting this shoulder of beef as Hank James derivative, that side of pork as sub-Jimmy Joyce. I saw myself no longer a perplexed freelancer with an unpredictable income, balancing this magazine assignment, that film job, against the time it would buy me. No sir. Sipping Tio Pepe in the faculty club, snug in my leather wing-backed chair, in the cherished company of other disinterested scholars, speculating on the significance of the comparable Frederick Philip Grove, I would not, given the assurance of a monthly cheque, chat about anything so coarse as money.

– Why don't you, um, write a novel yourself this summer, Professor Richler?

– Well, Dr. Lemming, like you, I have too much respect for the tradition to sully it with my own feeble scribblings.

– Quite.

– Just so.

Alas, academe, like girls, whisky, and literature, promised better than it paid. I now realize, after riding the academic gravy train for a season, that vaudeville hasn't disappeared or been killed by TV, but merely retired to smaller circuits, among them, the universities. Take the poets, for instance. Applying for Canada Council grants today, they no longer catalogue their publications (the accomplishments of obsolete linear man), but, instead, like TV actors on the make, they list their personal appearances, the campuses where they have read aloud. Wowsy at Simon Fraser

U., hotsy at Carleton. Working wrinkles out of the act in the stix, with a headliner coming up in the veritable Palace of the campus circuit, the U. of T.

If stand-up comics now employ batteries of gag writers because national TV exposure means they can only use their material once, then professors, playing to a new house every season, can peddle the same one-liners year after year, improving only on timing and delivery. For promos, they publish. Bringing out journals necessary to no known audience, but essential to their advancement.

Put plainly, these days everybody's in show business, all trades are riddled with impurities. And so, after a most enjoyable (and salaried) year in academe – a reverse sabbatical, if you like – I now return, refreshed, to the uncertain world of the free-lance writer, where nobody, as James Thurber once wrote, sits at anybody else's feet unless he's been knocked there.

Why do you write?

Doctors are seldom asked why they practice, shoemakers how come they cobble, or baseball players why they don't drive a coal truck instead, but again and again writers, like house-breakers, are asked why they do it.

Orwell, as might be expected, supplies the most honest answer in his essay, *Why I Write*.

"1. Sheer egoism. Desire to seem clever, to be talked about, to be remembered after death, to get your own back on grown-ups who snubbed you in childhood, etc. etc." To this I would add egoism informed by imagination, style, and a desire to be known, yes, *but only on your own conditions*.

Nobody is more embittered than the neglected writer and, obviously, allowed a certain recognition, I am a happier and more generous man than I would otherwise be. But nothing I have done to win this recognition appalls me, has gone against my nature. I fervently believe that all a writer should send into the marketplace to be judged is his own work; the rest should remain private. I deplore the writer as a personality, however large and undoubted the talent, as is the case with Norman Mailer. I also do not believe in special licence for the so-called artistic temperament. After all, basically, my problems, as I grudgingly come within spitting distance of middle age, are the same as anybody else's. Easier maybe. I can bend my anxieties to subversive uses. Making stories of them. When I'm not writing, I'm a husband and a father of five. Worried about air pollution. The population explosion. My sons' report cards.

"2. Aesthetic enthusiasm. Perception of beauty in the external world, or, on the other hand, in words and their right arrangement." The agonies involved in creating a novel, the unsatisfying draft that follows unsatisfy-ing draft, the scenes you never get right, are redeemed by those rare and memorable days when, seemingly without reason, everything falls right. Bonus days. Blessed days when, drawing on sources unsuspected, you pluck ideas and prose out of your skull that you never thought yourself capable of.

Such, such are the real joys.

Unfortunately, I have never been able to sustain such flights for a novel's length. So the passages that flow are balanced with those which were forced in the hothouse. Of all the novels I've written, it is *The Apprenticeship of Duddy Kravitz* and *Cocksure,* which come closest to my intentions and therefore give me the most pleasure. I should add that I'm still lumbered with the characters and ideas, the social concerns, I first attempted in *The Acrobats.* Every serious writer has one theme, many variations to play on it.

Like any serious writer, I desperately want to write one novel that will last, something that will make me remembered after death, and so I am compelled to keep trying.

"3. Historical impulse. Desire to see things as they are . . ."

No matter how long I continue to live abroad, I do feel forever rooted in St. Urbain Street. This was my time, my place, and I have elected myself to get it exactly right.

"4. Political purpose – using the word 'political' in the widest possible sense. Desire to push the world in a certain direction, to alter other people's idea of the kind of society that they should strive after."

Not an overlarge consideration in my work, though I would say that any serious writer is a moralist, and only incidentally an entertainer.

Bambinger

I don't write many short stories for the excellent reason that I'm not very good at it. It doesn't suit my style. And there have been too many false starts. The trouble is I tend to overload a story with characters and incident, so that, whatever the original intention, it ends up choked, tangled, and more like a chapter in a novel. In fact most of my novels have their roots in failed short stories that gradually ballooned into the first draft of a book. *The Apprenticeship of Duddy Kravitz* began as a short story about Duddy, his school mates, and the undoing of a school master, Mr. MacPherson, and rested unpublished in a desk drawer for years before I plucked it out again to hammer a novel out of it. *Cocksure* also began as a short story, first published under the title, "It's Harder To Be Anybody." One of the writers I most admire, possibly because I lack the short story writer's gift myself, is the great short story writer Isaac Babel. It is also true that one of the best writers we have ever had in Canada, Morley Callaghan, is essentially a short story writer.

"Bambinger", like everything else I've done, went through many fat drafts before it finally emerged in its present slender form. It is auto-biographical only to the extent that we did rent rooms to refugees during World War II. But there was no Bambinger among them. He is an invention.

MORDECAI RICHLER

BIBLIOGRAPHY

The Acrobats. London: André Deutsch, 1954. (Out of print). [Novel]

Son of a Smaller Hero. London: André Deutsch, 1955. [Novel]

A Choice of Enemies. London: André Deutsch, 1957. [Novel]

The Apprenticeship of Duddy Kravitz. London: André Deutsch, 1959. [Novel]

The Incomparable Atuk. Toronto: McClelland and Stewart, 1963. [Novel] (Also published in the United States under the title *Stick Your Neck Out,* New York: Simon and Schuster, 1963.)

Cocksure. Toronto: McClelland and Stewart, 1968. [Novel]

The Street. Toronto: McClelland and Stewart, 1969. [Stories]

Hunting Tigers Under Glass. Toronto: McClelland and Stewart, 1969. [Essays]

Canadian Writing Today. Harmondsworth: Penguin Books, 1970. [An anthology edited by Richler]

BOOKS PUBLISHED IN PAPERBACK

Son of a Smaller Hero. (*New Canadian Library* Series.) Toronto: McClelland and Stewart, 1966. (Also available in Paperback Library, New York: 1968.)

A Choice of Enemies. London: Panther Books, 1971.

The Apprenticeship of Duddy Kravitz. (*New Canadian Library* Series.) Toronto: McClelland and Stewart, 1969. (Also available in Paperback Library, New York: 1968, and Penguin Books, Harmondsworth: 1964.)

The Incomparable Atuk. (*Canadian Bestseller Library* Series.) Toronto: McClelland and Stewart, 1965. (Out of print.)

Cocksure. New York: Bantam Books, 1968.

The Street. London: Panther Books, 1971.

Hunting Tigers Under Glass. London: Panther Books, 1971.

Canadian Writing Today. Harmondsworth: Penguin Books, 1970.

Alice Munro

Alice Munro was born in 1931 in Wingham, a small town in western
Ontario. She later attended the University of Western Ontario in
London. She married in 1951 and moved to British Columbia. She
lived in Vancouver for several years but now lives in Victoria with
her husband and three daughters. She has worked as a waitress,
domestic, tobacco picker, library clerical and housewife. Her
husband owns a bookstore in Victoria where, she says, "we live in
a big old house with an antique furnace and a garden the tourist
buses try not to notice."

In 1968 Alice Munro was the winner of the Governor-General's
Award for Literature.

An Ounce of Cure

My parents didn't drink. They weren't rabid about it, and in fact I remember that when I signed the pledge in grade seven, with the rest of that superbly if impermanently indoctrinated class, my mother said, "It's just nonsense and fanaticism, children of that age." My father would drink a beer on a hot day, but my mother did not join him, and – whether accidentally or symbolically – this drink was always consumed *outside* the house. Most of the people we knew were the same way, in the small town where we lived. I ought not to say that it was this which got me into difficulties, because the difficulties I got into were a faithful expression of my own incommodious nature – the same nature that caused my mother to look at me, on any occasion which traditionally calls for feelings of pride and maternal accomplishment (my departure for my first formal dance, I mean, or my hellbent preparations for a descent on college) with an expression of brooding and fascinated despair, as if she could not possibly expect, did not ask, that it should go with me as it did with other girls; the dreamed-of spoils of daughters – orchids, nice boys, diamond rings – would be borne home in due course by the daughters of her friends, but not by me; all she could do was hope for a lesser rather than a greater disaster – an elopement, say, with a boy who could never earn his living, rather than an abduction into the White Slave trade.

But ignorance, my mother said, ignorance, or innocence if you like, is not always such a fine thing as people think and I am not sure it may not be dangerous for a girl like you; then she emphasized her point, as she had a habit of doing, with some quotation which had an innocent pomposity and odour of mothballs. I didn't even wince at it, knowing full well how it must have worked wonders with Mr. Berryman.

The evening I baby-sat for the Berrymans must have been in April. I had been in love all year, or at least since the first week in September, when a boy named Martin Collingwood had given me a surprised, appreciative, and rather ominously complacent smile in the school assembly. I never knew what surprised him; I was not looking like anybody but me; I had an old blouse on and my home-permanent had turned out badly. A few weeks after that he took me out for the first time, and kissed me on the dark side of the porch – also, I ought to say, on the mouth; I am sure it was the first time anybody had ever kissed me effectively, and I know that I did not wash my face that night or the next morning, in order to keep the imprint of those kisses intact. (I showed the most painful banality in the conduct of this whole affair, as you will see.) Two months, and a few amatory stages later, he dropped me. He had fallen for the girl who played opposite him in the Christmas production of *Pride and Prejudice*.

I said I was not going to have anything to do with that play, and I got another girl to work on Makeup in my place, but of course I went to it after all, and sat down in front with my girl friend Joyce, who pressed my hand when I was overcome with pain and delight at the sight of Mr. Darcy in the white breeches, silk waistcoat, and sideburns. It was surely seeing Martin as Darcy that did for me; every girl is in love with Darcy anyway, and the part gave Martin an arrogance and male splendour in my eyes which made it impossible to remember that he was simply a high-school senior, passably good-looking and of medium intelligence (and with a reputation slightly tainted, at that, by such preferences as the Drama Club and the Cadet *Band*) who happened to be the first boy, the first really presentable boy, to take an interest in me. In the last act they gave him a chance to embrace Elizabeth (Mary Bishop, with a sallow complexion and no figure, but big vivacious eyes) and during this realistic encounter I dug my nails bitterly into Joyce's sympathetic palm.

That night was the beginning of months of real, if more or less self-inflicted, misery for me. Why is it a temptation to refer to this sort of thing lightly, with irony, with amazement even, at finding oneself involved with such preposterous emotions in the unaccountable past? That is what we are apt to do, speaking of love; with adolescent love, of course, it's practically obligatory; you would think we sat around, dull afternoons, amusing ourselves with these tidbit recollections of pain. But it really doesn't make me feel very gay – worse still, it doesn't really surprise me – to remember all the stupid, sad, half-ashamed things I did, that people in love always do. I hung around the places where he might be seen, and then pretended not to see him; I made absurdly roundabout approaches, in conversation, to the bitter pleasure of casually mentioning his name. I daydreamed endlessly; in fact if you want to put it mathematically, I spent perhaps ten times as many hours thinking about Martin Collingwood – yes, pining and weeping for him – as I ever spent with him; the idea of him dominated my mind relentlessly and, after a while, against my will. For if at first I had dramatized my feelings, the time came when I would have been glad to escape them; my well-worn daydreams had become depressing and not even temporarily consoling. As I worked my math problems I would torture myself, quite mechanically and helplessly, with an exact recollection of Martin kissing my throat. I had an exact recollection of *everything*. One night I had an impulse to swallow all the aspirins in the bathroom cabinet, but stopped after I had taken six.

* * *

My mother noticed that something was wrong and got me some iron pills. She said, "Are you sure everything is going all right at school?" *School!* When I told her that Martin and I had broken up all she said was, "Well so much the better for that. I never saw a boy so stuck on himself." "Martin has enough conceit to sink a battleship," I said morosely and went upstairs and cried.

The night I went to the Berrymans was a Saturday night. I baby-sat for them quite often on Saturday nights because they liked to drive over to Baileyville, a much bigger, livelier town about twenty miles away, and perhaps have supper and go to a show. They had been living in our town only two or three years – Mr. Berryman had been brought in as plant manager of the new door-factory – and they remained, I suppose by choice, on the fringes of its society; most of their friends were youngish couples like themselves, born in other places, who lived in new ranch-style houses on a hill outside town where we used to go tobogganing. This Saturday night they had two other couples in for drinks before they all drove over to Baileyville for the opening of a new supper-club; they were all rather festive. I sat in the kitchen and pretended to do Latin. Last night had been the Spring Dance at the High School. I had not gone, since the only boy who had asked me was Millerd Crompton, who asked so many girls that he was suspected of working his way through the whole class alphabetically. But the dance was held in the Armouries, which was only half a block away from our house; I had been able to see the boys in dark suits, the girls in long pale formals under their coats, passing gravely under the street-lights, stepping around the last patches of snow. I could even hear the music and I have not forgotten to this day that they played "Ballerina," and – oh, song of my aching heart – "Slow Boat to China." Joyce had phoned me up this morning and told me in her hushed way (we might have been discussing an incurable disease I had) that yes, M.C. *had* been there with M.B., and she had on a formal that must have been made out of somebody's old lace tablecloth, it just *hung*.

When the Berrymans and their friends had gone I went into the living room and read a magazine. I was mortally depressed. The big softly lit room, with its green and leaf-brown colours, made an uncluttered setting for the development of the emotions, such as you would get on a stage. At home the life of the emotions went on all right, but it always seemed to get buried under the piles of mending to be done, the ironing, the children's jigsaw puzzles and rock collections. It was the sort of house where people were always colliding with one another on the stairs and listening to hockey games and Superman on the radio.

I got up and found the Berrymans' "Danse Macabre" and put it on the record player and turned out the living-room lights. The curtains were only partly drawn. A street light shone obliquely on the windowpane, making a rectangle of thin dusty gold, in which the shadows of bare branches moved, caught in the huge sweet winds of spring. It was a mild black night when the last snow was melting. A year ago all this – the music, the wind and darkness, the shadows of the branches – would have given me tremendous happiness; when they did not do so now, but only called up tediously familiar, somehow humiliatingly personal thoughts, I gave up my soul for dead and walked into the kitchen and decided to get drunk.

No, it was not like that. I walked into the kitchen to look for a coke or something in the refrigerator, and there on the front of the counter were three tall beautiful bottles, all about half full of gold. But even after I had looked at them and lifted them to feel their weight I had not decided to get drunk; I had decided to have a drink.

Now here is where my ignorance, my disastrous innocence, comes in. It is true that I had seen the Berrymans and their friends drinking their highballs as casually as I would drink a coke, but I did not apply this attitude to myself. No; I thought of hard liquor as something to be taken in extremities, and relied upon for extravagant results, one way or another. My approach could not have been less casual if I had been the Little Mermaid drinking the witch's crystal potion. Gravely, with a glance at my set face in the black window above the sink, I poured a little whisky from each of the bottles (I think now there were two brands of rye and an expensive Scotch) until I had my glass full. For I had never in my life seen anyone pour a drink and I had no idea that people frequently diluted their liquor with water, soda, et cetera, and I had seen that the glasses the Berrymans' guests were holding when I came through the living room were nearly full.

I drank it off as quickly as possible. I set the glass down and stood looking at my face in the window, half expecting to see it altered. My throat was burning, but I felt nothing else. It was very disappointing, when I had worked myself up to it. But I was not going to let it go at that. I poured another full glass, then filled each of the bottles with water to approximately the level I had seen when I came in. I drank the second glass only a little more slowly than the first. I put the empty glass down on the counter with care, perhaps feeling in my head a rustle of things to come and went and sat down on a chair in the living room. I reached up and turned on a floor lamp beside the chair, and the room jumped on me.

When I say that I was expecting extravagant results I do not mean that I was expecting this. I had thought of some sweeping emotional change, an upsurge of gaiety and irresponsibility, a feeling of lawlessness and escape, accompanied by a little dizziness and perhaps a tendency to giggle out loud. I did not have in mind the ceiling spinning like a great plate somebody had thrown at me, nor the pale green blobs of the chairs swelling, converging, disintegrating, playing with me a game full of enormous senseless inanimate malice. My head sank back; I closed my eyes. And at once opened them, opened them wide, threw myself out of the chair and down the hall and reached – thank God, thank God – the Berrymans' bathroom, where I was sick everywhere, everywhere, and dropped like a stone.

From this point on I have no continuous picture of what happened; my memories of the next hour or two are split into vivid and improbable segments, with nothing but murk and uncertainty between. I do remember lying on the bathroom floor looking sideways at the little six-sided white tiles, which lay together in such an admirable and logical pattern, seeing them with the brief broken gratitude and sanity of one who has just been torn to pieces with vomiting. Then I remember sitting on the stool in front of the hall phone, asking weakly for Joyce's number. Joyce was not home. I was told by her mother (a rather rattlebrained woman, who didn't seem to notice a thing the matter – for which I felt weakly, mechanically grateful) that she was at Kay Stringer's house. I didn't know Kay's number so I just asked the operator; I felt I couldn't risk looking down at the telephone book.

Kay Stringer was not a friend of mine but a new friend of Joyce's. She had a vague reputation for wildness and a long switch of hair, very oddly, though naturally, coloured – from soap-yellow to caramel-brown. She knew a lot of boys more exciting than Martin Collingwood, boys who had quit school or been imported into town to play on the hockey team. She and Joyce rode around in these boys' cars, and sometimes went with them – having lied of course to their mothers – to the Gay-la dance hall on the highway north of town.

I got Joyce on the phone. She was very keyed-up, as she always was with boys around, and she hardly seemed to hear what I was saying.

"Oh, I can't tonight," she said. "Some kids are here. We're going to play cards. You know Bill Kline? He's here. Ross Armour – "

"I'm *sick*," I said trying to speak distinctly; it came out an inhuman croak. "I'm *drunk*. Joyce!" Then I fell off the stool and the receiver dropped out of my hand and banged for a while dismally against the wall.

I had not told Joyce where I was, so after thinking about it for a moment she phoned my mother, and using the elaborate and unnecessary subterfuge that young girls delight in, she found out. She and Kay and the boys –

there were three of them – told some story about where they were going to Kay's mother, and got into the car and drove out. They found me still lying on the broadloom carpet in the hall; I had been sick again, and this time I had not made it to the bathroom.

It turned out that Kay Stringer, who arrived on this scene only by accident, was exactly the person I needed. She loved a crisis, particularly one like this, which had a shady and scandalous aspect and which must be kept secret from the adult world. She became excited, aggressive, efficient; that energy which was termed wildness was simply the overflow of a great female instinct to manage, comfort and control. I could hear her voice coming at me from all directions, telling me not to worry, telling Joyce to find the biggest coffeepot they had and make it full of coffee (*strong* coffee, she said), telling the boys to pick me up and carry me to the sofa. Later, in the fog beyond my reach, she was calling for a scrub-brush.

Then I was lying on the sofa, covered with some kind of crocheted throw they had found in the bedroom. I didn't want to lift my head. The house was full of the smell of coffee. Joyce came in, looking very pale; she said that the Berryman kids had wakened up but she had given them a cookie and told them to go back to bed, it was all right; she hadn't let them out of their room and she didn't believe they'd remember. She said that she and Kay had cleaned up the bathroom and the hall though she was afraid there was still a spot on the rug. The coffee was ready. I didn't understand anything very well. The boys had turned on the radio and were going through the Berrymans' record collection; they had it out on the floor. I felt there was something odd about this but I could not think what it was.

Kay brought me a huge breakfast mug full of coffee.

"I don't know if I can," I said. "Thanks."

"Sit up," she said briskly, as if dealing with drunks was an everyday business for her, I had no need to feel myself important. (I met, and recognized, that tone of voice years later, in the maternity ward.) "Now drink," she said. I drank, and at the same time realized that I was wearing only my slip. Joyce and Kay had taken off my blouse and skirt. They had brushed off the skirt and washed out the blouse, since it was nylon; it was hanging in the bathroom. I pulled the throw up under my arms and Kay laughed. She got everybody coffee. Joyce brought in the coffeepot and on Kay's instructions she kept filling my cup whenever I drank from it. Somebody said to me with interest. "You must have really wanted to tie one on."

"No," I said rather sulkily, obediently drinking my coffee. "I only had two drinks."

108

Kay laughed, "Well it certainly gets to you, I'll say that. What time do you expect *they'll* be back?" she said.

"Late, after one I think."

"You should be all right by that time. Have some more coffee."

Kay and one of the boys began dancing to the radio. Kay danced very sexily, but her face had the gently superior and indulgent, rather cold look it had when she was lifting me up to drink the coffee. The boy was whispering to her and she was smiling, shaking her head. Joyce said she was hungry, and she went out to the kitchen to see what there was – potato chips or crackers, or something like that, that you could eat without making too noticeable a dint. Bill Kline came over and sat on the sofa beside me and patted my legs through the crocheted throw. He didn't say anything to me, just patted my legs and looked at me with what seemed to me a very stupid, half-sick, absurd and alarming expression. I felt very uncomfortable; I wondered how it had ever got around that Bill Kline was so good looking, with an expression like that. I moved my legs nervously and he gave me a look of contempt, not ceasing to pat me. Then I scrambled off the sofa, pulling the throw around me, with the idea of going to the bathroom to see if my blouse was dry. I lurched a little when I started to walk, and for some reason – probably to show Bill Kline that he had not panicked me – I immediately exaggerated this, and calling out, "Watch me walk a straight line!" I lurched and stumbled, to the accompaniment of everyone's laughter, towards the hall. I was standing in the archway between the hall and the living room when the knob of the front door turned with a small matter-of-fact click and everything became silent behind me except the radio of course and the crocheted throw inspired by some delicate malice of its own slithered down around my feet and there – oh, delicious moment in a well-organized farce – there stood the Berrymans, Mr. and Mrs., with expressions on their faces as appropriate to the occasion as any old-fashioned director of farces could wish. They must have been preparing those expressions, of course; they could not have produced them in the first moment of shock; with the noise we were making, they had no doubt heard us as soon as they got out of the car; for the same reason, we had not heard them. I don't think I ever knew what brought them home so early – a headache, an argument – and I was not really in a position to ask.

Mr. Berryman drove me home. I don't remember how I got into that car, or how I found my clothes and put them on, or what kind of a good-night, if any, I said to Mrs. Berryman. I don't remember what happened to my friends, though I imagine they gathered up their coats and fled, covering up the ignominy of their departure with a mechanical roar of defiance. I remember Joyce with a box of crackers in her hand, saying that I had become terribly sick from eating – I think she said *sauerkraut* – for supper, and that I had called them for help. (When I asked her later what they made of this she said, "It wasn't any use. You *reeked*.") I remember also her saying, "Oh, no, Mr. Berryman I beg of you, my mother is a terribly nervous person I don't know what the shock might do to her. I will go down on my knees to you if you like but *you must not phone my mother*." I have no picture of her down on her knees – and she would have done it in a minute – so it seems this threat was not carried out.

Mr. Berryman said to me, "Well I guess you know your behaviour tonight is a pretty serious thing." He made it sound as if I might be charged with criminal negligence or something worse. "It would be very wrong of me to overlook it," he said. I suppose that besides being angry and disgusted with *me*, he was worried about taking me home in this condition to my strait-laced parents, who could always say I got the liquor in his house. Plenty of Temperance people would think that enough to hold him responsible, and the town was full of Temperance people. Good relations with the town were very important to him from a business point of view.

"I have an idea it wasn't the first time," he said. "If it was the first time, would a girl be smart enough to fill three bottles up with water? No. Well in this case, she *was* smart enough, but not smart enough to know I could spot it. What do you say to that?" I opened my mouth to answer and although I was feeling quite sober the only sound that came out was a loud, desolate-sounding giggle. He stopped in front of our house. "Light's on," he said. "Now go in and tell your parents the straight truth. And if you don't, remember I will." He did not mention paying me for my baby-sitting services of the evening and the subject did not occur to me either.

I went into the house and tried to go straight upstairs but my mother called to me. She came into the front hall, where I had not turned on the light, and she must have smelled me at once for she ran forward with a cry of pure amazement, as if she had seen somebody falling, and caught me by the shoulders as I did indeed fall down against the bannister, overwhelmed by my fantastic lucklessness, and I told her everything from the start, not omitting even the name of Martin Collingwood and my flirtation with the aspirin bottle, which was a mistake.

On Monday morning my mother took the bus over to Baileyville and found the liquor store and bought a bottle of Scotch whiskey. Then she had to wait for a bus back, and she met some people she knew and she was

110

not quite able to hide the bottle in her bag; she was furious with herself for not bringing a proper shopping-bag. As soon as she got back she walked out to the Berrymans'; she had not even had lunch. Mr. Berryman had not gone back to the factory. My mother went in and had a talk with both of them and made an excellent impression and then Mr. Berryman drove her home. She talked to them in the forthright and unemotional way she had, which was always agreeably surprising to people prepared to deal with a mother, and she told them that although I seemed to do well enough at school I was extremely backward – or perhaps eccentric – in my emotional development. I imagine that this analysis of my behaviour was especially effective with Mrs. Berryman, a great reader of Child Guidance books. Relations between them warmed to the point where my mother brought up a specific instance of my difficulties, and disarmingly related the whole story of Martin Collingwood.

Within a few days it was all over town and the school that I had tried to commit suicide over Martin Collingwood. But it was already all over school and the town that the Berrymans had come home on Saturday night to find me drunk, staggering, wearing nothing but my slip, in a room with three boys, one of whom was Bill Kline. My mother had said that I was to pay for the bottle she had taken the Berrymans out of my baby-sitting earnings, but my clients melted away like the last April snow, and it would not be paid for yet if newcomers to town had not moved in across the street in July, and needed a baby sitter before they talked to any of their neighbours.

My mother also said that it had been a great mistake to let me go out with boys and that I would not be going out again until well after my sixteenth birthday, if then. This did not prove to be a concrete hardship at all, because it was at least that long before anybody asked me. If you think that news of the Berrymans adventure would put me in demand for whatever gambols and orgies were going on in and around that town, you could not be more mistaken. The extraordinary publicity which attended my first debauch may have made me seem marked for a special kind of ill luck, like the girl whose illegitimate baby turns out to be triplets: nobody wants to have anything to do with her. At any rate I had at the same time one of the most silent telephones and positively the most sinful reputation in the whole High School. I had to put up with this until the next fall, when a fat blonde girl in grade ten ran away with a married man and was picked up two months later, living in sin – though not with the same man – in the city of Sault Ste. Marie. Then everybody forgot about me.

But there was a positive, a splendidly unexpected, result of this affair: I got completely over Martin Collingwood. It was not only that he at once

said, publicly, that he had always thought I was a nut; where he was concerned I had no pride, and my tender fancy could have found a way around
that, a month, a week, before. What was it that brought me back into the
world again? It was the terrible and fascinating reality of my disaster; it
was *the way things happened*. Not that I enjoyed it; I was a self-conscious
girl and I suffered a good deal from all this exposure. But the development
of events on that Saturday night – that fascinated me; I felt that I had had
a glimpse of the shameless, marvellous, shattering absurdity with which
the plots of life, though not of fiction, are improvised. I could not take my
eyes off it.

And of course Martin Collingwood wrote his Senior Matric that June,
and went away to the city to take a course at a school for Morticians, as I
think it is called, and when he came back he went into his uncle's under-
taking business. We lived in the same town and we would hear most
things that happened to each other but I do not think we met face to face
or saw one another, except at a distance, for years. I went to a shower for
the girl he married, but then everybody went to everybody else's showers.
No, I do not think I really saw him again until I came home after I had
been married several years, to attend a relative's funeral. Then I saw him;
not quite Mr. Darcy but still very nice-looking in those black clothes. And
I saw him looking over at me with an expression as close to a reminiscent
smile as the occasion would permit, and I knew that he had been surprised
by a memory either of my devotion or my little buried catastrophe. I gave
him a gentle uncomprehending look in return. I am a grown-up woman
now; let him unbury his own catastrophes.

Boys and Girls

My father was a fox farmer. That is, he raised silver foxes, in pens; and in
the fall and early winter, when their fur was prime, he killed them and
skinned them and sold their pelts to the Hudson's Bay Company or the
Montreal Fur Traders. These companies supplied us with heroic calendars
to hang, one on each side of the kitchen door. Against a background of
cold blue sky and black pine forests and treacherous northern rivers,
plumed adventurers planted the flags of England or of France; magnifi-
cent savages bent their backs to the portage.

For several weeks before Christmas, my father worked after supper
in the cellar of our house. The cellar was whitewashed, and lit by a
hundred-watt bulb over the worktable. My brother Laird and I sat on the
top step and watched. My father removed the pelt inside-out from the

body of the fox, which looked surprisingly small, mean and rat-like, deprived of its arrogant weight of fur. The naked, slippery bodies were collected in a sack and buried at the dump. One time the hired man, Henry Bailey, had taken a swipe at me with this sack, saying, "Christmas present!" My mother thought that was not funny. In fact she disliked the whole pelting operation – that was what the killing, skinning, and preparation of the furs was called – and wished it did not have to take place in the house. There was the smell. After the pelt had been stretched inside-out on a long board my father scraped away delicately, removing the little clotted webs of blood vessels, the bubbles of fat; the smell of blood and animal fat, with the strong primitive odour of the fox itself, penetrated all parts of the house. I found it reassuringly seasonal, like the smell of oranges and pine needles.

Henry Bailey suffered from bronchial troubles. He would cough and cough until his narrow face turned scarlet, and his light blue, derisive eyes filled up with tears; then he took the lid off the stove, and, standing well back, shot out a great clot of phlegm – hsss – straight into the heart of the flames. We admired him for this performance and for his ability to make his stomach growl at will, and for his laugher, which was full of high whistlings and gurglings and involved the whole faulty machinery of his chest. It was sometimes hard to tell what he was laughing at, and always possible that it might be us.

After we had been sent to bed we could still smell fox and still hear Henry's laugh, but these things, reminders of the warm, safe, brightly lit downstairs world, seemed lost and diminished, floating on the stale cold air upstairs. We were afraid at night in the winter. We were not afraid of *outside* though this was the time of year when snowdrifts curled around our house like sleeping whales and the wind harassed us all night, coming up from the buried fields, the frozen swamp, with its old bugbear chorus of threats and misery. We were afraid of *inside*, the room where we slept. At this time the upstairs of our house was not finished. A brick chimney went up one wall. In the middle of the floor was a square hole, with a wooden railing around it; that was where the stairs came up. On the other side of the stairwell were the things that nobody had any use for any more – a soldiery roll of linoleum, standing on end, a wicker baby carriage, a fern basket, china jugs and basins with cracks in them, a picture of the Battle of Balaclava, very sad to look at. I had told Laird, as soon as he was old enough to understand such things, that bats and skeletons lived over there; whenever a man escaped from the county jail, twenty miles away, I imagined that he had somehow let himself in the window and was hiding behind the linoleum. But we had rules to keep us safe. When the light was on, we were safe as long as we did not step off the square of worn carpet which defined our bedroom-space; when the light was off no place was safe but the beds themselves. I had to turn out the light kneeling on the end of my bed, and stretching as far as I could to reach the cord.

In the dark we lay on our beds, our narrow life rafts, and fixed our eyes on the faint light coming up the stairwell, and sang songs. Laird sang "Jingle Bells," which he would sing any time, whether it was Christmas or not, and I sang "Danny Boy." I loved the sound of my own voice, frail and supplicating, rising in the dark. We could make out the tall frosted shapes of the windows now, gloomy and white. When I came to the part, *When I am dead, as dead I well may be* – a fit of shivering caused not by the cold sheets but by pleasurable emotion almost silenced me. *You'll kneel and say, an Ave there above me* – What was an Ave? Every day I forgot to find out.

Laird went straight from singing to sleep. I could hear his long, satisfied, bubbly breaths. Now for the time that remained to me, the most perfectly private and perhaps the best time of the whole day, I arranged myself tightly under the covers and went on with one of the stories I was telling myself from night to night. These stories were about myself, when I had grown a little older; they took place in a world that was recognizably mine, yet one that presented opportunities for courage, boldness and self-sacrifice, as mine never did. I rescued people from a bombed building (it discouraged me that the real war had gone on so far away from Jubilee). I shot two rabid wolves who were menacing the schoolyard (the teachers cowered terrified at my back). I rode a fine horse spiritedly down the main street of Jubilee, acknowledging the towns-people's gratitude for some yet-to-be-worked-out piece of heroism (nobody ever rode a horse there, except King Billy in the Orangemen's Day parade). There was always riding and shooting in these stories, though I had only been on a horse twice – bareback because we did not own a saddle – and the second time I had slid right around and dropped under the horse's feet; it had stepped placidly over me. I really was learning to shoot, but I could not hit anything yet, not even tin cans on fence posts.

Alive, the foxes inhabited a world my father made for them. It was surrounded by a high guard fence, like a medieval town, with a gate that was padlocked at night. Along the streets of this town were ranged large, sturdy pens. Each of them had a real door that a man could go through, a wooden ramp along the wire, for the foxes to run up and down on, and a kennel – something like a clothes chest with airholes – where they slept and stayed in winter and had their young. There were feeding and water-

114

ing dishes attached to the wire in such a way that they could be emptied and cleaned from the outside. The dishes were made of old tin cans, and the ramps and kennels of odds and ends of old lumber. Everything was tidy and ingenious; my father was tirelessly inventive and his favourite book in the world was Robinson Crusoe. He had fitted a tin drum on a wheelbarrow, for bringing water down to the pens. This was my job in summer, when the foxes had to have water twice a day. Between nine and ten o'clock in the morning, and again after supper, I filled the drum at the pump and trundled it down through the barnyard to the pens, where I parked it, and filled my watering can and went along the streets. Laird came too, with his little cream and green gardening can, filled too full and knocking against his legs and slopping water on his canvas shoes. I had the real watering can, my father's, though I could only carry it three-quarters full.

The foxes all had names, which were printed on a tin plate and hung beside their doors. They were not named when they were born, but when they survived the first year's pelting and were added to the breeding stock. Those my father had named were called names like Prince, Bob, Wally and Betty. Those I had named were called Star or Turk, or Maureen or Diana. Laird named one Maud after a hired girl we had when he was little, one Harold after a boy at school, and one Mexico, he did not say why.

Naming them did not make pets out of them, or anything like it. Nobody but my father ever went into the pens, and he had twice had blood-poisoning from bites. When I was bringing them their water they prowled up and down on the paths they had made inside their pens, barking seldom – they saved that for nighttime, when they might get up a chorus of community frenzy – but always watching me, their eyes burning, clear gold, in their pointed, malevolent faces. They were beautiful for their delicate legs and heavy, aristocratic tails and the bright fur sprinkled on dark down their backs – which gave them their name – but especially for their faces, drawn exquisitely sharp in pure hostility, and their golden eyes.

Besides carrying water I helped my father when he cut the long grass, and the lamb's quarter and flowering money-musk, that grew between the pens. He cut with the scythe and I raked into piles. Then he took a pitchfork and threw fresh-cut grass all over the top of the pens, to keep the foxes cooler and shade their coats, which were browned by too much sun. My father did not talk to me unless it was about the job we were doing. In this he was quite different from my mother, who, if she was feeling cheerful, would tell me all sorts of things – the name of a dog she had had when she was a little girl, the names of boys she had gone out with later on when she was grown up, and what certain dresses of hers had looked like – she

115

could not imagine now what had become of them. Whatever thoughts and stories my father had were private, and I was shy of him and would never ask him questions. Nevertheless I worked willingly under his eyes, and with a feeling of pride. One time a feed salesman came down into the pens to talk to him and my father said, "Like to have you meet my new hired man." I turned away and raked furiously, red in the face with pleasure.

"Could of fooled me," said the salesman. "I thought it was only a girl."

After the grass was cut, it seemed suddenly much later in the year. I walked on stubble in the earlier evening, aware of the reddening skies, the entering silences, of fall. When I wheeled the tank out of the gate and put the padlock on, it was almost dark. One night at this time I saw my mother and father standing talking on the little rise of ground we called the gangway, in front of the barn. My father had just come from the meathouse; he had his stiff bloody apron on, and a pail of cut-up meat in his hand.

It was an odd thing to see my mother down at the barn. She did not often come out of the house unless it was to do something – hang out the wash or dig potatoes in the garden. She looked out of place, with her bare lumpy legs, not touched by the sun, her apron still on and damp across the stomach from the supper dishes. Her hair was tied up in a kerchief, wisps of it falling out. She would tie her hair up like this in the morning, saying she did not have time to do it properly, and it would stay tied up all day. It was true, too; she really did not have time. These days our back porch was piled with baskets of peaches and grapes and pears, bought in town, and onions and tomatoes and cucumbers grown at home, all waiting to be made into jelly and jam and preserves, pickles and chili sauce. In the kitchen there was a fire in the stove all day, jars clinked in boiling water, sometimes a cheesecloth bag was strung on a pole between two chairs, straining blue-black grape pulp for jelly. I was given jobs to do and I would sit at the table peeling peaches that had been soaked in the hot water, or cutting up onions, my eyes smarting and streaming. As soon as I was done I ran out of the house, trying to get out of earshot before my mother thought of what she wanted me to do next. I hated the hot dark kitchen in summer, the green blinds and the flypapers, the same old oilcloth table and wavy mirror and bumpy linoleum. My mother was too tired and preoccupied to talk to me, she had no heart to tell about the Normal School Graduation Dance; sweat trickled over her face and she was always counting under her breath, pointing at jars, dumping cups of sugar. It seemed to me that work in the house was endless, dreary and peculiarly depressing; work done out of doors, and in my father's service, was ritualistically important.

I wheeled the tank up to the barn, where it was kept, and I heard my mother saying, "Wait till Laird gets a little bigger, then you'll have a real help."

What my father said I did not hear. I was pleased by the way he stood listening, politely as he would to a salesman or a stranger, but with an air of wanting to get on with his real work. I felt my mother had no business down here and I wanted him to feel the same way. What did she mean about Laird? He was no help to anybody. Where was he now? Swinging himself sick on the swing, going around in circles, or trying to catch caterpillars. He never once stayed with me till I was finished.

"And then I can use her more in the house," I heard my mother say. She had a dead-quiet, regretful way of talking about me that always made me uneasy. "I just get my back turned and she runs off. It's not like I had a girl in the family at all."

I went and sat on a feedbag in the corner of the barn, not wanting to appear when this conversation was going on. My mother, I felt, was not to be trusted. She was kinder than my father and more easily fooled, but you could not depend on her, and the real reasons for the things she said and did were not to be known. She loved me, and she sat up late at night making a dress of the difficult style I wanted, for me to wear when school started, but she was also my enemy. She was always plotting. She was plotting now to get me to stay in the house more, although she knew I hated it (*because* she knew I hated it) and keep me from working for my father. It seemed to me she would do this simply out of perversity, and to try her power. It did not occur to me that she could be lonely, or jealous. No grown-up could be; they were too fortunate. I sat and kicked my heels monotonously against a feedbag, raising dust, and did not come out till she was gone.

At any rate, I did not expect my father to pay any attention to what she said. Who could imagine Laird doing my work – Laird remembering the padlock and cleaning out the watering-dishes with a leaf on the end of a stick, or even wheeling the tank without it tumbling over? It showed how little my mother knew about the way things really were.

I have forgotten to say what the foxes were fed. My father's bloody apron reminded me. They were fed horsemeat. At this time most farmers still kept horses, and when a horse got too old to work, or broke a leg or got down and would not get up, as they sometimes did, the owner would call my father, and he and Henry went out to the farm in the truck. Usually they shot and butchered the horse there, paying the farmer from five to twelve dollars. If they had already too much meat on hand, they would bring the horse back alive, and keep it for a few days or weeks in our stable, until the meat was needed. After the war the farmers were buying tractors and gradually getting rid of horses altogether, so it sometimes happened that we got a good healthy horse, that there was just no use for any more. If this happened in the winter we might keep the horse in our stable till spring, for we had plenty of hay and if there was a lot of snow – and the plow did not always get our road cleared – it was convenient to be able to go to town with a horse and cutter.

The winter I was eleven years old we had two horses in the stable. We did not know what names they had had before, so we called them Mack and Flora. Mack was an old black workhorse, sooty and indifferent. Flora was a sorrel mare, a driver. We took them both out in the cutter. Mack was slow and easy to handle. Flora was given to fits of violent alarm, veering at cars and even at other horses, but we loved her speed and high-stepping, her general air of gallantry and abandon. On Saturdays we went down to the stable and as soon as we opened the door on its cosy, animal-smelling darkness Flora threw up her head, rolled her eyes, whinnied despairingly and pulled herself through a crisis of nerves on the spot. It was not safe to go into her stall; she would kick.

This winter also I began to hear a great deal more on the theme my mother had sounded when she had been talking in front of the barn. I no longer felt safe. It seemed that in the minds of the people around me there was a steady undercurrent of thought, not to be deflected, on this one subject. The word *girl* had formerly seemed to me innocent and unburdened, like the word *child*; now it appeared that it was no such thing. A girl was not, as I had supposed, simply what I was; it was what I had to become. It was a definition, always touched with emphasis, with reproach and disappointment. Also it was a joke on me. Once Laird and I were fighting, and for the first time ever I had to use all my strength against him; even so, he caught and pinned my arm for a moment, really hurting me. Henry saw this, and laughed, saying, "Oh, that there Laird's gonna show you, one of these days!" Laird was getting a lot bigger. But I was getting bigger too.

My grandmother came to stay with us for a few weeks and I heard other things. "Girls don't slam doors like that." "Girls keep their knees together when they sit down." And worse still, when I asked some questions, "That's none of girls' business." I continued to slam the doors and sit as awkwardly as possible, thinking that by such measures I kept myself free.

When spring came, the horses were let out in the barnyard. Mack stood against the barn wall trying to scratch his neck and haunches, but Flora trotted up and down and reared at the fences, clattering her hooves against the rails. Snow drifts dwindled quickly, revealing the hard grey and brown earth, the familiar rise and fall of the ground, plain and bare after the fantastic landscape of winter. There was a great feeling of opening-out, of release. We just wore rubbers now, over our shoes; our feet felt ridiculously light. One Saturday we went out to the stable and found all the doors open, letting in the unaccustomed sunlight and fresh air. Henry was there, just idling around looking at his collection of calendars which were tacked up behind the stalls in a part of the stable my mother had probably never seen.

"Come to say goodbye to your old friend Mack?" Henry said. "Here, you give him a taste of oats." He poured some oats into Laird's cupped hands and Laird went to feed Mack. Mack's teeth were in bad shape. He ate very slowly, patiently shifting the oats around in his mouth, trying to find a stump of a molar to grind it on. "Poor old Mack," said Henry mournfully. "When a horse's teeth's gone, he's gone. That's about the way."

"Are you going to shoot him today?" I said. Mack and Flora had been in the stable so long I had almost forgotten they were going to be shot.

Henry didn't answer me. Instead he started to sing in a high, trembly, mocking-sorrowful voice, *Oh, there's no more work, for poor Uncle Ned, he's gone where the good darkies go.* Mack's thick, blackish tongue worked diligently at Laird's hand. I went out before the song was ended and sat down on the gangway.

I had never seen them shoot a horse, but I knew where it was done. Last summer Laird and I had come upon a horse's entrails before they were buried. We had thought it was a big black snake, coiled up in the sun. That was around in the field that ran up beside the barn. I thought that if we went inside the barn, and found a wide crack or a knothole to look through, we would be able to see them do it. It was not something I wanted to see; just the same, if a thing really happened, it was better to see it, and know.

My father came down from the house, carrying the gun.

"What are you doing here?" he said.

"Nothing."

"Go on up and play around the house."

He sent Laird out of the stable. I said to Laird, "Do you want to see them shoot Mack?" and without waiting for an answer led him around to the front door of the barn, opened it carefully, and went in. "Be quiet or they'll hear us," I said. We could hear Henry and my father talking in the stable, then the heavy, shuffling steps of Mack being backed out of his stall.

In the loft it was cold and dark. Thin, crisscrossed beams of sunlight fell through the cracks. The hay was low. It was a rolling country, hills and hollows, slipping under our feet. About four feet up was a beam going around the walls. We piled hay up in one corner and I boosted Laird up and hoisted myself. The beam was not very wide; we crept along it with our hands flat on the barn walls. There were plenty of knotholes, and I found one that gave me the view I wanted – a corner of the barnyard, the gate, part of the field. Laird did not have a knothole and began to complain.

I showed him a widened crack between two boards. "Be quiet and wait. If they hear you you'll get us in trouble."

My father came in sight carrying the gun. Henry was leading Mack by the halter. He dropped it and took out his cigarette papers and tobacco; he rolled cigarettes for my father and himself. While this was going on Mack nosed around in the old, dead grass along the fence. Then my father opened the gate and they took Mack through. Henry led Mack away from the path to a patch of ground and they talked together, not loud enough for us to hear. Mack again began searching for a mouthful of fresh grass, which was not to be found. My father walked away in a straight line, and stopped short at a distance which seemed to suit him. Henry was walking away from Mack too, but sideways, still negligently holding on to the halter. My father raised the gun and Mack looked up as if he had noticed something and my father shot him.

Mack did not collapse at once but swayed, lurched sideways and fell, first on his side; then he rolled over on his back and, amazingly, kicked his legs for a few seconds in the air. At this Henry laughed, as if Mack had done a trick for him. Laird, who had drawn a long, groaning breath of surprise when the shot was fired, said out loud, "He's not dead." And it seemed to me it might be true. But his legs stopped, he rolled on his side again, his muscles quivered and sank. The two men walked over and looked at him in a businesslike way; they bent down and examined his forehead where the bullet had gone in, and now I saw his blood on the brown grass.

"Now they just skin him and cut him up," I said. "Let's go." My legs were a little shaky and I jumped gratefully down into the hay. "Now you've seen how they shoot a horse," I said in a congratulatory way, as if I had seen it many times before. "Let's see if any barn cat's had kittens in the hay." Laird jumped. He seemed young and obedient again. Suddenly I remembered how, when he was little, I had brought him into the barn and told him to climb the ladder to the top beam. That was in the spring, too, when the hay was low. I had done it out of a need for excitement, a desire for something to happen so that I could tell about it. He was wearing a little bulky brown and white checked coat, made down from one of mine. He went all the way up, just as I told him, and sat down on the top beam with the hay far below him on one side, and the barn floor and some old machinery on the other. Then I ran screaming to my father, "Laird's up on the top beam!" My father came, my mother came, my father went up the ladder talking very quietly and brought Laird down under his arm, at which my mother leaned against the ladder and began to cry. They said to me, "Why weren't you watching him?" but nobody ever knew the truth. Laird did not know enough to tell. But whenever I saw the brown and white checked coat hanging in the closet, or at the bottom of the rag bag, which was where it ended up, I felt a weight in my stomach, the sadness of unexorcized guilt.

I looked at Laird who did not even remember this, and I did not like the look on his thin, winter-pale face. His expression was not frightened or upset, but remote, concentrating. "Listen," I said, in an unusually bright and friendly voice, "you aren't going to tell, are you?"

"No," he said absently.

"Promise."

"Promise," he said. I grabbed the hand behind his back to make sure he was not crossing his fingers. Even so, he might have a nightmare; it might come out that way. I decided I had better work hard to get all thoughts of what he had seen out of his mind – which, it seemed to me, could not hold very many things at a time. I got some money I had saved and that afternoon we went into Jubilee and saw a show, with Judy Canova, at which we both laughed a great deal. After that I thought it would be all right.

Two weeks later I knew they were going to shoot Flora. I knew from the night before, when I heard my mother ask if the hay was holding out all right, and my father said, "Well, after to-morrow there'll just be the cow, and we should be able to put her out to grass in another week." So I knew it was Flora's turn in the morning.

This time I didn't think of watching it. That was something to see just one time. I had not thought about it very often since, but sometimes when I was busy, working at school, or standing in front of the mirror combing my hair and wondering if I would be pretty when I grew up, the whole scene would flash into my mind: I would see the easy, practised way my father raised the gun, and hear Henry laughing when Mack kicked his legs in the air. I did not have any great feeling of horror and opposition, such as a city child might have had; I was too used to seeing the death of animals as a necessity by which we lived. Yet I felt a little ashamed, and there was a new wariness, a sense of holding-off, in my attitude to my father and his work.

It was a fine day, and we were going around the yard picking up tree branches that had been torn off in winter storms. This was something we had been told to do, and also we wanted to use them to make a teepee. We heard Flora whinny, and then my father's voice and Henry's shouting, and we ran down to the barnyard to see what was going on.

The stable door was open. Henry had just brought Flora out, and she had broken away from him. She was running free in the barnyard, from one end to the other. We climbed up on the fence. It was exciting to see her running, whinnying, going up on her hind legs, prancing and threatening like a horse in a Western movie, an unbroken ranch horse, though she was just an old driver, an old sorrel mare. My father and Henry ran after her and tried to grab the dangling halter. They tried to work her into a corner, and they had almost succeeded when she made a run between them, wild-eyed, and disappeared around the corner of the barn. We heard the rails clatter down as she got over the fence, and Henry yelled, "She's into the field now!"

That meant she was in the long L-shaped field that ran up by the house. If she got around the center, heading towards the lane, the gate was open; the truck had been driven into the field this morning. My father shouted to me, because I was on the other side of the fence, nearest the lane, "Go shut the gate!"

I could run very fast. I ran across the garden, past the tree where our swing was hung, and jumped across a ditch into the lane. There was the open gate. She had not got out, I could not see her up on the road; she must have run to the other end of the field. The gate was heavy. I lifted it out of the gravel and carried it across the roadway. I had it half-way across when she came in sight, galloping straight towards me. There was just time to get the chain on. Laird came scrambling through the ditch to help me.

Instead of shutting the gate, I opened it as wide as I could. I did not make any decision to do this, it was just what I did. Flora never slowed down; she galloped straight past me, and Laird jumped up and down, yelling, "Shut it, shut it!" even after it was too late. My father and Henry appeared in the field a moment too late to see what I had done. They only saw Flora heading for the township road. They would think I had not got there in time.

They did not waste any time asking about it. They went back to the barn and got the gun and the knives they used, and put these in the truck; then they turned the truck around and came bouncing up the field toward us. Laird called to them, "Let me go too, let me go too!" and Henry stopped the truck and they took him in. I shut the gate after they were all gone.

I supposed Laird would tell. I wondered what would happen to me. I had never disobeyed my father before, and I could not understand why I had done it. Flora would not really get away. They would catch up with her in the truck. Or if they did not catch her this morning somebody would see her and telephone us this afternoon or tomorrow. There was no wild country here for her to run to, only farms. What was more, my father had paid for her, we needed the meat to feed the foxes, we needed the foxes to make our living. All I had done was make more work for my father who worked hard enough already. And when my father found out about it he was not going to trust me any more; he would know that I was not entirely on his side. I was on Flora's side, and that made me no use to anybody, not even to her. Just the same, I did not regret it; when she came running at me and I held the gate open, that was the only thing I could do.

I went back to the house, and my mother said, "What's all the commotion?" I told her that Flora had kicked down the fence and got away. "Your poor father," she said, "now he'll have to go chasing over the countryside. Well, there isn't any use planning dinner before one." She put up the ironing board. I wanted to tell her, but thought better of it and went upstairs and sat on my bed.

Lately I had been trying to make my part of the room fancy, spreading the bed with old lace curtains, and fixing myself a dressing-table with some leftovers of cretonne for a skirt. I planned to put up some kind of barricade between my bed and Laird's, to keep my section separate from his. In the sunlight, the lace curtains were just dusty rags. We did not sing at night any more. One night when I was singing Laird said, "You sound silly," and I went right on but the next night I did not start. There was not so much need to anyway, we were no longer afraid. We knew it was just old furniture over there, old jumble and confusion. We did not keep to the rules. I still stayed awake after Laird was asleep and told myself stories, but even in these stories something different was happening, mysterious alterations took place. A story might start off in the old way, with a spectacular danger, a fire or wild animals, and for a while I might rescue people; then things would change around, and instead, somebody would be rescuing me. It might be a boy from our class at school, or even Mr. Campbell, our teacher, who tickled girls under the arms. And at this point the story concerned itself at great length with what I looked like – how long my hair was, and what kind of dress I had on; by the time I had these details worked out the real excitement of the story was lost.

It was later than one o'clock when the truck came back. The tarpaulin was over the back, which meant there was meat in it. My mother had to heat dinner up all over again. Henry and my father had changed from their bloody overalls into ordinary working overalls in the barn, and they washed their arms and necks and faces at the sink, and splashed water on their hair and combed it. Laird lifted his arm to show off a streak of blood. "We shot old Flora," he said, "and cut her up in fifty pieces."

"Well I don't want to hear about it," my mother said. "And don't come to my table like that."

My father made him go and wash the blood off.

We sat down and my father said grace and Henry pasted his chewing-gum on the end of his fork, the way he always did; when he took it off he would have us admire the pattern. We began to pass the bowls of steaming, overcooked vegetables. Laird looked across the table at me and said proudly, distinctly, "Anyway it was her fault Flora got away."

"What?" my father said.

"She could of shut the gate and she didn't. She just open' it up and Flora run out."

"Is that right?" my father said.

Everybody at the table was looking at me. I nodded, swallowing food with great difficulty. To my shame, tears flooded my eyes.

My father made a curt sound of disgust. "What did you do that for?"

I did not answer. I put down my fork and waited to be sent from the table, still not looking up.

But this did not happen. For some time nobody said anything, then Laird said matter-of-factly, "She's crying."

"Never mind," my father said. He spoke with resignation, even good humour, the words which absolved and dismissed me for good. "She's only a girl," he said.

I didn't protest that, even in my heart. Maybe it was true.

"An Ounce of Cure" is a story I found ready-made, the only story I ever found like that. A friend told me an anecdote; there it was. Of course I used a lot of my own memories, my own teenage self, my own home-town. One thing in it I think is interesting, now that I look back on it: when the girl's circumstances become hopelessly messy, when nothing is going to go right for her, she gets out of it by looking at the way things happen – by changing from a participant into an observer. This is what I used to do myself, it is what a writer does; I think it may be one of the things that make a writer in the first place. When I started to write the dreadful things I did write when I was about fifteen, I made the glorious leap from being a victim of my own ineptness and self-conscious miseries to being a godlike arranger of patterns and destinies, even if they were all in my head; I have never leapt back.

"Boys and Girls" is a very different sort of story. I wrote it rather too purposefully perhaps, to show something, to show what happens to girls and women, then found I had to write about something that happens to boys too. It is one of my favourite stories but not at all one of the most successful; there is some disjointedness about it I have not been able to mend.

This is what I was trying to say: Up until the time she is twelve or thirteen years old a girl feels free, able to think of her future in terms of action, to dream of adventure, heroism, power. With the full realization of her sexual nature a change is forced on her, partly from within, mostly from without. (This was true in my generation and, it goes without saying, in previous generations; I have hopes it is much less true today.) She understands that, for her, participation in the world of action is not impossible, but does hold great dangers, the greatest danger being that it will make her not splendid, but grotesque. She must go back inside the house, inside herself, wait, dream of being beautiful rather than courageous. The full human powers she thought she had are seen to be illusory. She cannot make herself; a definition of herself, as a woman, is waiting for her. Unless she has fantastic strength or stubbornness she is going to accept that definition or at least compromise with it. This is painful; something crippling is happening to her.

But this very denial of action, of full responsibility to the girl, gives her a kind of freedom the young male in most societies must give up. To be accepted, to be fully male, he cannot criticize, he must sometimes participate in, whatever bloodstained practices his society believes necessary to itself; that, or become a revolutionary. In this story the family is economically dependent on the systematic killing of animals; if the boy wants into his father's world, he must learn to take part in this. It is the girl, already half shut-out, becoming mutinous, confused, critical, who is permitted the gesture of refusal. She is permitted it because she is "only a girl".

That is how the story ends. What it says is something like this: it is permissible to have fine feelings, impractical sympathies, if you are a girl, because what you say or do does not finally count. On the other hand, if you are a boy, certain feelings are not permissible at all. So taking on these roles, whichever you get, is a hard and damaging thing.

Perhaps that is a big chunk of message for a slight story. Most readers seem to think the story is a nostalgia-piece and there are things in it that come from my own childhood. I did want very much to get the "feel" of this life, of the economically isolated family, their self-contained world. I wanted to get the sense of childhood horrors, imaginary horrors which are a premonition of the real ones. When I read this story over I have a feeling of failure and despair; I feel that there's so much more that should be there, a whole world really, and I have strained it out into this little story and cannot tell if I got what matters. With "An Ounce of Cure", on the other hand, I got everything down just as I meant to, there's no shadowy world unrealized behind it, so I'm satisfied, but I don't like it half as well.

It seems to me this is what writing is, when it's real – a straining of something immense and varied, a whole dense vision of the world, into whatever confines the writer has learned to make for it, and this process, unless you are Shakespeare or Tolstoy, must be accompanied by regret; fortunately it is often accompanied by gleeful satisfactions as well.

ALICE MUNRO

BIBLIOGRAPHY

Dance of the Happy Shades: Stories by Alice Munro. (Foreword by Hugh Garner.) Toronto: The Ryerson Press, 1968.

Shirley Faessler

Shirley Faessler was born of immigrant Jewish parents, on Walnut or Chestnut Street in Toronto. She attended King Edward School where she did not bring herself into notice for scholarship. After a repeat year in Grade 8 under Miss Chalmers, she was discharged, sent packing — with the comment from the principal of the school to the teacher: "To keep her a third year would be pointless, she's been in your class long enough to teach."

Grade 8 (failed) is the extent of her academic education.

—S.F.

A Basket of Apples

This morning Pa had his operation. He said I was not to come for at least two or three days, but I slipped in anyway and took a look at him. He was asleep, and I was there only a minute before I was hustled out by a nurse.

"He looks terrible, nurse. Is he all right?"

She said he was fine. The operation was successful, there were no secondaries, instead of a bowel he would have a colostomy, and with care should last another –

Colostomy. The word has set up such a drumming in my ears that I can't be sure now whether she said another few years or another five years. Let's say she said five years. If I go home and report this to Ma she'll fall down in a dead faint. She doesn't even know he's had an operation. She thinks he's in the hospital for a rest, a checkup. Nor did we know – my brother, my sister, and I – that he'd been having a series of X-rays.

"It looks like an obstruction in the lower bowel," he told us privately, "and I'll have to go in the hospital for a few days to find out what it's all about. Don't say anything to Ma."

"I have to go in the hospital," he announced to Ma the morning he was going in.

She screamed.

"Just for a little rest, a checkup," he went on, patient with her for once.

He's always hollering at her. He scolds her for a meal that isn't to his taste, finds fault with her housekeeping, gives her hell because her hair isn't combed in the morning and sends her back to the bedroom to tidy herself.

But Ma loves the old man. "Sooner a harsh word from Pa than a kind one from anyone else," she says.

"You're not to come and see me, you hear?" he cautioned her the morning he left for the hospital. "I'll phone you when I'm coming out."

I don't want to make out that my pa's a beast. He's not. True, he never speaks an endearing word to her, never praises her. He loses patience with her, flies off the handle and shouts. But Ma's content. Poor man works like a horse, she says, and what pleasures does he have. "So he hollers at me once in a while, I don't mind. God give him the strength to keep hollering at me, I won't repine."

Night after night he joins his buddies in the back room of an ice-cream parlor on Augusta Avenue for a glass of wine, a game of klaber-jass, pinochle, dominoes: she's happy he's enjoying himself. She blesses him on his way out. "God keep you in good health and return you in good health."

But when he is home of an evening reading the newspaper and comes across an item that engages his interest, he lets her in on it too. He shows her a picture of the Dionne quintuplets and explains exactly what happened out there in Callander, Ontario. This is a golden moment for her – she and Pa sitting over a newspaper discussing world events. Another time he shows her a picture of the Irish Sweepstakes winner. He won a hundred and fifty thousand, he tells her. She's entranced. *Mmm-mm-mm!* What she couldn't do with that money. They'd fix up the bathroom, paint the kitchen, clean out the backyard. *Mmm-mm-mm!* Pa says if we had that kind of money we could afford to put a match to a hundred-dollar bill, set fire to the house and buy a new one. She laughs at his wit. He's so clever, Pa. Christmas morning King George VI is speaking on the radio. She's rattling around in the kitchen, Pa calls her to come and hear the King of England. She doesn't understand a word of English, but pulls up a chair and sits listening. "He stutters," says Pa. This she won't believe. A king? Stutters? But if Pa says so it must be true. She bends an ear to the radio. Next day she has something to report to Mrs. Oxenberg, our next-door neighbour.

I speak of Pa's impatience with her; I get impatient with her too. I'm always at her about one thing and another, chiefly about the weight she's putting on. Why doesn't she cut down on the bread, does she have to drink twenty glasses of tea a day? No wonder her feet are sore, carrying all that weight. (My ma's a short woman a little over five feet and weighs almost two hundred pounds.) "Go ahead, keep getting fatter," I tell her. "The way you're going you'll never be able to get into a decent dress again."

But it's Pa who finds a dress to fit her, a Martha Washington Cotton size 52, which but for the length is perfect for her. He finds a shoe she can wear, Romeo Slippers with elasticized sides. And it's Pa who gets her to soak her feet, then sits with them in his lap scraping away with a razor blade at the callouses and corns.

Ma is my father's second wife, and our step-mother. My father, now sixty-three, was widowed thirty years ago. My sister was six at the time, I was five, and my brother was four when our mother died giving birth to a fourth child who lived only a few days. We were shunted around from one family to another who took us in out of compassion, till finally my father went to a marriage broker and put his case before him. He wanted a woman to make a home for his three orphans. An honest woman with a

129

good heart, these were the two and only requirements. The marriage broker consulted his lists and said he thought he had two or three people who might fill the bill. Specifically, he had in mind a young woman from Russia, thirty years old, who was working without pay for relatives who had brought her over. She wasn't exactly an educated woman; in fact, she couldn't even read or write. As for honesty and heart, this he could vouch for. She was an orphan herself and as a child had been brought up in servitude.

Of the three women the marriage broker trotted out for him, my father chose Ma, and shortly afterward they were married.

A colostomy. So it is cancer . . .

As of the second day Pa was in hospital I had taken to dropping in on him on my way home from work. "Nothing yet," he kept saying, "maybe tomorrow they'll find out."

After each of these visits, four in all, I reported to Ma that I had seen Pa. "He looks fine. Best thing in the world for him, a rest in the hospital."

"Pa's not lonesome for me?" she asked me once, and laughing, turned her head aside to hide her foolishness from me.

Yesterday Pa said to me, "It looks a little more serious than I thought. I have to have an operation tomorrow. Don't say anything to Ma. And don't come here for at least two or three days."

I take my time getting home. I'm not too anxious to face Ma – grinning like a monkey and lying to her the way I have been doing the last four days. I step into a hospital telephone booth to call my married sister. She moans. "What are you going to say to Ma?" she asks.

I get home about half past six, and Ma's in the kitchen making a special treat for supper. A recipe given her by a neighbour and which she's recently put in her culinary inventory – pieces of cauliflower dipped in batter and fried in butter.

"I'm not hungry, Ma. I had something in the hospital cafeteria." (We speak in Yiddish; as I mentioned before, Ma can't speak English.)

She continues scraping away at the cauliflower stuck in the bottom of the pan. (Anything she puts in a pan sticks.) "You saw Pa?" she asks without looking up. Suddenly she thrusts the pan aside. "The devil take it, I put in too much flour." She makes a pot of tea, and we sit at the kitchen table drinking it. To keep from facing her I drink mine leafing through a magazine. I can hear her sipping hers through a cube of sugar in her mouth. I can feel her eyes on me. Why doesn't she ask me, How's Pa? Why doesn't she speak? She never stops questioning me when I come from hospital, drives me crazy with the same questions again and again.

I keep turning pages, she's still sucking away at that cube of sugar – a maddening habit of hers. I looked up. Of course her eyes are fixed on me, probing, searching.

I lash out at her. "Why are you looking at me like that!"

Without answer she takes her tea and dashes it in the sink. She spits the cube of sugar from her mouth. (Thank God for that; she generally puts it back in the sugar bowl.) She resumes her place, puts her hands in her lap, and starts twirling her thumbs. No one in the world can twirl his thumbs as fast as Ma. When she gets them going they look like miniature windmills whirring around.

"She asks me why I'm looking at her like that," she says addressing herself to the twirling thumbs in her lap. "I'm looking at her like that because I'm trying to read the expression in her face. She tells me Pa's fine, but my heart tells me different."

Suddenly she looks up, and thrusting her head forward, splays her hands out flat on the table. She has a dark-complexioned strong face, masculine almost, and eyes so black the pupil is indistinguishable from the iris.

"Do you know who Pa is!" she says. "Do you know who's lying in the hospital? I'll tell you who. The captain of our ship is lying in the hospital. The emperor of our domain. If the captain goes down, the ship goes with him. If the emperor leaves his throne, we can say goodbye to our domain. That's who's lying in the hospital. Now ask me why do I look at you like that."

She breaks my heart. I want to put my arms around her, but I can't do it. We're not a demonstrative family, we never kiss, we seldom show affection. We're always hollering at each other. Less than a month ago I hollered at Pa. He had taken to dosing himself. He was forever mixing something in a glass, and I became irritated at the powders, pills and potions lying around in every corner of the house like mouse droppings.

"You're getting to be a hypochondriac!" I hollered at him, not knowing what trouble he was in.

I reach out and put my hand over hers. "I wouldn't lie to you, Ma. Pa's fine, honest to God."

She holds her hand still a few seconds, then eases it from under and puts it over mine. I can feel the weight of her hand pinioning mine to the table, and we sit a moment in an unaccustomed gesture of tenderness, with locked hands.

"You know I had a dream about Pa last night?" she says. "I dreamt he came home with a basket of apples. I think that's a good dream?"

* * *

Ma's immigration to Canada had been sponsored by her Uncle Yankev. Yankev at the time he sent for his niece was in his mid-forties and had been settled a number of years in Toronto with his wife, Danyeh, and their six children. They made an odd pair, Yankev and Danyeh. He was a tall two-hundred-and-fifty-pound handsome man, and Danyeh, whom he detested, was a lackluster little woman with a pockmarked face, maybe weighing ninety pounds. Yankev was constantly abusing her. Old Devil, he called her to her face and in the presence of company.

Ma stayed three years with Yankev and his family, working like a skivvy for them and without pay. Why would Yankev pay his niece like a common servant? She was one of the family, she sat at table with them and ate as much as she wanted. She had a bed and even a room to herself, which she'd never had before. When Yankev took his family for a ride in the car to Sunnyside, she was included. When he bought ice-cream cones, he bought for all.

She came to Pa without a dime in her pocket.

Ma has a slew of relatives, most of them émigrés from a remote little village somewhere in the depths of Russia. They're a crude lot, loud-mouthed and coarse and my father had no use for any of them. The Russian Hordes, he called them. He was never rude; anytime they came around to visit he simply made himself scarce.

One night I remember in particular; I must have been about seven. Ma was washing up after supper and Pa was reading a newspaper when Yankev arrived, with Danyeh trailing him. Pa folded his paper, excused himself, and was gone. The minute Pa was gone Yankev went to the stove and lifted the lids from the two pots. Just as he thought – *mamaliga* in one pot, in the other one beans, and in the frying pan a piece of meat their cat would turn its nose up at. He sat himself in the rocking chair he had given Ma as a wedding present, and rocking, proceeded to lecture her. He had warned her against the marriage, but if she was satisfied, he was content. One question and that's all. How had she bettered her lot? True, she was no longer an old maid. True, she was now mistress of her own home. He looked around and snorted. A hovel. "*And* three snot-nose kids," he said, pointing to us.

Danyeh, hunched over in a kitchen chair, her feet barely reaching the floor, said something to him in Russian, cautioning him, I think. He told her to shut up, and in Yiddish continued his tirade against Ma. He had one word to say to her. To *watch* herself. Against his advice she had married this no-good Rumanian twister, this murderer. The story of how he had kept his first wife pregnant all the time was now well known. Also well known was the story of how she had died in her ninth month with a

132

fourth child. Over an ironing board. Ironing his shirts while he was out playing cards with his Rumanian cronies and drinking wine. He had buried one wife, and now was after burying a second. So Ma had better *watch* herself, that's all.

Ma left her dishwashing and with dripping wet hands took hold of a chair and seated herself facing Yankev. She begged him not to say another word. "Not another word, Uncle Yankev, I beg you. Till the day I die I'll be grateful to you for bringing me over. I don't know how much money you laid out for my passage, but I tried my best to make up for it in the three years I stayed with you, by helping you in the house. But maybe I'm still in your debt? Is this what gives you the right to talk against my husband?"

Yankev, rocking, turned up his eyes and groaned. "*You* speak to her," he said to Danyeh. "It's impossible for a *human being* to get through to her."

Danyeh knew better than to open her mouth.

"Uncle Yankev," Ma continued, "every word you speak against my husband is like a knife stab in my heart." She leaned forward, thumbs whirring away. "*Mamaliga*? Beans? A piece of meat your cat wouldn't eat? A crust of *bread* at his board, and I will thank God every day of my life that he chose me from the other two the *shadchan* showed him."

In the beginning my father gave her a hard time. I remember his bursts of temper at her rough ways in the kitchen. She never opened a kitchen drawer without wrestling it – wrenching it open, slamming it shut. She never put a kettle on the stove without its running over at the boil. A pot never came to stove without its lid being inverted, and this for some reason maddened him. He'd right the lid, sometimes scalding his fingers – and all hell would break loose. We never sat down to a set or laid table. As she had been used to doing, so she continued; slamming a pot down on the table, scattering a handful of cutlery, dealing out assorted-size plates. More than once, with one swipe of his hand my father would send the plates crashing to the floor, and stalk out. She'd sit a minute looking at our faces, one by one, then start twirling her thumbs and talking to herself. What had she done now?

"Eat!" she'd admonish us, and leaving table would go to the mirror over the kitchen sink and ask herself face to face, "What did I do now?" She would examine her face profile and front and then sit down to eat. After, she'd gather up the dishes, dump them in the sink, and running water over them, would study herself in the mirror. "He'll be better," she'd tell herself, smiling. "He'll be soft as butter when he comes home. You'll see," she'd promise her image in the mirror.

Later in life, mellowed by the years perhaps (or just plain defeated – there was no changing her), he became more tolerant of her ways and was kinder to her. When it became difficult for her to get around because of her poor feet, he did her marketing. He attended to her feet, bought her the Martha Washingtons, the Romeo slippers, and on a summer's evening on his way home from work, a brick of ice cream. She was very fond of it.

Three years ago he began promoting a plan, a plan to give Ma some pleasure. (This was during Exhibition time.) "You know," he said to me, "it would be very nice if Ma could see the fireworks at the Exhibition. She's never seen anything like that in her life. Why don't you take her?"

The idea of Ma going to the Ex for the fireworks was so preposterous, it made me laugh. She never went anywhere.

"Don't laugh," he said. "It wouldn't hurt you to give her a little pleasure once in a while."

He was quite keen that she should go, and the following year he canvassed the idea again. He put money on the table for taxi and grandstand seats. "Take her," he said.

"Why don't you take her?" I said. "She'll enjoy it more going with you."

"Me? What will I do at the Exhibition?"

As children, we were terrified of Pa's temper. Once in a while he'd belt us around, and we were scared that he might take the strap to Ma too. But before long we came to know that she was the only one of us not scared of Pa when he got mad. Not even from the beginning when he used to let fly at her was she intimidated by him, not in the least, and in later years was even capable of getting her own back by taking a little dig at him now and then about the "aristocracy" – as she called my father's Rumanian connections.

Aside from his buddies in the back room of the ice-cream parlour on Augusta Avenue, my father also kept in touch with his Rumanian compatriots (all of whom had prospered), and would once in a while go to them for an evening. We were never invited, nor did they come to us. This may have been my father's doing, I do not know. I expect he was ashamed of his circumstances, possibly of Ma, and certainly of how we lived.

Once in a blue moon during Rosh Hashanah or Yom Kippur after shul, they would unexpectedly drop in on us. One time a group of four came to the house, and I remember Pa darting around like a gadfly, collecting glasses, wiping them, and pouring a glass of wine he'd made himself. Ma shook hands all around, then went to the kitchen to cut some slices of her honey cake, scraping off the burnt part. I was summoned to take the plate in to "Pa's gentle folk." Pretending to be busy, she rattled around the kitchen a few seconds, then seated herself in the partially open door, inspecting them. Not till they were leaving did she come out again, to wish them a good year.

The minute they were gone, my father turned on her. "Russian peasant! Tartar savage, you! Sitting there with your eyes popping out. Do you think they couldn't see you?"

"What's the matter? Even a cat may look at a king?" she said blandly.

"Why didn't you come out instead of sitting there like a caged animal?"

"Because I didn't want to shame you," she said, twirling her thumbs and swaying back and forth in the chair Yankev had given her as a wedding present.

My father busied himself clearing table, and after a while he softened. But she wasn't through with him yet. "Which one was Falik's wife?" she asked in seeming innocence. "The one with the beard?"

This drew his fire again. "No!" he shouted.

"Oh, the other one. The pale one with the hump on her back," she said wickedly.

So . . . notwithstanding the good dream Ma had of Pa coming home with a basket of apples, she never saw him again. He died six days after the operation.

It was a harrowing six days, dreadful. As Pa got weaker, the more disputatious we became – my brother, my sister, and I – arguing and snapping at each other outside his door, the point of contention being should Ma be told or not.

Nurse Brown, the special we'd put on duty, came out once to hush us. "You're not helping him by arguing like this. He can hear you."

"Is he conscious, nurse?"

"Of course he's conscious."

"Is there any hope?"

"There's always hope," she said. "I've been on cases like this before, and I've seen them rally."

We went our separate ways, clinging to the thread of hope she'd given us. The fifth day after the operation I had a call from Nurse Brown: "Your father wants to see you."

Nurse Brown left the room when I arrived, and my father motioned me to undo the zipper of his oxygen tent. "Ma's a good woman," he said, his voice so weak I had to lean close to hear him. "You'll look after her? Don't put her aside. Don't forget about her –"

135

"What are you talking about!" I said shrilly, then lowered my voice to a whisper. "The doctor told me you're getting better. Honest to God, Pa, I wouldn't lie to you," I whispered.

He went on as if I hadn't spoken. "Even a servant if you had her for thirty years, you wouldn't put aside because you don't need her any-more –"

"Wait a minute," I said, and went to the corridor to fetch Nurse Brown. "Nurse Brown, will you tell my father what you told me yesterday. You remember? About being on cases like this before, and you've seen them rally. Will you tell that to my father, please. He talks as if he's –"

I ran from the room and stood outside the door, bawling. Nurse Brown opened the door a crack. "*Ssh!* You'd better go now; I'll call you if there's any change."

At five the next morning, my brother telephoned from hospital. "You'd better get down here," he said. "I think the old man's checking out. I've already phoned Gertie."

My sister and I arrived at the hospital within seconds of each other. My brother was just emerging from Pa's room. In the gesture of a baseball umpire he jerked a thumb over his shoulder, signifying OUT.

"Is he dead?" we asked our brother.

"Just this minute," he replied.

Like three dummies we paced the dimly-lit corridor, not speaking to each other. In the end we were obliged to speak; we had to come to a decision about how to proceed next.

We taxied to the synagogue of which Pa was a member, and roused the shamus. "As soon as it's light I'll get the rabbi," he said. "He'll attend to everything. Meantime go home."

In silence we walked slowly home. Dawn was just breaking, and Ma, a habitually early riser, was bound to be up now and in the kitchen. Quietly we let ourselves in and passed through the hall leading to the kitchen. We were granted an unexpected respite; Ma was not yet up. We waited ten minutes for her, fifteen – an agonizing wait. We decided one of us had better go and wake her; what was the sense in prolonging it? The next minute we changed our minds. To awaken her with such tidings would be inhuman, a brutal thing to do.

"Let's stop whispering," my sister whispered. "Let's talk in normal tones, do something, make a noise, she'll hear us and come out."

In an excess of activity we busied ourselves. My sister put the kettle on with a clatter; I took teaspoons from the drawer, clacking them like castanets. She was bound to hear, their bedroom was on the same floor at the front of the house – but five minutes elapsed and not a sound from the room.

"Go and see," my sister said, and I went and opened the door to that untidy bedroom Pa used to rail against.

Ma, her black eyes circled and her hair in disarray, was sitting up in bed. At the sight of me she flopped back and pulled the feather tick over her head. I approached the bed and took the covers from her face. "Ma –"

She sat up. "You are guests in my house now?"

For the moment I didn't understand. I didn't know the meaning of her words. But the next minute the meaning of them was clear – with Pa dead, the link was broken. The bond, the tie that held us together. We were no longer her children. We were now guests in her house.

"When did Pa die?" she asked.

"How did you know?"

"My heart told me."

Barefooted, she followed me to the kitchen. My sister gave her a glass of tea, and we stood like mutes, watching her sipping it through a cube of sugar.

"You were all there when Pa died?"

"Just me, Ma," my brother said.

She nodded. "His kaddish. Good."

I took a chair beside her, and for once without constraint or self-consciousness, put my arm around her and kissed her on the cheek.

"Ma, the last words Pa spoke were about you. He said you were a good woman. 'Ma's a good woman,' that's what he said to me."

She put her tea down and looked me in the face. "Pa said that? He said I was a good woman?" She clasped her hands. "May the light shine on him in paradise," she said, and wept silently, putting her head down to hide her tears.

Eight o'clock the rabbi telephoned. Pa was now at the funeral parlor on College near Augusta, and the funeral was to be at eleven o'clock. Ma went to ready herself, and in a few minutes called me to come and zip up her black crepe, the dress Pa had bought her six years ago for the Applebaum wedding.

The Applebaums, neighbours, had invited Ma and Pa to the wedding of their daughter, Lily. Right away Pa declared he wouldn't go. Ma kept coaxing. How would it look? It would be construed as unfriendly, un-neighbourly. A few days before the wedding he gave in, and Ma began scratching through her wardrobe for something suitable to wear. Nothing she exhibited pleased him. He went downtown and came back with the black crepe and an outsize corset.

I dressed her for the wedding, combed her hair, and put some powder on her face. Pa became impatient; he had already called a cab. What was I doing? Getting her ready for a beauty contest? The taxi came, and as Pa held her coat he said to me in English, "You know, Ma's not a bad-looking woman?"

For weeks she talked about the good time she'd had at the Applebaum wedding, but chiefly about how Pa had attended her. Not for a minute had he left her side. Two hundred people at the wedding and not one woman among them had the attention from her husband that she had had from Pa. "Pa's a gentleman," she said to me, proud as proud.

Word of Pa's death got around quickly, and by nine in the morning people began trickling in. First arrivals were Yankev and Danyeh. Yankev, now in his seventies and white-haired, was still straight and handsome. The same Yankev except for the white hair and an asthmatic condition causing him to wheeze and gasp for breath. Danyeh was wizened and bent over, her hands hanging almost to her knees. They approached Ma, Danyeh trailing Yankev. Yankev held out a hand and with the other one thumped his chest, signifying he was too congested to speak. Danyeh gave her bony hand to Ma and muttered a condolence.

From then on there was a steady influx of people. Here was Chaim the schnorrer! We hadn't seen him in years. Chaim the schnorrer, stinking of fish and in leg wrappings as always, instead of socks. Rich as Croesus he was said to be, a fish-peddling miser who lived on soda crackers and milk and kept his money in his leg wrappings. Yankev, a minute ago too congested for speech, found words for Chaim. "How much money have you got in those *gutkess*? The truth, Chaim!"

Ma shook hands with all, acknowledged their sympathy, and to some she spoke a few words. I observed the Widow Spector, a gossip and trouble-maker, sidling through the crowd and easing her way toward Ma. "The Post" she was called by people on the street. No one had the time of day for her; even Ma used to hide from her.

I groaned at the sight of her. As if Ma didn't have enough to contend with. But No! here was Ma welcoming the Widow Spector, holding hand out to her. "Give me your hand, Mrs. Spector. Shake hands, we're partners now. Now I know the taste, I'm a widow too." Ma patted the chair beside her. "Sit down partner. Sit down."

At a quarter to eleven the house was clear of people. "Is it time?" Ma asked, and we answered, Yes, it was time to go. We were afraid this would be the breaking point for her, but she went calmly to the bedroom and took her coat from the peg on the door and came to the kitchen with it, requesting that it be brushed off.

The small funeral parlor was jammed to the doors, every seat taken but for four up front left vacant for us. On a trestle table directly in front of our seating was the coffin. A pine box draped in a black cloth, and in its center a white Star of David.

Ma left her place, approached the coffin, and as she stood before it with clasped hands I noticed the uneven hemline of her coat, hiked up in back by that mound of flesh on her shoulders. I observed that her lisle stockings were twisted at the ankles, and was embarrassed for her.

She stood silently a moment, then began to speak. She called him her dove, her comrade, her friend.

"Life is a dream," she said. "You were my treasure. You were the light of my eyes. I thought to live my days out with you – and look what it has come to." (She swayed slightly, the black shawl slipping from her head – and I observed that could have done with a brushing too.) "If ever I offended you or caused you even a twinge of discomfort, forgive me for it. As your wife I lived like a queen. Look at me now. I'm nothing. You were my jewel, my crown. With you at its head my house was a palace. I return now to a hovel. Forgive me for everything, my dove. Forgive me."

("Russian peasant," Pa used to say to her in anger, "Tartar savage." If he could see her now as she stood before his bier mourning him. Mourning him like Hecuba mourning Priam and the fall of Troy. And I a minute ago was ashamed of her hiked-up coat, her twisted stockings and dusty shawl.)

People were weeping; Ma resumed her place dry-eyed, and the rabbi began the service.

It is now a year since Pa died, and as he had enjoined me to do, I am looking after Ma. I have not put her aside. I get cross and holler at her as I always have done, but she allows for my testiness and does not hold it against me. I'm a spinster, an old maid now approaching my thirty-seventh year, and she pities me for it. I get bored telling her again and again that Pa's last words were Ma's a good woman, and sometimes wish I'd never mentioned it. She cries a lot, and I get impatient with her tears. But I'm good to her.

This afternoon I called Moodey's, booked two seats for the grand-stand, and tonight I'm taking her to the Ex and she'll see the fireworks.

AUTHOR'S COMMENTARY

"A Basket of Apples" was an attempt to re-create in short story form the emotional impact on me of my father's death. It was written at a remove of many years after the event and instead of telling of my reaction to his death, which was my intention, it tells of my stepmother's reaction. Instead of it being a commemorative remembrance of my father, which was my intention, it turned out to be a memorial to my stepmother.

At the finish of the story I was reminded (because of the turn it had taken) of a three frame cartoon I had seen in *Writer's Digest*. First frame the writer sits at his typewriter, typing away. Second frame typescript is flying, sheets piling up. Third frame writer slumps in his chair, appalled. The cut line reads: "My God, what have I done! I've killed my hero –"

I come of poor people. I grew up in a poor neighbourhood on a poor street. When I was nine or ten I discovered in myself a talent for mimicry, and became the show-off I was. I clowned, mimed, and mimicked in the school yard, winning for myself a following. I played the fool, the jester at the houses of girl-friends, getting the parents to laugh. I was generous with my talent, I never accepted an invitation to a meal without singing for my supper. Unasked, I performed for strangers. It was only my family who were denied the benefit of my talent. At home I was spleeny, glum.

I married young and had a child within a year of my marriage. I took pleasure in my child, but domestic routine on the whole I found a bore, tiresome. Instead of making my bed, I read a book. Books since childhood have been a passion with me. I used to take books from the library and start one on the way home, reading it in the street.

My first attempt to break into print was through the medium of the love pulps. I bought a stack of magazines and read them through, story after story, studying the formula, the technique. I applied my mind to the course of true love, personal love, intimate love, exciting love, unrestrained love, unrequited love – then went to work. In eight days I had a story running to 25,000 words (which would be a record even for Simenon), and ready to be shipped. Its title *Be a Good Girl*. I sent it air mail. It made a heavy parcel and cost a lot to dispatch by air – but I was eager for it to reach the market with a minimum of delay. I began another story right away, this one titled *I Married an Artist*, which I thought (considering the literary genre) was gorgeous. Both came back. Which was discouraging, I was so sure they'd be bought.

I returned to my books. There was more pleasure in reading than writing. Especially if I was not going to be published.

140

For years now – at parties, suppers, and dinners – I have been telling stories. Stories of my stepmother, my stepmother's relatives (whom my father called the Russian Hordes), stories of my sister, my brother, myself. I established a reputation as a raconteur and it was flattering to be sought after, to be coaxed to tell again the story of Mrs. Baskin's love affair with Katz the fishmonger; the story of the two prostitutes who rented a room with the Oxenbergs next door to us, claiming they were office workers; the story of Mrs. Spinner who, while her husband (an amputee) was still in hospital, had gambled away at rake-off five card stud poker the money he had put aside for an artificial limb.

Singing for my supper was a habit, a carry over from childhood.

When it came time to write my stories I knew that the telling of a story has no relation whatever with the writing of a story. It has taken me a long time to evolve a style which enables me to express in writing what I want to say; and I am still learning. There is not a short story writer of any account whose work I have not read, studied, and tried to analyze. The late Flannery O'Connor once said, "asking me to talk about story-writing is just like asking a fish to lecture on swimming. The more stories I write, the more mysterious I find the process and the less I find myself capable of analyzing it."

I know there is no greater pleasure for me than a piece of work that's going well. Conversely, nothing can sink me quicker than a piece of work that is not going well.

At present I am revising two completed short stories, and I am also at work on a novel. A collection of my stories, with the related theme of my background and childhood, will be published as soon as I am able to complete enough of them. I am a slow worker, and it worries me some-times when I think of the backlog of stories I have in my head, waiting to be written. But I find I can't work any other way except by reworking, rewriting, revising – and rereading! Frank O'Connor says, in his book *The Lonely Voice*, "the writer should never forget that he is also a reader, though a prejudiced one, and if he cannot read his own work a dozen times he can scarcely expect a reader to look at it twice." So far, in this respect, and in all others pertaining to writing, I have been lucky.

SHIRLEY FAESSLER

BIBLIOGRAPHY

Shirley Faessler has had the honour of having all the stories she has so far written published in *The Atlantic Monthly*. One of her stories, "Maybe Later It Will Come Back To My Mind", was reprinted in Robert Weaver's *Canadian Short Stories* (Second Series, Toronto: Oxford University Press, 1968). Her first collection of stories is eagerly awaited.

Alden Nowlan

Alden Nowlan was born near Windsor, Nova Scotia, on January 25th 1933. He left school early and did a variety of jobs mostly manual, menial, or both, before becoming a newspaper reporter at the age of nineteen. He was formerly night news editor of *The Telegraph-Journal*, Saint John, and is currently writer in residence at the University of New Brunswick Fredericton, N.B. (Earlier jobs included pulp cutter, sawmill worker, and manager of a country and western orchestra.)

In 1967 Alden Nowlan was a Guggenheim Fellow and during that year went to Ireland and England; he has twice received Canada Council awards and in 1968 won the Governor-General's Award for Poetry.

He has published eight collections of poetry, the latest of which is entitled *The Mysterious Naked Man,* and one collection of short stories, *Miracle at Indian River*. He writes a weekly column for *The Telegraph-Journal*. Alden Nowlan's poems have been translated into Russian, French and Spanish, and published in the U.S.A., England, Switzerland, France, Australia, New Zealand, and India.

The Girl Who Went to Mexico

Ordinarily Sam Baxter heard a car stopping in front of his house in time to take a look out the kitchen window to see who was coming. He liked to be prepared for visitors. Not that he had anything to fear, but he was a shy man and surprises, including pleasant surprises, made him uncomfortable.

But that day he was cooking his supper, something he had had to do since his mother's death the previous year. He was frying steak with plenty of onions, steeping tea, warming up biscuits he had made a couple of days earlier, setting the table, listening to Don Messer and his Islanders on the radio, and rather enjoying all this noise and rushing about – when, happening to look up, he saw a girl standing in the doorway.

"Good afternoon, sir," said the girl, whom Sam had never seen before. "Could you tell me your name, please? If I get just ten more names on my list, I'll win a free trip to Mexico."

"My name?" stammered Sam. "Why, my name's Bam Saxter. I mean Sam Baxter. I mean what you want to know for? I mean what you up to, anyway, scaring a man pretty near to death that way?"

"Oh, you poor darling!" the girl wailed. "Did I really frighten you? I'm awfully sorry. I really am. I knocked, but you couldn't have heard me. I feel so silly I could just die!"

She was a pretty little blonde, about twenty years old, wearing what Sam remembered afterwards as a very pretty and rather daring dress, although actually Sam never quite dared look at a woman closely enough to notice the style and texture, or even the colour, of her clothes.

"Don't worry about it," Sam said. "You didn't really scare me. Now what did you say you was selling?"

"Oh, no! I'm not selling anything. All I want is your name. You see –"

The girl talked, very rapidly and charmingly, while Charlie Chamberlain sang "McNamara's Band" and "An Irish Lullaby" and "Beyond the Sunset," and Sam's steak went from medium-rare, which he preferred, to well done. In the end, as the result of a process that still baffled him when he tried next day to reassemble it in his mind, Sam found himself paying three dollars for a year's subscription to a weekly magazine called *The Canadian Yeoman*.

The only other periodical to which Sam subscribed was *The Connaught County and Environs World Intelligencer* which most of its readers referred to, not without affection, as *The Blat*. So the arrival of his first copy of *The Canadian Yeoman* was a bit of an event in his life. As an Orangeman and a Royal Black Knight of Ireland, sworn to uphold the British connection, he was pleased that the cover carried a handsome colour portrait of the Queen and Prince Philip in the regalia of the Order of the Garter. In fact, he liked the portrait so much that he tacked it on the kitchen wall and, once or twice, even considered putting it in the gilt frame in the living room that now contained a sampler in purple and gold needlework reading: *What Is Home Without a Mother?*

Being a farmer who raised purebred Lacombe hogs, Shorthorn cattle and twenty-five acres of potatoes, he read most of the articles on agriculture. Since he had to prepare his own meals he occasionally clipped out a recipe. And, often, he felt a little electric tingle of nostalgia when he glanced at the page devoted to republishing old songs; when, for instance, he read:

> *My name is Peter Emberley*
> *As you must understand,*
> *I was born on Prince Edward Island,*
> *Nearby the ocean's strand...*

Soon, as he went to bed on Tuesday nights, Sam was thinking, well, tomorrow's the day my paper comes. And he stayed up later than usual on Wednesdays, sometimes until ten-thirty or eleven, enjoying his magazine, smoking his pipe of Old Virginia tobacco, and listening to country and western music from Wheeling, West Virginia and Nashville, Tennessee. This became his private little weekly festival. In time he got into the habit of finishing the evening with a little toddy of rum, hot water and sugar.

New covers were tacked up: Bobby Hull working in a hayfield, Prince Philip at the Royal Winter Fair, Brahma bull riding at the Calgary Stampede, wheat ripening in Saskatchewan, the RCMP musical ride. One week the cover pictured a group of Israeli farm girls in very tight shirts and shorts, but after a few days Sam took this one down and slid it under the radio.

Then, one Wednesday, the magazine didn't arrive.

"Oh, well, it will be here tomorrow, I guess," Sam said to himself when he found his mailbox empty. But that night he had nothing to read and he felt very lonely, just sitting there, smoking and listening to the radio.

At last he resentfully picked up the previous week's issue and, since he had already read everything else, found himself perusing the classified advertisements that occupied several of the back pages.

Farms For Sale, New and Used Clothing, Agents Wanted, Missing Persons, In Memoriam, Personal.

145

It was the column headed "Personal" that changed Sam Baxter's way of life.

Next day, when the current issue arrived, he hardly glanced at the cover, which showed a Scottish shepherd, his dog and a flock of sheep, before turning to the classified columns.

"Elijah coming before Christ," he read aloud. "Wonderful book free."

And there was an address, just as there were addresses in all the other advertisements in the "Personal" column.

There were notices inserted by the Millenial Dawn Movement, the Christadelphians, the Rosicrucians, the Theosophists, the Socialist Labour Party, the Christian Nationalist Crusade, the Commonwealth Association for the Restoration of the House of Stuart, the Church of Jesus Christ of Latter Day Saints, the Unitarians, the Universalists, the Anti-Vivisectionists, the Baha'i World Faith, the Society for Herbal Medicine, the Knights of Columbus – each of them offering books, pamphlets, magazines or correspondence courses in exchange for a postcard.

Sam drove his half-ton truck into Hainesville and bought six postcards.

"Looks as though you're planning on catching up on your correspondence," said Albion Greeley, the postmaster, eyeing him curiously through his rimless glasses.

"Thought maybe I would," Sam answered.

"Suppose you're going to write to that brother of yours out in Detroit. Haven't seen any letters from him in a coon's age. And maybe you'll drop a line to your Uncle Bythie down Boston-way? You write him you tell him Albion Greeley was asking about him – hey?"

"Don't know as I'll be writing to either of them," Sam said.

"Well, I'd sooner be bit by a dog than poke my snout into somebody else's business," said Albion, turning away.

It took Sam most of an evening to write his messages and address his cards. The actual writing didn't take long, but he spent hours deciding which advertisements looked most interesting. After the cards were mailed, he walked to his mailbox every day with the same eagerness he had felt as a boy visiting his rabbit snares.

The replies came – first a trickle, then a flood. Before long he was receiving literature even from organizations to which he had not written.

He read it all, every word of it. He read the books of Charles Taze Russell, who maintained that the Great Pyramid was not an Egyptian tomb but a Hebrew prophecy. He read Helena Petrovna Blavatsky and learned about the transmigration of souls and the secret doctrines of the ascended masters. He read Gerald L. K. Smith, Daniel DeLeon, Baha'u'llah and the Book of Mormon. He read that sunflower seeds cured

146

constipation and that his rightful sovereign was a Bavarian duke named Albrecht Von Wittlesbach.

"That Sam Baxter's got himself mixed up with one of them screwball religions," Albion Greeley reported. "Don't know which one of them it is for sure. Jehovah Witness, maybe. He may even be a Communist. Some of the stuff that fellow gets in the mail would scare you. The stuff I could tell about some people around here if I wasn't a civil servant sworn to secrecy! Wouldn't surprise me none, though, if the Mounties was around asking about Sam one of these days. No, sir, wouldn't surprise me one bit."

On the infrequent occasions when Sam went to town to buy livestock feed or replace worn-out parts on his tractor or potato digger, those who knew him pointed him out to those who didn't and whispered "There goes the Mormon," or "That there's Sam Baxter, he's some kind of a Communist."

As for Sam, he was hardly aware that each of the books and pamphlets he devoured was designed to convert him to a Cause. He was a Tory, because his parents had been Tories, and his grandparents, too, for all he knew, and because he suspected the Grits of being sympathetic to the Church of Rome. If he had been asked his religion he would have hesitated for an instant and then answered "Baptist," because while his mother had attended the United Church of Canada, the only church within walking distance of the Baxter farm for close to forty years, both she and his father had been raised as Baptists and, to the end of their lives, had believed that God had delivered a greater measure of His truth to the Baptists than He had chosen to entrust to Methodists, Presbyterians or anybody else.

He was neither baffled nor confused when in the same evening he dipped into *Isis Unveiled* and *The Secret Doctrine* and thumbed through the lastest issues of *The Weekly People* and *The Cross and the Flag*. Astral bodies, Devachan, the Four Noble Truths of the Compassionate Buddha, the international bankers' conspiracy, industrial democracy through worker control of the means of production, the secret return of Jesus in 1914, the martyrdom of The Bab and the Prophet Joseph Smith – these were not things he tried to understand or relate in any way to his own life. His reading was a kind of dreaming. He was not a convert or a student, but an adventurer.

Eventually, he wearied of this adventure and embarked on a more daring one.

The personal column of *The Canadian Yeoman* contained advertisements of another kind.

Middle-aged Ukrainian farmer, well-to-do, Catholic, wishes to correspond with Catholic widow, with view to matrimony. No objection to one or two children.

Woman, 46, considered attractive, good cook, wishes to hear from lonely bachelor or widower with means. Enclose photo in first letter. No triflers, please.

Man, 50, owner of successful small business, non-drinker, non-smoker, invites letters from middle-aged woman, Protestant church-goer with some private means preferred. Enclose snapshot, please.

Childless widow, 41, with small bank account, blue eyes, natural blonde, wants to hear from white Protestant between 40 and 60, preferably with means. No objection to one child. Object: matrimony, if suited.

The old Sam Baxter would never have dreamed of answering such an advertisement. But the new Sam Baxter thought of himself as a rather reckless man.

At Steadman's 5¢ to $1.00 Store in Hainesville, he bought a nineteen-cent ballpoint pen, a tablet of pale blue paper and a package of white, blue-lined envelopes. Furtively he slipped in and out of a curtained booth in which he sat in semi-darkness, looking at himself in a mirror, while a coin-operated camera, its light flashing off and on, took his picture. When the machine coughed out a strip of four photographs, not much bigger than postage stamps, he put them in his wallet very quickly and did not take them out until he got home, where he examined them through his mother's old-fashioned reading glass and decided, finally, that, well, he must have been behind the door when good looks were handed out but at least he'd never scare a cat into having a miscarriage.

Then, slowly, almost painfully, he composed his letter:

Dear Madam,

Having seen your ad in The Canadian Yeoman my favourite paper I am dropping you a line to tell you I am a farmer here in New Brunswick a very beautiful place to live and guess I am an old bachelor (ha ha) because I had to look after Mother after Father died and don't see many women here my age that are not married although am not as old as all that either, will be 46 next Sept. 26 if God lets me live, and am lucky enough to have my health, which I think you will agree is the most important thing there is, and they say life begins at 40 (ha ha.) Am sending you snap which you can use to scare the mice away (ha ha again.) Own 260 acres of land here in Connaught County which I think is God's Country although that does not mean I have anything against Ontario where you live but when you are born somewhere that makes it different. Have 25 acres in potatoes

148

which this year are $5 a barrel so am doing pretty good (knock on wood) although not rich or anything. Also have Lacombe hogs best breed there is and Shorthorn cattle. Hope I am not talking too much about farming but think farmer most important man there is in a way because if it wasn't for the farmer, everybody would starve, if you know what I mean. Am Protestant, Orangeman, and great admirer of Mr. Diefenbaker. Read a lot because reading is a great pastime and also you learn a lot that way. I am well and trust you are the same. Drop a line when you have time.

Yours Truly, Sam Baxter

When the reply came, he was afraid to open it, so afraid that he tore the unopened letter into four sections, intending to destroy it, and later had to put it back together like a jigsaw puzzle.

This is what it said:

Dear Sam,

I can see by your picture that you are a very kind man and by reading between the lines I can tell you are a very lonely one. I have been very lonely myself these last five years since my husband passed away. He was a conductor on the CPR so I get a small pension and don't have to worry about where the next meal is coming from, which is a blessing. And I like to play Bingo and watch wrestling on the television, which helps pass the time away. But to tell the truth I can't seem to get used to living alone.

From your letter, you sound a lot like Harry (my husband) and your picture even looks something like him. You have the same shy, gentle look he did. Something tells me that you and I have a lot in common and would like one another very much if we had a chance to get to know each other better.

Please don't think I write to every strange man like this, or make a habit of writing to strange men. Most of the letters I got after The Canadian Yeoman came out with my ad in it I didn't even bother answering. Some of them were enough to scare a woman to death. But I can tell that you are a gentleman.

I am sending you a picture of myself. In case you are interested, I am five feet four inches tall and weigh 135 pounds. Have brown hair and dark brown eyes. Before I was married I was a stenographer in Oshawa.

Harry and I never had any children, which is too bad in a way, because they sure would of been a great comfort to me this last few years. But it was God's will, I guess, so it must have been for the best.

Write soon and tell me more about yourself.

Yours Sincerely,
Mrs. Amelia Brady.

Here is how Sam began his three-page reply:

Dear Amelia,

Maybe I should be writing dear Mrs. Brady instead of dear Amelia never having met you but after I read your letter I felt I knew you better than some people I've known all my life which may sound like a strange thing to say to a stranger but it is the way I feel and I can't help telling you so because Mother when she was alive used to say the time to give people roses is when they're alive and kicking and not wait until they're dead and gone. . . .

And here is how he ended it:

. . . so be sure and drop me a line as soon as you have time and feel like it and I'll be watching the mailbox every day just like a little kid waiting for a letter from Santa Claus (ha ha) except of course you're a lot prettier than Santa Claus (ha ha again) not that I judge people by their looks because beauty is only skin deep and handsome is as handsome does but I liked your letter so much I can hardly wait to hear from you again.

Her answer came by return mail, and this time he did not tear it apart. They exchanged a letter a week, then two letters a week, and then three. Baha'u'llah and his Letters to the Kings, the Prophet Joseph and his Pearl of Great Price, the ravings of Billy James Hargis and the papal bulls of Marxism were all but forgotten. When new leaflets arrived they were tossed in the woodbox and, the following morning, used to kindle the fire. When Sam's subscription to *The Canadian Yeoman* expired, he almost decided not to renew it. Nowadays the only articles he ever read were those on potatoes, hogs and cattle, and most of the time he skipped even those. A second and much larger photograph of Amelia sat on the table beside his bed.

When she wrote that she wished to meet him, he shut himself in the barn and sat there for a long time with his hands over his eyes.

His letters had been truthful enough, yet he felt like a man who has told a very long and complicated lie and discovers that he has been found out.

It was not so much fear he felt, as guilt. "She'll despise me," he thought irrationally, "and I deserve to be despised."

He thought of suicide, but like most people who think of suicide he did not want to be dead, but only to die.

He considered running away, of hiding in the woods and living on trout and venison.

150

"What a fool I am," he thought. "I wish somebody would shoot me."

Then he realized that if he did not write to her again she would not dare invade his privacy – for that is how he regarded her now, as an intruder.

"Why can't the silly bitch leave things the way they are?" he wondered. "Why do women always have to come barging in where they're not wanted!"

So her letter went unanswered and when she wrote again he threw the unopened envelope in the stove. Weeks passed. Then one night, his telephone rang.

"Long distance calling Mr. Samuel Baxter."

"Huh?"

"Is Mr. Baxter there, please?"

"Who's calling?"

"May we speak with Mr. Baxter, please?" The tone of the operator's voice did not change from one of boredom to one of impatience; it simply became more bored.

"This is Sam Baxter speaking," Sam Baxter said.

"Sam! Is that you, Sam? This is Amelia."

What was there for him to say?

"Are you still there, Sam? It's Amelia Brady. I haven't heard from you for so long that I got worried. How are you, Sam? Operator, I think I've been disconnected. Operator!"

"Hello," said Sam, weakly.

"Sam, there's nothing wrong is there? You haven't been answering my letters. I've been worrying myself sick."

"Well, I been feeling kind of poorly lately if you want to know the truth."

"You poor man! I'm coming right down there to look after you. Don't worry about a thing, you hear me! Let me see, what day is this? Tuesday. I'll be coming in on the train Thursday. What time does the train from Montreal get in there?"

"Six o'clock. Six o'clock in the evening, there's a CPR dayliner stops at Hainesville."

"Good enough. Well, you be waiting for that train, Sam Baxter!"

"Yes," said Sam, "I'll be there."

And he *was* there – standing on the station platform in his blue suit with the white pin-stripe, his red and green-striped necktie and tweed cap.

"Taking a little trip, are you, Sam?" asked Albion Greeley, who was there to pick up the Montreal mail bags.

"No," Sam answered. "Waiting for somebody."

151

"Your brother, I bet? Can't be your Uncle Bythie for this train don't bring no passengers from down Boston-way. Your brother Benjy's coming home, is he? Well, sir, everybody will be some glad to see Benjy again."

"Not my brother," said Sam. "Not my uncle neither."

"Well, now, I'd be the last man to nose into another man's business. If people took care of their own affairs the way they should they wouldn't have time to poke into other people's affairs is what I always say."

"Don't mind telling you," Sam said. "Everybody will know soon enough. I'm going to get myself married."

"You're going to get married! Did you say you were going to get married?"

"Yep," said Sam, rather proudly. "You see there was this girl that wanted to go to Mexico and –"

AUTHOR'S COMMENTARY

Why do I write? I doubt if I'd ever put that question to myself if others didn't ask it so frequently. Why do I like knackwurst and sauerkraut and dislike lemon meringue pie? Why am I six feet three inches tall? Why do I almost never swear except when I'm driving a car? I think it was Paul Verlaine who said that he wrote to kill time. That's as good an answer as any. I started writing poems and stories when I was eleven years old, and I continue to write poems and stories at thirty-six. Why do I write? Almost any answer I could offer you would be true.

I am a Canadian, and a child of the twentieth century, yet the Nova Scotia village in which I spent my early childhood now seems almost as remote as Byzantium. My people were dispossessed peasants or wild Celtic brigands. The men worked themselves to death in sawmills or the lumber woods, sailed around Cape Horn in tern schooners they'd built with their own hands, posed as Indian guides to fleece American hunters, fought with guns when there was a war and with their boots and fists when there wasn't. The women, like the wives of peasants and brigands everywhere, mostly worked and waited.

Their lives were pervaded with Christian mythology. Curiously, it was mythology almost devoid of theology or morality. They weren't puritans. In fact, to them, the New Morality of the 1960's would have seemed tame, middle class and prudish. (I know a lot about puritanism, too, but I didn't encounter that until I was nineteen and went to work in a little Loyalist market town in New Brunswick, an experience somewhat similar to that of an eighteenth-century Highland Scot descending to the dour Lowlands.)

Since they were nominally protestant, the crux of their mythology was a book, the Bible. But it's important for you to realize that almost none of them actually read it. For that matter, they were rather afraid of reading it, or of hearing it read. It was as though they believed it contained powerful and generally benign but potentially dangerous charms.

So, as a child, I went to the Bible not as a sanctimonious little Calvinist, but as a kind of sorcerer's apprentice, seeking power rather than piety. I dreamed of growing up to be a prophet, and of adding books to the canon, books beginning, "The words which the Lord God of Abraham, and of Isaac, and of Jacob spake unto His servant, Alden . . ."

Those nurtured in a society that believes God is contained in a book will always, provided they're imaginative, retain an almost mystical feeling about the written and printed word. I suppose that in my unconscious

153

mind I still harbour the delusion that all books, including comics and movie fan magazines, are chapters in one enormous Bible. Well, even atheists can *conceive* of God inspiring a book. But who among us can imagine God producing a television show?

So I began writing because I wanted to be a prophet? It would be equally true – possibly a great deal more true – to say that I wrote for the same reason that some of my friends stole hub caps and, a little later, broke into filling stations. "One sheds one's sicknesses in books," D. H. Lawrence said. Part of my childhood was spent in a slum. At least three of my friends later served time in penitentiaries. I kept on writing words in scribblers.

It might be still truer to say that I wrote because I needed to talk to someone and there was nobody to listen. So perhaps I wrote for the same reason that some children invent imaginary playmates. Maybe even today I write for an imaginary playmate. For there's a sense in which all writers, all artists, are grown-up children.

If, when I was younger, there had been anyone at all with whom I could have talked honestly and fearlessly I might not have continued to write. But, then, I'm not certain that utterly honest and wholly fearless communication is possible, outside of art. What was it Anne Frank wrote in her diary? "Paper is more patient than people."

And, of course, I read. I can remember so vividly the excitement with which I discovered Guy de Maupassant when I was, oh, thirteen or fourteen, the sheer *physical* excitement of it as I giggled, clapped my hands, knuckled my temples and, at intervals, jumped to my feet and walked back and forth, reading things like "Simeon's Papa," "Madame Tellier's Excursion," and the other tales about Norman peasants who were at once so like and so unlike the people I knew. The first adult novel I remember reading was Gene Fowler's *Trumpet in the Dust* – I've never seen a copy of it since and hope that I never do: it meant so much to me once that I never want to confirm my suspicion that it was a very weak novel indeed. And perhaps my suspicion is incorrect. Perhaps it's a neglected masterpiece. I would like to hope so.

My father, sometimes when he was drunk, would recite Robert Service – "The Shooting of Dan McGrew" and "The Cremation of Sam McGee." My father, my grandmothers and many of my uncles and aunts sang folk songs – sentimental ballads about leaving Ireland, rousing songs about Irish rebellions, dirges for lumbermen drowned or crushed to death on the great river log drives, songs that purported to be the confessions of contrite murderers. Probably that, too, went into making me a writer.

154

I suspect the truth of the matter is that everything that has gone into making me a man has also gone into making me a writer.

And perhaps I write because it is the only thing I do well.

Man is the only animal that creates forms that don't exist in nature. The longer I live, the more I write, the more convinced I am that the great function of the writer is to create form, to impose order on chaos. I strongly suspect that, ultimately, the universe is not only formless but meaningless. Or if there is any absolute form and meaning I doubt the human mind is capable of comprehending it. I agree with Charles Fort who wrote: "Nothing ever has been proved, because there is nothing to prove. Nothing has ever been finally found out, because there is nothing final to find out." (He also wrote that "every attempt to achieve beauty is an attempt to give to the local the attribute of the universal." I agree with him there, too.)

My consciousness of formlessness and meaninglessness doesn't cause me to despair. On the contrary. I not only accept the mystery of my existence, but welcome it. For one thing, men will cease to kill one another over ideological differences once they acknowledge that all forms and meanings are fragmentary and tentative and that, ultimately, as I've written in a poem, "all truths are half-truths."

No writer can ever be truly successful simply because no work of art, no poem, no story, no novel, no painting, no music can ever be more than a tiny polished fragment from the infinitely and eternally formless reality that inspired it.

All of a sudden, I'm afraid that you, reading this, will find the last several paragraphs excessively philosophical or even, worst of all, pretentious. I gather that most of this book's readers will be students. Myself, I'm not altogether certain that students should be required to study poems and stories. Sometimes I think that once they've mastered the alphabet they should be allowed to find their way to poetry and fiction on their own.

I don't have a great deal to say about my story, "The Girl Who Went to Mexico." I tried to make it both funny and sad. And, perhaps to a greater degree than in some of my other stories, I tried to make it entertain. Some readers see the ending as a defeat for Sam Baxter, some see it as a victory. It will be up to you to make up your own mind about that.

Many of you will live in an urban environment very different from the setting for this story. And you will be young, where Sam Baxter is aging, if he is not already old. I hope you won't let those essentially superficial differences distract you. There are young people living in cities who are as shy and lonely as Sam Baxter and, like him, prisoners of forces they can neither understand nor wholly control.

Finally, with Andre Gide and Norman Mailer, I'd like to ask a favour of you, and that is:

"Do not understand me too quickly."

ALDEN NOWLAN

BIBLIOGRAPHY

The Rose and the Puritan. Fredericton, N.B.: Fiddlehead Poetry Books, 1958. (Out of Print) [Poetry]

A Darkness in the Earth. Eureka, California: Hearse Press, 1959. (Out of Print) [Poetry]

Wind in a Rocky Country. Toronto: Emblem Books, 1961. (Out of Print) [Poetry]

Under the Ice. Toronto: Ryerson Press, 1961 [Poetry]

The Things Which Are. Toronto: Contact Press, 1962. (Out of Print) [Poetry]

Bread, Wine and Salt. Toronto: Clarke, Irwin and Co. Ltd., 1967. [Poetry]

A Black Plastic Button and a Yellow Yoyo. (Limited edition.) Toronto: 1968. Charles Pachter. (Out of Print) [Poetry]

Miracle at Indian River. Toronto: Clarke, Irwin and Co. Ltd., 1969. [Short Stories]

The Mysterious Naked Man. Toronto: Clarke, Irwin and Co. Ltd., 1969. [Poetry]

Playing the Jesus Game. Trumansburg, N.Y.: New Books, 1970 [A selection of poems]

George Bowering

George Bowering was born on December 1, 1935, in Penticton, British Columbia. He went to high school in Oliver, B.C. and college at Victoria College, UBC, and the University of Western Ontario.

He has worked as a timber cruiser, photographer, sportswriter, farm worker and aerial photographer. During 1967-68 he was writer in residence at Sir George Williams University in Montreal; currently he is a member of the English Department of Sir George Williams University.

George Bowering was the founding editor of the important west coast poetry newsletter *Tish* from 1961 till its 19th issue. Currently, he is the editor of *Imago*, an international magazine for longer poems.

In 1962 he married Angel Luoma. They have no children.

He speaks Spanish and travels to Mexico and Europe. He is currently the Canadian contact for people in the U.S.A. who want to get books to Cuba.

In 1970 Mr. Bowering received the Governor-General's Award for poetry. The award cited his books *Rocky Mountain Foot* and *The Gangs of Kosmos*.

Time and Again

Being back in Lawrence was an experience of isolation. He had been a boy there, he had gone to school there, he had started to read novels there, and it was there that he had first thought about writing – sports stories; he would be a baseball writer for the St. Louis *Post Dispatch*, he had even sent a letter to J. Roy Stockton, the sports editor, and asked what he should do, and J. Roy had said go to a journalism college and look him up when he was through St. Louis, home of the enemy Cardinals – he would have been afraid to approach the thing directly, that is write to a paper in Brooklyn.

The paper in Lawrence was a weekly sheet he had written basketball stories for when he was in grades eleven and twelve – WILDCATS DEMOLISH RED DEVILS, Selkirk Leads Winners With 25 Points – and when he had been away at college he had sent the odd story "of special interest to Lawrence residents," by George Delsing, formerly of Lawrence.

Now back in Lawrence, noted in the social page of the weekly, Delsing was back in town, nobody noticing, the victor returning; not noticed by you boobs, who's to care? But somebody could. Frances for instance, off somewhere, not even known where this summer, married or separated, with one child two years old now; how could it be that he was once the theoretical father of that planned-for child, and now somewhere in a space, not knowing the other juncture?

In the café he had gone to see Bud and have a Coke. They said the same things they had said last winter, and Bud said he's seen Donna. So he has. I guess I better go see what they're going to feed me at home, he said, and walked out to the sidewalk, passing people he knew, all of them, and they all looked past him, a stranger, or not consequential here now in the middle of the peach season. Aw, well.

He looked up and down the street, greengrocers with aprons carrying paper cups of coffee into stores with crude handwritten sale signs scotch-taped to the window, cool Indians, in from the reserve, playing pool and drinking beer in the middle of peach season, riding ponies by night up on Coyote Ridge, old Jack Berk, out of jail it seems, this time wearing a dirty fluorescent hunter's cap, pinning someone and telling about the invincibility of the Brooklyn Dodgers, daffy as a ram; the Dodgers have moved to Los Angeles while Jack was in jail for exposing himself somewhere. All the same. He turned and headed up the hill, home. The truth was, it suited him fine nobody knew about him, or cared, here, except his folks suddenly more friendly and man-to-manly now that he was a man of the outer world. Why be appreciated in Lawrence? Take umbrage if someone claims you as a Lawrence boy. That's fine. Up the hill.

Remembering now in the heavy steps up the steep sidewalk how damn hot it gets in this country; and that sinks into your shoulders with a familiar grace, an ease, like the dogs yapping here at the front door, no matter how softly you sneak up the walk.

His brother Reggie was sitting at the kitchen table, tall lean kid; what? thirteen years old, reading a hot-rod magazine, gloating over chromium tailpipes to a red thought of a car, as George, Dels, did years before with sports magazines, knowing the batting average of Eddie Stanky, unable to remember his mother sent him downtown with a shopping list; unwilling to get work, but working like hell if it caught up to him.

"When I was your age I was working nine hours a day in an orchard, my son," he said to Reggie, who flipped the page to a reconditioned Essex Super Six.

"Ha, ha, ha," interjected his mother, standing at the sink coring the dripping stones out of a sinkful of peaches.

He snuck over beside her and grabbed a sticky handful of sliced peaches and crammed them in his mouth.

"You've got a handy memory," said his mother. "You can remember any amazing legend of stuff if it recounts the hard life and times of George Delsing."

"The favourite son," he added.

"The first son, perhaps unwisely claimed." His mother had grown more adept at jabbing that way, which was fun, but she would never understand the things he had stayed up to tell her the night before, elbows on the late-night kitchen table, everyone else in bed, telling how he would steal money to keep from toiling while he wrote a great long novel on the blatant secret lives of three thousand people in Lawrence and other places, yours included. His mother had sat there, smoking cigarettes, listening to brashness, reserving motherly knowledge about first son George later to marry and take a job and settle down, maybe in middle age bringing out poems for relatives to see, collecting fine music and books as recompense, staying close to the artist life, which after all does not inhere in people from Lawrence, but is the drawing-room air of people in mythical European cities located somewhere far off, at the Atlantic Ocean probably. A hobby is okay, as long as it does not obsess a mature man away from the business of making a way, keeping up with expectations for age brackets, paying debts, establishing a post whence to get weekly letters, like all the relatives, immediately Delsing, with trace of Lawrence, modified by the job and the new town.

159

"I would abandon my children and deny my father if they got in the way of what I'm going to do."

And goodnight – forgotten but submerged visible the next day.

"The ironic thing," he said, "is that I'm writing immense novels and poems about all the people of this town, and they don't know it. For them I am a goof-off, with brains, but a goof-off, who will probably amount to something medium, and not deserve that much. There will be great pages and chapters written about this little town, known to every hamlet in the nation except itself."

His mother peeled a peach, the skin pulling off in utter silence belonging to the world of sweet tree-fruit.

"Put yourself in the position of a Lawrence orchardist. Would you care?" she said.

And was right, as always, this is a hard fact to shake, no matter how intelligent and insightful he might become in the swirl outside the valley.

"I suppose not. That's why I feel no compunction in giving them life or killing them mercilessly. Except I never do it mercilessly," he added.

"In fact, I wonder if you have ever put yourself in the place of an orchardist, for example," she said. "I wonder if you can, seriously."

He had been wondering lately, once in a while.

"I will go out and see an orchardist," he said, grabbing a freshly washed peach on his way out.

The highway between the overhanging orchards, it was a groove deep in the sensual part of his mind, the motor of the car running smooth along it, leading him down the white line of earlier drunken auto races when the road narrowed and the trees crowded in close, pushing against the edges of the windshield. He knew where he was going, turned in at the weeping willow tree that hung to the ground over half of the dirt road winding a weedy edged trail up to the house, where he stopped the car and looked. The old house still needed painting, and the screen that darkened the long verandas was still loose at the edges. But the flowers still crowded the wooden steps, and the screen door was propped open with an old wicker armchair.

He got out of the car after the dust had settled because he had his new canvas shoes on, and walked around to the back. She was there as always, digging in the garden with little green tools, Mrs. Ackerman, skinny old grey woman with amazing pink face, hair knotted and stained yellow in spots at the back of her head, heavy man's boots on her feet, cigarette hanging from the side of her mouth.

Seventy-one when I left, she's seventy-six now, he thought.

160

She looked up when he walked across the lawn, squinting at him as he stood between her and the sun.

"Georgie Delsing!" she said, and got up from her crouch as quickly as she could, brushed the dry soil off her hand before she extended it to him. That was the way she was, not like a man – an eager force, strength.

"Hi, Mrs. Ackerman. I told you I'd be back to see you," he said, not embarrassed.

"Five years ago," she said. She was right on, not like old folks.

He didn't have to say he was sorry. "I heard about Mr. Ackerman. I'm feeling kind of strange not hearing him." Mr. Ackerman used to sit and whistle loudly, filling the air of the orchard he couldn't see.

She rubbed the back of her wrist across her forehead, a gesture of habit. She was too old to sweat.

"He just fell on his face straight out of his chair on the grass. Dead as a doornail," she said in the manner that she knew unsettled George.

"How do you make out here by yourself? I mean, don't you have any help around the house?" It was six or seven years ago that he would join the small desperate crew trying to get her peaches off the trees before they got ripe.

"Oh, I certainly miss all the heavy work Walter used to do for me," she said, dumping the garden tools into the green box with the curled up hose.

He remembered coming to the house and seeing her standing on a sawhorse to reach the end of the twisted clothesline, her straight spindly legs, and Mr. Ackerman in his chair, whistling an opera tune with all the short piccolo noises.

"Come on in the house and eat up all my peanut butter cookies," she said, clumping with her boots up the wooden steps to the kitchen.

She poured the tea, much too weak, the English way, and he dropped his cigarette into the wood-stove.

"There's talk in town that you inherited a whole lot of insurance money," he said, putting it accusingly, the old way, with the precarious delight of being able to talk to an old woman without making allowances for her oldness.

"In that town," she said, as if it were a hundred miles away, past the weeping willow tree, and it was true – the occasion when she would be seen on the street was some kind of visit, or visitation, from the duchess, old Mrs. Ackerman, never forgotten out there four miles from town; but mysterious, a kind of local belief, like an abandoned silver mine. "In that town you could start a story that Bismark was living as a recluse in the hospital basement, among the mops and furnaces." She enjoyed the idea. He filed it in his mind, then forgot it.

161

"Come on, Mrs. Ackerman . . ."

"Well, to tell the truth, I'm not poor, Georgie, we never really were. You never thought of that, did you?"

He hadn't. And that showed what? That he hadn't really examined all the hours he'd spent talking with them, in fact he never thought of an encounter that way – it made a sense record in his head, and that was all. So the peril here – he'd thought of the Ackermans as types, replying to the condition they lived in, as he'd seen it. Expectations become fact too quick if you get comfortable.

"I'll take another cookie, that being the case." He wasn't looking at her now, rather down, in the tea leaves in the bottom of his cup. "That is, how – why didn't you ever . . .?" He didn't know what he was asking, but she did.

She laughed lightly, in the tone that was as clearly dry and ridged as her cheeks, and he lifted his head.

"Have another cup of tea, and I'll tell you." (He didn't like tea generally, at least never a second cup, but he had always waived that when it was worth it, paid some attention to the fancy cup and the fancy silver spoon.) "In fact – have you got anywhere to go this afternoon? – fine, then – in fact, I'll go back to the beginning."

Which she had done on many occasions before, and he had settled back apprehensive at first, but later eagerly happy to sit and listen to her hard factual accounts of childhood farm days in some English shire of a greeny sound.

"I never told you how I met and married Walter, did I?" she asked, doing something evasive with a napkin, settling. Surprised he thought, no, by God, and then, quit interrupting, brain.

"I don't believe so," he said, settling.

"You've seen him sitting in his chair, whistling as loud as he can, filling the orchard with some sense he can trust – hear, because he never did like the sight of peaches on a tree, they were work growing and money coming in, that's all because what he wanted was to use work to get away from it. That has a lot to do with it.

"When I first met him, I was new over from the Old Country, and it was a good job I did find him, because it was the middle of the summer in the Niagara Peninsula, which can be a lonely time for someone not bred to the place or passing through on a honeymoon. He was wearing thick glasses then, those old round ones with the spidery legs clinging to the ears – I always swore his ears stuck out from the side of his head because of those glasses. And of course I loved him, for which I felt at first nonplussed, and

162

later guilty, because I knew I made him love me, not in the way girls in That Town do it now . . ."

She didn't blush, and she wasn't digressing into scorn, just telling hard facts.

". . . but the reason I felt guilty was becoming clear to me. He had been working all his thirty years to save up enough money to get to Europe – he came from an old family of Ontario Loyalists, and he told me all about Europe, what was waiting for him, for a fellow, over there, as if I had come from Ketchikan, Alaska. And of course when he married me he had to start all over again, which he did, thinking of no way to do it but to buy a farm, an orchard, in the Peninsula, and pay for that over the next fifteen years if the crops were good; which they were, from that time till six years later, the Great War, and he tried to get into the army, it was going to a sort of modern Europe, but they wouldn't take him; his eyes they said, but there was something about the farm too – not as if he was an oldest son, going off to fight for the peach blossoms.

"Then the next ten years were his own fault – the times were so profitable, even for orchardists, that he kept working and working, not now with the idea of a trip to Europe, but thinking about going there to live, which meant of course putting it off for a few years, and working extra hard, with a bigger orchard – so when the chance came to pick up a big piece of land in the Valley, he jumped at it, moving us out in 1922, in the old truck all the way across the country, the wrong direction, west, but he always said in those times, westward was the quickest route to Europe; and so when he got out here he realized that it would be a few years before the new trees yielded fruit, so we lost most of the little we had saved after buying the new place, and kept our heads above water by raising cucumbers and tomatoes, good ones, too – have another cookie."

He let the names of the years skid off his attention, all this before he was born, happening to two people, and hundreds of people whose faces he didn't know – he was born in 1935 – and he waited for her to get quickly up to that year, taking another cookie, and holding his cup out for tea in the meantime, third cup.

"All the time he was buying travel books, postcards, magazines, even road maps, marking the route between Paris and Vienna in red ink which after a while grew faded and even obsolete as the postwar highways cut across Europe in new swift lines. All the time telling me what we were going to see; he was always talking about buildings, parks, cities, bridges, farms, never mentioned the paintings and music festivals everyone else was pretending they longed to add to their memories.

"Then it was the Depression and he was in his fifties, and even the

163

farmers were in trouble, sometimes not having the money to pay their travelling peach pickers, and afraid the desperate-looking men would set fire to their houses. He would read the papers and say no Depression in Germany that's where we should have been long ago, in Germany. Then Germany started the war again and of course the orchard was mature and business was good again, and Walter said we would leave for Europe as soon as the war was over; but after the war business was even better, and the pictures of Europe were old piles of bricks with kids climbing on them looking for dirty heels of bread, so we said 1950 no later. In 1948 he was completely blind."

George was nervous. The tea was too strong now and it tasted like acid in his stomach. He lit two cigarettes and handed her one.

"So you didn't go," he said.

"Oh, yes, we went. We went in 1950, no later."

"But I mean –"

"He packed all the travel books and maps together, and off we went, sitting on the deck of the ship all the way, and he would get me to tell him what kind of sea it was and everything that happened on the deck in front of us. We stopped in England for a while and saw some of my relatives. Then we went over to Europe and stayed in Paris, and took the road from Paris to Vienna. And of course we didn't go to the music festivals, and we didn't go to the paintings. We used to sit at a table on the sidewalk, and I would tell him what the street looked like, and the buildings and the little French people walking by, and what the cars looked like, how heavy the traffic was. We went to every big city in Europe, and some of the towns and villages. Most of the time we walked along the sidewalks or sat for a cup of tea at a sidewalk café. It was very nice."

Then George remembered his feeling coming back into Lawrence, the walk up and down the sidewalk. The mountains were very close in Lawrence.

"It was then he started the whistling," he said.

"It was there he started it," she said. "But it was just once in a while, till we were back in Paris, waiting for our boat train. When we were back here, he whistled all the time."

"It's a funny thing," said George. "All the time I saw him sitting there whistling like that, I never once wondered what he was thinking. I suppose you usually guess or apprehend what a person is thinking when you see the expression – in their eyes."

Mrs. Ackerman had her own expression in her eyes. "I knew what he was thinking all the time. From about two months after he went totally blind till the day he died, he kept a diary."

164

"How?"

"On his little typewriter. He used to sit in his dark room with the type-writer on his lap and type out his diary every night. I could hear it right through the wall, very slow typing. I wanted to jump up and offer to help, it got on my nerves so much, but of course I couldn't do that, having caused him to go blind and get into the peach business and never see Europe and all that. So I used to read it the next day when he thought I was watering the front garden."

"Can I look at – ?"

"No."

She was right, of course, and it wasn't entirely because he was from and going to the town, and he knew why, was glad she had said that; that she knew, surprised even him who had thought he'd known how wise she was.

So he opened the car up on the highway back, not as he had done many times before, in fury and impatience to get home under the dark tree in the front yard, back inside the gates of the town where Frances was a stranger though she'd lived three miles from town more than half her life. Now it was that he was in a spirit like a casual hope, and the pedal underfoot was a direct connection to and from all gladland. So he sang, rocking his head back lustily as he hit the high distorted notes, propelling the car like a lateral rocket toward the little town of his youth.

AUTHOR'S COMMENTARY

Delsing & Me

I think that it is probably true that there are particular features of the short story, that it can be differentiated from other forms of writing, even other forms of fiction. Teachers talk about one single incident, and so forth. I've often thought that if you could see a novel as a rope made of many strands, you could see the short story as a cross section of a rope. But like most writers I get a lot of my fun (and writing has to be a form of playing) from breaking the rules, or just not thinking of them.

While I know that in writing a short story I'm doing something different from what I'm doing in a novel or a poem, I'm more interested in two things that I try to do all the time, in all three forms. I want to give a strong sense of place, and a strong sense of voice. When I talk to a stranger or an old friend from some place I've lived, I listen to how he talks in order to find out what his territory is like. I assume that other people want to know those things from me. So I read my stories out loud; and I write them to be read out loud. Sometimes when I read them at schools I'm told that people in the audience think they're poems. I like that. I guess what I want to write is lyric prose.

We tend to get a sense of a person from the way he does things, (including talking) more than from what he does, or what he talks about, I think. He might be telling a lie, but that doesn't stop us from finding out stuff about him. In literature, reality can come only from the way it is written. Even if I tell a story about something that really happened to me, the things in the story are made up – the real things happened earlier. But the language will go on being real if it originally came out of the author's response to life in a real fashion. For me that means writing the way I talk.

There's an old adage about writing: write about what you know. I would change that to "write the way you know." In any kind of writing, poetry or fiction, if I get a sense that the writer is adopting some special kind of rhetoric for the poem or story, I sense that he's faking it; so that I despair of getting any sense of something real. If it is not real for the author, how can it be real for the reader? Hence for me rhythm is all important. People are differentiated by their rhythms, and the differences are the reasons for writing, so that we can experience our imaginations. Our imaginations allow us to see from other people's eyes and listen with other people's ears. Each person has his own rhythm in his bloodbeat, his breathing, his walk (I recognize the "foot" in prose as much as in

166

poetry), his thinking, and of course his speech. Then, when things act on a person, and when he reacts, his rhythms change in his particular way. Try telling a story, and then try telling it after you've run up a flight of stairs. Something has happened, and it has made an effect on your rhythms, blood, breath, speech, etc. When something happens, you've got something to write a story about. To get it right, you have to pay attention to what has happened to your rhythms.

I spoke about place, too. Just as your blood, breath and so on have a place in your own body, I think that each place has its own rhythms. Obviously Toronto has a rhythm different from that of the road between two little towns in British Columbia. Different parts of Toronto have their different rhythms. You will feel the effects of the different rhythms while driving a car, or walking, or talking with the people on the sidewalks. The different patterns of weather and the seasons are differences in rhythm. If a writer can show me the intersection of his own rhythms and the external ones, he will interest me. He will awaken my imagination.

I've just read my story, "Time & Again", for the first time in a few years. It strikes me now as one of the most conventional stories I've ever written, and easy to pick apart as a short story – I mean you can relate Delsing's singing at the end of Mr. Ackerman's whistling, or you can relate Mr. Ackerman's blindness and Mrs. Ackerman's courage to Mrs. Delsing's advice to her son that he try to use his imagination to share the eyes and ears of an orchardist in the Valley. I guess I was subconsciously aware of these things when I wrote the story, and now if I were to teach it or write an essay on it, I could have a field day. You could have fun with the mere structure: there's a story within a story, and connections between the two, and there are suggestions that all this is taking place inside a larger story of which this is a section.

But I'd rather mention something else. Many writers get nervous if readers start asking them how autobiographical the stories are, who the people in them really are, and so forth. That's understandable. The writer doesn't want his reader to attend to that hopeless sense of "reality." Better to take the general stand that of course it's all made up – but if you write about people you can't help using the stuff you observe, just as a mountain in a story should share the characteristics of a mountain on your own real horizon. Reality is in the I of the beholder.

My character, George Delsing, has a name somewhat like my own. He is the narrator or central character or minor personage in almost all my fiction, novels and stories. He's not me – I am me. But he is a projection of myself more than anyone else is. His speech is very much like mine. His experiences are similar to mine, with the condition or

167

limitation that they will always be presented through my imagination, even when, as in my novel, *Mirror on the Floor,* the narrator is his best friend, Bob Small. The town of Lawrence is based on the village of Oliver, in the Okanagan Valley of British Columbia, where I grew up. Many of the people in the story (and other stories) are projections of people in Oliver. (In writing this, just now, I accidentally wrote "Lawrence" instead of "Oliver" – you see?)

Now, Mrs. Ackerman is not based on any one person I knew. Yet I hope that she is just as "real" as anyone else in the story. As I've suggested before, her reality will depend on how well I've managed to make her seem right in the place, and true to her language. More pertinently, she should be seen from Delsing's eyes.

For that reason, I don't try to describe scenes or people, but rather offer details that would appear to my character. So you don't get a description of Delsing because he doesn't ever look into a mirror here. You are told that the old house still needed painting; you aren't told what color it is. The fact is that the former would pass through Delsing's mind – he's not interested in telling some prospective audience the color because (1) it is not important, and (2) the details are meant to allow your imagination inside Delsing's head: the phrase says that time has passed, Delsing is in a familiar place, and Mrs. Ackerman is still Mrs. Ackerman. What information about Delsing's thoughts would be given if you were told that the house was green? Only that Delsing's eyes picked up some green color. You don't write a story to fill up space.

So, while you could treat "Time & Again" as a structure made of parts, I would entreat you to test it another way as well. Is the language interesting, for example? I'm more interested in perception than structure. That is why I treat the story as a few pages in the life of George Delsing. I think that my novels and stories are part of an open-ended testament to my lifetime on earth. If there's no end in mind, if I don't know when I will die, I don't know when the Delsing story will end. I must therefore pay attention to both lives moment by moment, and keep on doing so. I can't come back and fix it up when it's over. So I pay attention to the things that define it as I go along. To me that means telling you where I am at the moment, and watching my language as I do.

GEORGE BOWERING

BIBLIOGRAPHY

Sticks and Stones. Vancouver: Tishbooks, 1963. (Out of print.) [Poetry.]

Points on the Grid. Toronto: Contact Press, 1964. (Out of print.) [Poetry.]

The Man in Yellow Boots. Mexico: Edicone El Corno, 1965. (Out of print.) [Poetry.]

The Silver Wire. Kingston, Ontario: Quarry Press, 1966. [Poetry.]

Mirror on the Floor. Toronto: McClelland and Stewart, 1967. [Novel.]

Baseball. Toronto: Coach House Press, 1967. (Out of print.) [Poetry.]

Rocky Mountain Foot. Toronto: McClelland and Stewart, 1969. [Poetry.]

Two Police Poems. Vancouver: Talon Books, 1969. [Poetry.]

The Gangs of Kosmos. Toronto: House of Anansi, 1969. [Poetry.]

Sitting in Mexico. Montreal: Imago, 1970. [Poetry.]

George, Vancouver. Toronto: Weed/Flower Press, 1970. [Poetry.]

Alfred Purdy. Toronto: Copp Clark, 1970. [Criticism.]

David Helwig

David Helwig was born in Toronto in 1938. At the age of ten he moved to Niagara-on-the-Lake, where his father, a cabinet-maker, bought an antique shop. He attended the University of Toronto, spent summers working with the Straw Hat Players, and subsequently did two years of graduate work at the University of Liverpool. He now lives in Kingston, where he teaches English at Queen's. He is married and has two daughters.

David Helwig's poems and stories have appeared in most of the leading little magazines and literary quarteries. He is one of the editors of *Quarry*. He has won awards for a play, *A Time of Winter*, and a short story, "Something for Olivia's Scrapbook I Guess". The latter was included in Robert Weaver's *Canadian Short Stories* (Second Series, Toronto: Oxford University Press, 1968.)

He is currently working on a novel called *A Possible Truth*.

170

One Evening

Miss Machry looked in the mirror, straightened her dress and then sat down in a chair beside the open window and waved the old Japanese fan. She succeeded in washing away only a little of the oppressive heat. As she looked out the window and up the street, the leaves waved in the late sunlight. There was no sign of him yet. She went back to her fanning. It was an exacting task, for only by the gentlest of handling could she preserve the fan. It had been her mother's many years ago and treasured both as useful and exotic, an object to be placed on any table that needed a touch of colour and life. And after her mother was taken she had used it to fan her father as he rocked into his dotage on the front porch of the house. There was a twinge of pain as she thought of that awful summer, the hottest in years, with the air dry and dusty in the daytime and at night heavy with the scent of flowers. In those last months her father lay on the porch silent and paralyzed, a wreck in the painful sun. For hours she sat and fanned him and spoke to him and waited. Then, almost with the first cool breeze of fall, he died and left her, relieved and alone.

She stood up once more and looked in the mirror. Was the lipstick too bright? she wondered. Just in case, she blotted it once more and checked again before she threw the kleenex in the wastebasket. Now it was all right. With her hand she touched her hair. It had been a rush to get to the hairdresser's in time after work and then come home and change. She should have eaten a decent meal, she supposed, but she was in such a hurry and she really wasn't hungry. Perhaps a bit of bread and cheese right now. But she decided against it. Once more she checked her dress, spinning around to make sure her slip didn't show. The fan was still in her hand. When she had opened it again, she waved it gingerly. As she fanned, she looked up the street, which was growing dark in the shadow of the trees. It was silent and empty and for a moment she worried. He must have been kept late at the store. The boys were always ducking out early and leaving him to clean up. He was too kindhearted to complain to them about it. The thought of the boys made her feel personally injured. As if they were the only ones who were in a hurry to get out and go some-place. She hoped they would see them tonight. Restraining the urge to do a little dance step across the floor, she sat down in her chair. With a nailfile she carefully repeated her simple manicure. She decided that perhaps she was a little hungry. She set down the nailfile, looked at her dim reflection in the mirror for the last time and went downstairs.

In the kitchen, she opened the icebox and took out a block of cheese, cut off a little and put it away. She ate it, along with a piece of unbuttered bread from the end of the loaf in the breadbox. The glass of water with which she washed it down tasted of chlorine. Cheese was binding she knew and not at all good for anyone who was troubled with constipation, but it was so simple. Besides, it seemed almost immodest to admit that she was troubled that way. She checked her watch; he certainly was a little behind time.

Outside the window, the birds were calling through the hot air. So were the crickets and locusts. The whole garden, on the verge of darkness, was full of peace and stillness. She thought of the man who was on his way to her through the silent town and the dark streets and she knelt in front of the open window.

"Lord," she said, and her voice sounded strange in the empty room, "make me worthy of such happiness." For a few moments she knelt there with her eyes tight shut, not praying really, just listening to the sounds from the garden. Then she heard the sound of a car coming down the street, and she quickly got to her feet. It went on past the house. Miss Machry stood still, a little ashamed of her excitement and hurry. But there was no use kneeling again, and her knee-joints were a little sore anyway from the unaccustomed bending. Tomorrow in church she would be especially attentive to her prayers and make it up. She wondered vaguely whether they would be too late for her to make the early service. It would do no harm to go at eleven o'clock after such a special occasion, but it must not become a habit. Lost in her speculation, she was almost unaware of a car stopping in front of the house. When the knock on the door came, she suddenly realized that he was there, and for a moment she was panic-stricken. But she composed herself, brushed and straightened her dress and went to answer the door.

"Good evening, Edith," he said as he stood in the doorway. Miss Machry restrained an urge to look modestly away. Instead she looked straight into his eyes and smiled.

"Good evening, Jim." She almost made the mistake of asking whether the boys had kept him late at the store, but she caught herself in time and said only "Isn't it warm?"

"Yes," he replied. "I'm afraid that I'm a little late. The boys at the store skipped out early again." Miss Machry was glad he had mentioned it first. With a start she realized that they were still standing at the door.

"Do come in for a minute," she said. He nodded and entered. Now that they were in, what were they to do? She took his hat, temporized. There was no reason for her to be so excited. She had not been like this since the first time he had taken her out. But, after all, tonight was special.

"Would you like a glass of wine, Jim. Or a little something to eat? Perhaps some bread and cheese?" She almost wondered whether he was ever troubled with . . . but she caught herself and suppressed the thought before it had a chance to form.

"I wouldn't mind a glass of wine." She moved toward her bottle of ceremonial sherry with its accompanying wine-glasses.

"I don't know how you stand those boys," she said. "Children nowadays are so lazy." That was a regrettable thing to have said. It made her sound old.

"All children are much the same, I guess," he answered tolerantly. "I doubt if I was much better at that age." His answer put them on the same basis as far as age was concerned. He went on, "Whenever I feel like criticizing other people's children, I just ask myself whether I could have raised them any better if they'd been mine. I doubt if I could." The spectre of his dead wife was in the room for a few seconds then. She had been a sickly woman who was unable to give her husband children and died very young. Miss Machry poured the sherry, a glass for him and a taste for herself. She tried to decide whether it was at all improper to wonder if she could bear him children, and suddenly she was aware of her stomach pressing the edge of the sideboard. She stood a little straighter. When she handed Jim his glass, he smiled and asked what they should toast. She hesitated, then was seized by a moment of recklessness. Raising her glass, she said:

"To our adventure tonight."

"May it be a proper beginning," he continued. They touched glasses and drank solemnly. Miss Machry tried to make her wine last as long as his, but it was so little that it was soon gone. The glass was awkward in her hand. She set it down and moved toward the stairs.

"I'll be down in a minute," she said, "and we can leave." As she reached the stairs, she wondered painfully if he thought she was going to the toilet after her sudden rush to leave. It was too late to do much about her embarrassment. She turned back toward him.

"I think I'd better close the windows. It smells a little like rain." All she really wanted to do was to check once more, see that she looked alright. When she reached the head of the stairs, she turned on the bedroom light and closed the windows, noisily so that he could hear. Then she went to the mirror and checked once again. She looked at the dress on her thin figure, her hands, her pale, ashen face with the hair a little grey on the temples. Everything seemed in order, so she shut off the light and went downstairs. He had finished his wine and rose as she came into the room.

"All set?" he asked.

"Yes," she said, "all ready." They went toward the door. Mentally Miss Machry checked to see that she hadn't left any lights on upstairs. She would leave the light in the hall burning so the house didn't look too empty. When they reached the car, he helped her in. Then they drove off down the street, leaving a cloud of dust. They sat close together on the seat of the car as they drove through town, feeling like conspirators. Their courtship was a carefully guarded secret, which up till now they had chosen to reveal to no one. Jim checked his watch.

"Seems a little early yet. We should wait awhile till the crowd gets there. Maybe we'll drive around for a while first."

"All right, Jim," she replied and rested her hand on his arm for a moment.

They drove out into the country along highways and back roads. For awhile they parked by the lake and watched the moon on the water glittering and moving with the ripples. In silence they watched. Once Jim turned to her and put his hand gently on her hair and took it away again. She thrilled with pleasure, but she hoped he hadn't mussed her hair. He checked his watch.

"We'll go now." Miss Machry nodded. They drove back to town and up to the main street. As they passed along through the strange shadows thrown by the leaves and the streetlights, their excitement mounted. They neared the park and began to run into heavy traffic. All the young people in town were out at the dance. Miss Machry had a bad moment as they parked the car. She grew dizzy and thought she was going to be ill. But then they got out and Jim took her hand and it was all right again. As they walked through the park, they could hear a saxophone wailing in its throat on the bandstand. They could see the young people, young men, soldiers and girls standing against the trees in the light. All the single boys and girls and a few of the young married couples came here on summer Saturday nights. The boys from Jim's store would probably be here; the thought gave Miss Machry some satisfaction and she held his hand a little more tightly. Then they emerged into the light and walked up to the counter. Grace, the woman at the counter who sold the tickets and refreshments, looked at them and tried to hide her surprise. Several of the young men and girls stopped their conversations and looked around.

"Two tickets please, Grace," Jim said in a strong, confident voice. Miss Machry was shivering with fear. They took their tickets and walked into the dancehall. Fantastic couples shuffled under the weird yellow light. Miss Machry thought she could see a tremor run through the crowd when they walked in. But she decided it was an illusion. However, there were a few of the youngsters who turned and looked at them standing there hand in hand, a little at a loss for something to say or do. She was filled with dismay and almost disgust as she watched the boy who danced in front of them sliding his hand across the back of the girl he was dancing with. Then Jim turned to her and took hold of her and they began to dance.

The music was slower than she found comfortable, and they danced awkwardly. She felt like part of an archaic monster as they turned across the floor. Some of the youngsters stood and watched their ungainly progress. Miss Machry's face burned as she thought of the stories they would tell their parents. Then she looked at Jim, his long, tired face and greying hair looking strange in the yellow light, and she didn't care any more.

She was afraid the dancing was making her sweat. There was a dampness along her back where Jim's hand was resting. The night seemed to be growing hotter and hotter. Over Jim's shoulder, she saw one of the boys from the store approaching. When he got a little closer he spoke.

"Hello, Mr. Cameron."

Jim was startled by the sudden voice, stopped and looked back over his shoulder. Miss Machry couldn't stop turning and lost her balance. The room whirled around as she fell over Jim's leg, tripping him and throwing him down. There was a sudden pain in her hip when she hit the floor. She heard herself give an ugly grunt. Her dress was above her knees, and she was trying to hold it down when Jim fell on top of her, hurting her hip again. She saw a line of the legs of people who stood around looking on.

"Golly, Mr. Cameron, I'm sorry," the boy from the store was saying. "I didn't mean to do that." He helped Jim up. His girl knelt down beside Miss Machry. She was a stranger. Miss Machry wished she would go away.

"I'm so sorry, Mrs. Cameron," she said. Miss Machry winced. "Are you all right?" She helped her up. Miss Machry was afraid she was going to cry or be sick.

"Are you all right, Edith?" Jim said.

"Yes," she said, "But perhaps we'd better go now." They moved toward the door. He didn't speak again. She was afraid that he was angry; she wished they hadn't come.

"I'm very sorry, Mr. Cameron." The boy was still there. Why didn't he go away? It was awful enough without his sympathy.

"That's all right, Jake," Jim answered. "It was my own fault."

Miss Machry was thinking ahead to tomorrow and the stares of the people in church. Perhaps she would stay away. When they arrived outside, it seemed strange that the world hadn't changed. A dog ran up the street and barked as he passed. Old Mr. and Mrs. Gordon still sat on their porch and tried to rock away the heat. Miss Machry reached over to take Jim's arm. She missed and stumbled. He caught her and held her by the elbow. Without a word, the two of them walked to the car and got in. As they drove home, Miss Machry could feel the pain in her hip where she had fallen. She had to sit toward one side. She was angry with herself for spoiling everything. Perhaps Jim was angry with her. The car stopped in front of her house. They got out and walked to the door. As they stood there in silence, Jim smiled down at her.

"I'm glad we did it," he said. Then he put his arms around her and kissed her on her lips that were dry and cracked from the heat. His thin arms were strong around her and she closed her eyes tight. He held her for a long time, until she became conscious of sweat on her back and the pain from her hip. Then he loosened his arms and she opened her eyes. He looked down at her, kissed her lightly once again and said goodnight. She watched him go down the walk. He climbed into his car. As she went into the house, she could hear him driving away. She went up the stairs to her bedroom. Strangely, it was just the way she had left it. Bed, dresser, curtains, her mother's fan. She walked to the window and looked out. The town was silent under the shadow of the great old trees. There was no wind, no motion except a moth which fluttered around the streetlight, struggling to reach the bulb. As Miss Machry watched it, tears were running down her face. But underneath she was smiling and smiling.

I started to write "One Evening" in the spring of 1958, sometime around my twentieth birthday, when I was a student at the University of Toronto. It began, I think, with the desire to evoke a place and a feeling, the town of Niagara-on-the-Lake where I'd lived for several years, and the feeling of a summer evening in the town. I think the first version of the story was little more than a descriptive passage.

I don't remember just when the characters came into being, but they were the kind of people I knew from the years I'd spent working in a grocery store and singing in a church choir, and they represented to me something about the town, some combination of age and quietness, that I wanted to embody. There were not real people, but I couldn't have imagined them without knowing real people who belonged to their world.

At that time I was just beginning to write stories, and there was a period in the development of this one when I had the place and the feeling and the people, but lacked any central focus, an event that would give the story a shape. Puzzling over this one night, I imagined them going to the dance in the park, and that event gave me the combination of the unusual and the ordinary that I needed. I finished the story, in much its present form, early in the summer, a month or so after I'd started it.

I sent it to *Canadian Forum* and left for Stoney Lake where I was working for the summer and where, a few weeks later, I heard that *Forum* had accepted the story. When it appeared a few months later, it was my first publication outside of student magazines. I also sold the story to the C.B.C. for broadcast on their program "Anthology." These two appearances of the story, along with the sale of another I wrote later the same year, allowed me to take myself seriously as a writer for the first time.

Naturally I have a kind of attachment to the story because it was my first publication, but when I look back at it now, I find myself asking questions about it. That bottle of sherry, for example, did Miss Machry buy it for herself? I can't imagine her walking into the liquor store in Niagara-on-the-Lake. Perhaps it had been around since before her father's death. Perhaps he bought it many years before. Or did Jim buy it?

The fact that I go back to question myself about that bottle of sherry suggests the kind of story I was trying to write, one in which the reader is drawn into the world of a character or group of characters who seem like the people he sees around him every day, but are known differently, from the inside, with the reader living the character's situation while reading the story. Miss Machry's life is defined by the things around her, and these things must be right, so that in the course of a few pages they'll make the reader understand her past, her present, her feelings about what happens.

Particular things, a time, a place, things seen or heard or remembered, the interplay of people with each other and their surroundings, these produce in me the kind of excitement that makes me start to write. I sometimes want my writing to go beyond them, but again and again, they are my starting point.

As I work through a story, what I want to do is to invent, organize, and select in such a way that the particular experience of the characters takes on life in the reader's imagination; things that are what they are, but mean more.

DAVID HELWIG

BIBLIOGRAPHY

Figures in a Landscape. Ottawa: Oberon Press, 1968. (Out of print) [Poems and plays]

The Sign of the Gunman. Ottawa: Oberon Press, 1969. [Poems]

The Streets of Summer. Ottawa: Oberon Press, 1969. [Stories]

John Metcalf

John Metcalf was born in Carlisle, England, in 1938. He attended Bristol University and came to Canada a year after graduating. He has worked as a teacher of English in various high schools in and around Montreal. In 1965 he married Gale Courey; they have a daughter, Elizabeth.

He has been awarded two Canada Council Bursaries. His story "The Estuary," was awarded the President's Medal of the University of Western Ontario for the best single story of 1969.

He enjoys violent private-eye stories and poetry. His favourite short story writers are Ernest Hemingway, Katherine Mansfield, Ring Lardner, Alice Munro, Margaret Laurence, and Richard Yates.

He is currently lecturing in English at Loyola College in Montreal and working on a collection of stories.

A Bag of Cherries

Astrella the pert-breasted slave girl murdered by lust-crazed drooling Gerentius, Martullus Roman-deathing himself on the battlefield – David skipped through the last few pages and pushed the paperback into his raincoat pocket. For the reviewer quoted on the back, the book had brought the last days of the Roman Empire glowingly to life. The best part of it for David had been the picture on the cover.

As he leaned over in the seat to get at his cigarettes, he looked up at his suitcase. He wondered, as he always did, if it was completely safe. Luggage racks were, of course, so constructed that the angle of the case prevented even the possibility. . . But what if the netting broke, if the wooden bar was rotten, or the screws holding the brackets. . . He got up and tested the case. It was quite safe. Just like his mother, he thought, feeling annoyed with himself. Just like his mother checking the gas taps on the stove before she went to bed and then getting up half an hour later to see whether they were turned off.

Bored now he had finished the book and, bored by the prospect of another two hours on the train, he turned to look secretly at his fellow passengers reflected in that phantom coach between the window and the darkness of the night. A fat, middle aged man crumpled asleep in his overcoat. A soldier reading a comic. A woman knitting, spectacles and her hat on, her ball of wool in a brown paper bag.

The young woman had got out at the last stop, Reedminster, over half an hour before. She'd been wearing a tight linen skirt and a black blouse. The crossings and recrossings of her legs had interrupted the last days of the Roman Empire since she'd got into the carriage at Brampton Junction.

She'd been useful between the Junction and Reedminster. Not really the most suitable material – he'd had to ignore her copy of *Reader's Digest* and the earrings – but better than nothing. She'd done well enough to start the story.

It was the story itself which was important and the story was always the same. It had reached its perfected form when he had been about fifteen. But much earlier than that, ever since the beginnings of his hot grammar school days when he'd got excited on buses, he'd been obsessed with the idea that on a journey, on a train, hitch-hiking perhaps, he'd meet a rich, lonely young woman of taste and sophistication.

180

They fell easily into a light and bantering conversation. Her voice was deep and slightly husky. Her hands gesturing, long fingers, on her wrist a massive silver bracelet. She listened with growing fascination as he talked about his art. Her eyes admired him as he described the tonalities, the silences, the *reverberations* he was striving for and which now seemed within his reach.

Ineluctible modalities of vision. Etc. Etc.

The apparatus of her life quickly sketched:

The Park.

Stately oak trees bordering the sweep of the drive.

An ivy-grown folly.

A herd of fallow deer.

And in the west wing, her father, the wounded colonel.

But her room! A deep, black carpet. White walls. Rich saffon curtains reaching to the floor. Commanding and stark against the white walls, set within niches, primitive carvings from the Congo. On the wall above the couch a Byzantine Christ on a wood panel.

As she refilled the wine glasses, he wandered over to the Sheraton table and glanced at the books lying there. One, bound in green crushed Morocco, was a privately printed and illustrated edition of Huysman's *A Rebours*. The other, in a white bible binding and blind-stamped with a cross, was De Sade's *Les crimes de l'amour*.

A subtle fragrance of incense, light and dry like the wine, scented the air...

Candle light. The whisper of silk...

David grinned at his reflection in the rattling window. His sole sexual experience on a train had consisted of a conversation which might have been suggestive, or merely friendly, and she had been about forty and had got off at Leamington Spa.

The conductor's call and the sound of carriage doors slamming was coming closer.

"Have your tickets ready! All tickets, please!"

David felt in his inside pocket. He had put the ticket inside a letter which he had received that morning. As the carriage door rolled back, letting in a rush of cold air, the man opposite him started from his sleep with a strangled snort and began searching through his pockets as the conductor impatiently tapped his clippers against the frame of the door. David pushed the envelope with its familiar writing back into his pocket. As he settled back in his seat and the comfortable warmth began to build up again he could feel the letter pressing against him with each movement of the train.

Although he'd opened the letter when it arrived he hadn't bothered reading more than the first few sentences. He knew what it would say – a reworking of what it always said. Had he received the parcel? Don't leave off a wool vest because warmer weather *seems* to be coming. Spring winds treacherous. Did he remember so and so – a *very* nice boy – a regular church-goer – married last week to *such* a nice girl. A nurse. Also a church-goer. The bulbs were beginning to sprout in the bowls and promised a brave show for the spring. His father poorly again – pain in his back – and ignoring the doctor's advice. Pipe smoking just as harmful as cigarettes and quite probably the cause of father's pain. Father obstinate and stubborn. These scientists didn't know *everything*. *All* smoking harmful. Hoped *he* was smoking less. Was he making his grant last out better this term? Money didn't grow on trees. He would have more money if he didn't smoke. Remember Mr. Micawber's advice. Was the girl he had mentioned in his last letter a *nice* girl?

Each letter, he thought, a mirror of his mother's world; a world made up of fat armchairs, bowls of bulbs, *nice* murder stories from *Boot's Library,* starched tablecloths, warm underwear, the intrigue and gossip culled from meetings of the Ladies' Social Hour at the Methodist Church – a world symbolized for him by the Missionary Boxes which stood about the house each picturing a beaming, mother hubbarded, wooly-haired piccaninny.

When he arrived home his mother would pursue the monologue, of which her letters were a part, trotting between the scullery and kitchen, rattling crockery, piling the table with food, talking, incessantly talking. His grandmother, who never moved from her chair by the fire, would sit glaring at him. After half an hour or so she would break her senile and malignant silence to say, "As big as you. And still at school. Ought to be working. You ought to be out at work." And his mother would say, "Not school, mother. *University.*" And his grandmother would twiddle with her hearing aid until it whined and crackled and would then belch loudly.

Later, in a way that had become a ritual, he would wander from room to room, taking stock, making an inventory, always ending up in the attic where his past was stored with the other lumber. And kneeling by the battered trunks and boxes he would look through old books and papers, toys and games; envelopes with *Important Papers: Private* written in red pencil, his butterfly collection, tobacco tins full of foreign coins, his big Scottish sword, a rusting sheath-knife and roller skates, a broken air rifle still in a box that said *Kills Vermin at Forty Yards,* marbles, dry tubes of oil paint, the big Oxo tin full of pairs of old spectacles, a John Bull Printing Set complete with eyeshade, a rubble of cigarette cards, lead soldiers, pencils, American *Superman* comics with the treasured DC stamp, cap guns and holsters and packets of cigarette papers for cigarettes he had never been able to roll.

But although going home was not exactly an adventure, he always felt an anticipation, in spite of himself a sense of excitement.

He looked at his watch. Another one and a half hours to go. There were no lights beyond the window, nothing to look at. Only the reflection of the carriage; the prim click and glint of the lady's knitting needles. The man in the overcoat was snoring. David stretched out his legs, taking care not to touch the sleeping man, and closed his eyes. The heavy rhythm of the train wheels began to dominate his mind and he found the irregular click-clicking of the knitting needles an annoyance.

The warmth, the soft sway and pull of the warm seat, lulled him into a doze. On the threshold of sleep he saw again, gleaming in the spotlight, the tilt and flash of the cymbal in the dark hall. Mary's face. The gleam of the cymbal, yellow and gold, and then its singing shatter died away and in the shapeless movements of his mind the cymbal became a sun, perfect with rays like a child's drawing, and the sun was stuck right in the middle of a sky, a sky of the purest blue.

He was walking through the village with his father. His father was laughing and instead of the black suit he always wore he was wearing grey flannels and a sports jacket and instead of the white dog-collar a red tie. And he was holding David's hand while they looked at the village pond and the stocks.

The stocks were bolted and clamped together by a rusty padlock. His father told him what they were and about Oliver Cromwell who had warts on his nose and destroyed churches. In the shallow pond they used to duck witches.

A steep white road climbed out of the village, the houses straggling, until it curved over the brow and out onto the open moors. At the last shop, which was dark and cluttered and smelled of cheese and paraffin and yellow soap, his father bought three pounds of cherries – they cost a florin – huge cherries on their stalks, black and juicy. And the paper bag turned black and sodden and gaped open, and together, hands piled full, they had climbed on up the hill spitting cherrystones and wiping their hands on their trousers.

And under the sky with the perfect sun they'd walked across the moors to an old house which was like a museum. And his father had said that a very great lady called Emily Bronte had lived there – a lady who wrote books and there was a low writing desk, its surface a sheen of light,

183

and on it a pewter inkstand with a goose feather curving out and the feather was called a quill pen.

Later, the sun lower in the sky and the wind colder, they had hunted in the rocks and heather for the plastic bases of hand-grenades left by the soldiers at practice. They were black and criss-cross knurled with War Office arrows on the bottom and they were for his mother to use as egg cups. David had stuffed his pockets with shining cartridge cases. He had found so many that his father had carried some too.

Running against its brakes, tempo changed, the train slowed towards the Longwell Tunnel. David stirred in his seat. Just before the train entered the tunnel it shuffled over points and the lights in the carriage flickered. David woke to the hollow rattle and sulphurous smoke which was blowing in through the small ventilation window. The soldier got up and slammed it shut.

The tunnel ran for half a mile and the Central Station was only minutes beyond. David checked the safety of his ticket again. Suddenly the roar and rattle of the train quieted and he could see the lights of the suburbs, the sign of the Odeon Cinema red and green against the sky and car lights on the London Road.

He pulled down his suitcase and put on his raincoat. The train was gliding in under the sodium lights of the station. As it jerked to a standstill with a clank and squealing of its couplings, David stepped down onto the empty, echoing platform.

Behind the ticket barrier he could see a small group of people waiting. Just behind them was a short figure in black. David felt a sudden surge of excitement and pleasure but, not knowing why he did so, pretended not to have seen him. He walked slowly down the platform towards the barrier and stopped to look at some creaking wicker baskets of racing pigeons. He looked up only as he was handing in his ticket, and pretended surprise. Then he was through and shaking hands with his father warmly. They stood looking at each other for a moment.

"Well," said his father, "have a good journey?"

"Yes. Fine." he said. "I had a seat all the way."

"Good," said his father. "That's good."

He bent to pick up David's suitcase and David said, "Don't be silly, Dad. Put it down. It's full of books."

"Are you sure you can manage?"

"Yes. Really. It's not too bad."

"Come along then," said his father. "I've got the car outside."

They walked across the booking hall and out into the car park.

"Had a good term?" said his father.

"Yes," said David. "I'm having to work pretty hard though."

184

"Well," said his father, "hard work never killed anyone. Here we are. Put the case in the back."

As they got in and slammed the doors his father said, "You always appreciate things more when you've had to work for them."

"How's the car been behaving?" asked David.

"It's never let me down. Not once. Not even in that cold snap a couple of weeks ago. You can't beat the old Morris."

His father started the car and edged out into the stream of traffic on the main road.

"That's the secret of buying a second-hand car – make sure you know who's owned it before."

He changed gear to tackle the hill and David said, "So how have you and mum been keeping?"

"Oh, your mother's fine. Tired, you know. She will insist on doing too much."

"And you?"

"I'm still on the tablets the doctor gave me but the pain's the same. I'll just have to get used to it, I suppose."

"Why?" said David. "Why don't you go to another doctor or to a specialist at the hospital?"

"There's a limit to what doctors can do, you know," said his father.

"Have you tried?" asked David.

"You can't argue with *facts*," said his father.

He changed gear to overtake a heavy truck. David glanced idly at the passing buildings. There was a silence.

"You'll certainly be able to see some changes in the house," said his father. "We repainted the kitchen and I've just finished putting new glass in the greenhouse. I've been thinking of running an extension cord out there and heating it more that way.

"Ummm," said David. "That's a good idea."

They passed the Rounding Road junction and turned down towards home.

"Yes," said his father, "The garden's going to look a real treat. Your mother's got daffs planted all along the side of the fence and I'm hoping for some tulips this year. In the centre beds, they'll go."

"That should look beautiful when they come out," said David.

"Yes," said his father. "It'll be as pretty as a picture."

David made an appreciative noise.

"Ah, well," said his father, "I expect you'll be about ready for a cup of tea."

"Yes," said David, staring at his father's profile, "a cup of tea would be very nice."

185

The Estuary

I sometimes think my tiredness is different from other people's. A different *kind* of thing. Once, I think it was in *Reader's Digest*, I saw the words *"depth fatigue"* and I'm pretty sure that's what I've got. Take the way I feel when I wake up in the morning. Apart from the specific things – dull headache, sore throat, inflamed eyelids and nausea – I feel chronically tired all over. It's as if all the cartilage has melted from between the bones and pads of tiredness have filled the spaces. And every morning these aching pads stiffen my back and legs and make it difficult for me to get out of bed.

The pain is in no way imaginary, I can assure you, although I *know* it's psychosomatic. The doctor I was using last year left me in no doubt about *that*. (Marvellous it was. I must have had about three weeks of working days off in trips to the hospital – allergy, lungs, heart, diabetes, ears, nose and throat – they tested everything before they threw me out.)

And so I took his pills – purple for go and blue for stop – until he refused to renew the prescription. He got rather moral towards the end and told me sternly that I ought to take myself in hand. And perhaps it was a good thing really because the purple ones only made me feel tired at a more active level.

I *know* it's psychosomatic but knowing *why* you're ill doesn't cure you. The important thing is to remove the cause. *As* I told him and which he didn't appreciate. (But I wasn't too bothered about that because he'd stopped giving me time off work anyway.) No, you've got to remove the cause and in my case that'd necessitate a pension – which creates certain problems when you're only twenty. I could present a case to the Ministry of Pensions that seems to me logically watertight – I'm tired because I'm bored and I'm bored because I hate working – but unfortunately they're not the most compassionate of institutions.

I'm sure my boredom's partly seasonal. Like tides. I offered that idea, which I consider quite original, to Dr. Cottle when I had to go and see him the other day but he's not a man who's attuned to the philosophic outlook. Oh, he's kind and well meaning but he's difficult to talk with. Though I'd rather one hour with him every two weeks than have done the thirty days.

His main fault is that he's obsessive. Every visit we get back to the same thing. *Why were you crying? Why were you shouting? What did the words mean?* But I always deny any knowledge; tell him I was too upset to remember.

Then he says, "You can't hold out for ever. You *need* to tell me." He is, of course, very wrong but I keep on going because – well lots of reasons. The probation officer from the court checks up. Mrs. Grice the welfare lady, who told me she prays for me. *And* the appointments are always on Thursdays when I'm low on cigarettes and he keeps on offering me *Players No. 3* which are a welcome change from tipped *Woodbines*.

Dr. Cottle interests me. The first few times I went he managed to control himself – he was using a Carl Rogers technique then – but the periods of silence seemed to eat his nerves raw. After a couple of visits I got a library book on Rogers and the non-directive method which gave me the whiphand. Since then, I've managed to bring him out quite a lot.

I think I disturb him. I chat away about my mother and father, my brother and sister, infancy and adolescence, work and relaxations, uncle tom cobbley and all. I offer him ideas and theories and I smoke his cigarettes.

And we sit there in his office. Two big leather armchairs. A small and expensively simple mahogany coffee-table. A Persian rug. Two Georgian sherry decanters. (One filled with *Harvey's Bristol Cream* and the other with *Tio Pepe*.) Vast glass ashtrays which slowly fill with butts. And on the just off-white wall a large, and in my opinion, rather pretentious, hard edge abstract.

And he always says – he's got one of those lazy, chocolate brown voices – "You can trust me, David. You know that, don't you?" And always at some point or other, "I'm not an officer of the court, you know." And whenever he says that I can always picture over by the door the small, discreet filing-cabinet (pastel; oyster grey, *of course*) and I say in *my* intense voice, "I know that, Doctor." He tries not to show it but it irritates him when I call him that.

And just before I go he always says, "Do you think you're feeling happier *in yourself?*" And I always reply, "I'm always happy *in myself.*" Then he usually smiles his roguish smile, which must have wreaked transference on Christ knows how many ladies, and says, "No more notions of doing anything silly?" (He's far too delicate to come right out with it. If he said the word "suicide" it'd embarrass him.)

And that's what I mean when I say he's difficult to talk with. I told him the very first time that I saw him that I hadn't been trying to commit suicide but there was no shaking him. He must have got a really strong line from the police and the two fishermen so I've given up arguing now.

I suppose the fishermen and the other man – I never did find out

187

whether he was a local or a visitor – I suppose they felt they had a stake in me after getting soaked to the armpits and hauling me ashore and nothing I could say was going to do them out of their moment of glory. So as far as Dr. Maximillian Cottle is concerned it was a desperate bid at self-destruction. The whole matter's basically too simple for him to understand though he's cottoned onto the fact that I'm hiding something. So every visit we get back to *Why were you crying? Why were you shouting? What did the words mean?*

The last time I went he abandoned all pretence of finesse. He was using his no nonsense, all cards on the table voice.

"When you were carried back to the beach," he said, having a quick refresher from my dossier, "you were crying in an hysterical manner."

PAUSE. Looks at me. Waits hopefully.

"The fishermen reported that when they first reached you, you were shouting, 'Don't go! Don't GO. Please don't go!' "

PAUSE. Looks up enquiringly and irritably scratches the back of his hand.

"On the beach you cried and said over and over again, and I quote, 'You can't leave me. You can't just go away.' "

The silence slowly builds.

And then I gave a little half shake of my head (I didn't want to overdo it because he watches me like a hawk) and I did my half embarrassed and half exasperated laugh and said, "I *really* can't remember. I really can't. I'm as mystified as you are."

Then he said, "I feel, David, that until you admit to yourself that you *were* shouting; until you explain your words; until you *acknowledge* them as yours you won't be able to enter into a period of adjustment."

So we sat there in the black armchairs, silently, and I tried to look as if I was struggling to remember. Every now and then, I breathed heavily through my nose. I frowned slightly. I pinched at my lower lip.

He lay stretched out in his chair staring at me and pressing his finger tips into a steeple; making his finger tips march up and down. Then after he'd played all the finger games he could think of he said, *very* reluctantly, "Perhaps you'd care to talk about something else . . . ?"

And so I told him again about being bored.

I told him about the No. 93 bus. About catching it every morning at 8:15 at the Canning Rd. terminus. About the people in the bus queue. A schoolboy with ginger hair. The woman who works as a char at the United Hospital and who doesn't sleep at night because of the pain in her legs. The girl who works in Josiah's Beauty Salon on Papermill Rd. whose hands are always raw from peroxide. A labourer, his boots white with cement dust. A small man, stooped in a shabby raincoat, carrying a cheap cardboard attaché case, who stands rigidly staring across the road at nothing. And every morning the same bus-conductor. An old man with white hair who has to stop half-way up the stairs to the top deck to catch his breath; who wears gloves with the fingers cut off. An old man whose fingers are so stiff and clumsy that they slip on the keys of his ticket machine.

Dr. Cottle seemed a bit restive so I said, "That's most important. Important to *me,* Dr. Cottle."

He said, "You feel the bus-conductor to be important?"

"Yes," I said. "I do."

He always regresses to an uninspired and dreary Rogers sort of response when he doesn't think he's getting anywhere. But I didn't give him a chance to try anything else. I bore on relentlessly. I told him all about the library again.

I told him about Miss Nevins. How her slip always shows at the back of her dress. A dress which ends only six or seven inches above the ankle. And how the slip is always mauve trimmed with mauve lace. And how she always has a hankie, trimmed with mauve lace, tucked into the sleeve of her cardigan. And how she always moves in a cloud of lavender like something put away in a winter drawer.

He crossed his legs carefully, making sure he didn't crush the crease in his trousers, and said, "I've heard this before, David. Do you think it's possible you're telling me this to avoid telling me something else?"

"Oh, no," I said. "This is more important than anything else."

And then I told him about explaining that with two tickets you could take out *one* Fiction and *one* Non-Fiction but not *two* Fiction or *two* Non-Fiction; that Fiction means a story book that isn't true and Non-Fiction means for example a book about history or science; and, no madam, biography is Non-Fiction although yes it *is* a story – the story of somebody's life – but the difference is that it's a true story and not an untrue story. Which *is* a funny way of dividing things up but no not even this once and the book must be replaced because the library has strict rules.

He'd been getting more and more restless as I'd been talking. He'd even done a few of his isometric exercises. And suddenly he said, "Really, David! You're indulging yourself again – enjoying your self-pity. I thought we'd got past all that. I'd really thought you were beginning to move into a more *constructive* phase."

I sneaked a flash at my watch – only twenty more minutes to fill in –

and said, "Well, you see, Doctor, I'm trying to fill in the way I *felt* – you know – *why* I went to Wales. I thought it might be helpful."

And I hurried on and told him about waking up in the morning with the tiredness where the cartilage used to be. And the impossible search for excuses. Colds. Influenza. Diarrhoea. Migraine. The repeated deaths of close relatives. Sprained ankles. Buses breaking down; the mechanical failure of my alarm clock. Ringing up with balls of paper in my mouth pretending to be my landlord. A sullen gathering of boredom which ripened every few weeks screaming for the lancet.

He broke in again and said, "David! David, I want you to stop and *think* about what you've just told me. You see that you're repeating a depressive pattern, don't you? I think it's obvious even to you. But I still feel that you're not quite prepared to break that pattern yet – to accept that your world is *necessarily* as it is. Umm? Do you think that's fair?"

"I do see what you mean, Doctor," I said.

He smiled his wise smile and said, "You have to want to adjust, David. You have to *commit* yourself. What you're just been telling me is obviously impossible as a way of life, isn't it?"

"Yes. I realize that now," I said.

"And," he said, "you have the future to think about."

I *didn't* tell him to what extent the future *did* possess me; how it shadowed each passing day; because that was precisely what he didn't want to hear. I didn't tell him how I feared the future which is only my present repeated CLICK click CLICK repeated. I didn't tell him that if I rolled round the strips of rubber on the date-stamp I would age with them. In November, January, April or May, this year, next year, each and every year the library floor would still gleam with polish; Miss Nevins' slip would still be peeping from beneath her withered dress; the electric clock would still be humming through the endless afternoon and my life would be slowly stamped away CLICK click CLICK of the date-stamp CLICK click CLICK stamping my life away two weeks from now two weeks from then two weeks from *then*. And fines for being late.

"Yes," I said. "Of course, you're right."

He smiled encouragingly and, pulling back inches of snowy cuff, looked at his watch. "We've about fifteen minutes left to us today. Shall we have another try at the events in Wales?" But he almost sighed as he said that.

He reached over for the folder which contained the notes on my case and as he picked it up some of the papers slipped out. I ducked to pick them up for him because I'd been wanting to get a glance at them for weeks. But he took them too quickly.

190

"Now then," he said. "On the day in question you'd overslept and were late for work. You were often late and as a result your relationship with Mr." – he checked the typescript – "with Mr. Prippet was not a happy one. And so, deciding that you might as well be hanged, as it were, for a sheep as a lamb, you took the whole day off. You went first to a café where you ate breakfast and then you sat in a park. Is that right? Am I leaving anything out?"

(There'd been an old man in the park muffled up against the cold. A huddled figure on a municipal bench staring over the neat gravel path and the trim lawn at the central bed of municipal flowers. And near his feet a grey sea of pigeons heaving and fluttering over a paper bag. The pigeons had horrid red feet – not pretty pink like coral – raw, red like sores. Like the hands of the girl in the bus queue.)

"No," I said. "That's what happened."

"And then you left the park and wandered around the streets for an hour or so. Quite by chance, you found yourself in front of the railway station and you went in, on impulse, and boarded the North Wales train without a ticket."

I nodded.

"Why North Wales? Had you been there before?"

"No," I said. "I don't really know why. There was an attractive poster outside. Mountains. A stream. I don't really know why."

"But didn't you think at all of the consequences of not being able to pay for the ticket?"

"No," I said. "I don't think it really crossed my mind."

"And it didn't cross your mind about what you were going to do when you got there? About paying for a hotel room and food?"

"No," I said. "I just wanted to go away."

"Was it, perhaps, because you knew before you went that there wasn't likely to *be* a reckoning? That your mind was filled with some rather silly notions . . . ?"

He leaned forward eagerly but I just shrugged and looked down at the patterns in the rug.

I'd enjoyed the journey on the train. Travelling always induces a wonderfully soothing state in me rather like a trance – a trance that seems to mingle past and present merging pictures from the passing landscape and images from memory. Thoughts without thinking.

The carriage had been empty most of the way and the click of the wheels and the clack-clacking of the knob of the window cord against the glass, irregular, sometimes fast, sometimes slow, shuffling with a blur and rattle over points, had echoed in my mind the sound of my father's

191

painful typing as he hammered out the Sunday sermon in his study. And I'd remembered – a flood of pictures – but strangely and insistently the summer-house at the bottom of the garden where I'd lock myself on summer evenings and light my stubs of candles. Sacks tacked over the windows. And the smell of jute and wood and oiled tools.

And moving aside my father's implements, forks, spades, dibbers, balls of twine, bundles of canes and pea-sticks, seed packets, trays of little plant pots, rags, paint cans and stiffened brushes, I'd take out my hidden bottles and range them on the broken cardtable. Bottles I'd found in the spinney near my house – Gin and Whiskey, Port, Sherry, Rum and Brandy. And I'd filled them all with lemonade made from *Robinson's Lemonade Crystals*. And in the warm light, sitting in an uncomfortable deckchair, I read Conan Doyle and Edgar Rice Burroughs and drank from each bottle pretending to be drunk.

Picture after picture – the past transfiguring the dingy carriage as the landscape changed and climbed towards Wales.

"The stop was an unscheduled stop," he said.

"Pardon?" I said.

"The stop – where you got off the train – it wasn't a regular station."

"No. That's right."

"You still remember these details?"

"Oh, yes," I said.

"Why did you choose to get out where you did?"

"Well the train stopped near a red signal – I think there was a tunnel ahead – and it seemed to wait there a long time and I could see the lights of a village below so – well I just got out."

"How did you feel? Resigned? Depressed?"

"I don't think I felt anything particularly," I said.

(It had been extremely cold after the warmth of the carriage and while I was standing by the side of the train as it started to move on into the tunnel a jet of white steam had burst from beneath one of the carriages to hang for a few moments in the blackness. By the time it had crumbled and whisped away into the night the train was only a distant rumble and the darkness had completely closed me in.

And I'd stood looking down at the spark and shine of the village lights and the soft movements of the moon on the sea. And I'd wanted to laugh out loud but didn't because of the silence.)

He checked his notes again and then said, "When you reached the village you went to the pub and asked the landlord – a Mr. Davies – for a room and dinner. We've no need to bother about *that* aspect of things. That's a legal matter – nothing to do with me – and was dealt with by the court." He smiled at me and said, "I merely render unto Caesar, as it were." I smiled back at him.

"But," he said, "what does concern us is this: you said a minute ago that when you got off the train you weren't feeling 'anything in particular.' You weren't unhappy. You weren't depressed. You've told me before that you went to bed immediately after you'd eaten and were soon sound asleep. You woke up fairly early and went for a walk along the beach. Yet the next thing we know is that you're being rescued from the sea. You're weeping and shouting hysterically. It doesn't make sense, does it, David?"

I made a selection of agreeing and being bewildered faces and inwardly cursed myself that I hadn't handled the matter in a more intelligent fashion. Right from the start I should have admitted to severe depression, attempted suicide, religious ecstasy and a vision of Jesus in a white gown appearing over the bay to carry me off in His arms. Then, gradually, he could have cured me of that and everyone would have been quite happy. But now I'd landed myself with amnesia or some sort of mental block and I couldn't see any end to this series of Happy Hours.

"We have to find out," he said, "or admit, what happened to make you feel desperate enough to – to become so disturbed. And when we do *that*, David, then. . . ."

"I can remember . . . " I said.

"Yes," he said.

"I can remember waking up and how quiet it was. And I can remember getting dressed and going out across the road to the beach and walking along the beach. . . ."

"Did you meet anyone?" he asked.

"No. Definitely. The street was deserted and I could see along the shore for miles."

"Go on."

"Well all I can remember is standing on some rocks."

"Yes."

"That's all."

"Nothing else at all?"

"No. Nothing."

"You were depressed," he said.

"I don't know. I just can't remember. There's nothing there."

"And that's all?"

"Well I remember being soaked and standing on the beach and a lot of people talking and shouting – but that must have been afterwards."

"You don't know why you were crying?" he said. "Or what you were shouting? 'Don't go! Don't GO. You can't just leave me.' This doesn't mean anything to you?"

I stared at him with my honest and troubled gaze and said, "I'm sorry, Doctor, I *know* how important it is but . . . well – there's just nothing *there*."

Another long silence.

I sighed.

But behind my frank and honest eyes, quite safe from Dr. Maximillian Cottle, I treasured the gleaming sweep of the estuary; and louder than his questions the sound of gulls.

And as near as the sound of gulls would allow I'd told him the truth. I had gone to bed early that night and it was certainly true that I *was* soon asleep. But I hadn't told him of the thick linen sheets and the engraving of General Picton at Waterloo which hung over the fireplace. Nor, just as I was falling asleep, of the sound of boots echoing along the road, each footstep caught and ringing for a second against the rock face of the mountain which towered sheer behind the houses.

And I'd kept from him, too, the beauty of the early morning. The estuary, gleaming like a sheet of old pewter, cradled by the humpy Welsh mountains, purple and grey, which disappeared into more distant ranges indistinguishable from cloud.

And the morning had been alive with sound. The soft slap of water against the sea-wall. The low tinkle and murmur of the ebb tide running, leaving the air sharp with the smell of mud and seaweed. And raucous crows and jackdaws circling the bare tree tops, squabbling and squawking as they wheeled and fluttered. And every few minutes a crow flaking away on black wings from the cliff face and drifting down over the street, wavering on the air like a walker on an invisible tight-rope, to suddenly swoop, and strut along the ebbing tide line.

As I'd stood gazing out over the estuary the sun had begun to glint on the water and tinge the grey rain clouds yellow like a fading bruise. A sandbank was slowly growing out of the water as the tide scoured out through the central channel and the moored yachts and dinghies turned and yawed at their ropes, creaking as the water rippled past them. And I watched the incredibly white gulls riding the tide and sitting on the boats as though they owned them.

Nearer to me, gulls were sitting stolidly on the posts of a ruined jetty which ran out towards the deeper water. I clapped my hands to see if they'd fly away but they wouldn't even turn their heads. Then I threw a pebble into the water near them to see if they'd swoop down but they were far too wise for such poor tourist tricks. And so I started to hunt along the beach for something that they'd eat.

I found a cabbage stalk and a piece of bread and it was when I straightened up and looked out towards the jetty again that I first saw them. Two black patches moving slowly through the water. At first, they looked like the dorsal fins of a big fish. I ran down to the edge of the water but whatever it was had moved under the piles of the jetty. Then I saw one of the black patches again just below one of the slimy posts. As I watched, the patch of blackness in the water grew larger and larger and I saw a creature's back like the swirl of a rolling black barrel. Then nothing. Nothing but grey water.

I continued staring at the spot where it had disappeared but suddenly, further up the beach, one of the things arched out of the water to vanish again with a loud splash. I hurried after it, scanning the surface of the estuary as I ran. And then, only yards from where I was standing, the water broke again and a porpoise curved into the air in a shower of spray.

Its bulk, black and shining, its glistening curve of a back, blotted out the sea and mountains. And in that second cold drops of water from its spray flicked my face. Then just before the water closed over it, I heard the warm huff and snort of its breath.

The pulse of my heart was knocking in my throat and I stood staring at the smooth water unable to move. I could feel the spray drops trickling down my cheek, following the curve of my lip, and I opened my mouth to taste the salt gift.

Then suddenly, further out, they both burst from the water, one of them jumping in a series of sleek curves, until the sea threshed around them. Leaping over each other, sliding, rolling, driving in towards the beach then gliding, after a sharp turn, towards the deeper water.

I followed their play as they forged up the estuary. I had to run to keep up with them. Sometimes they didn't surface for minutes on end and it was just as I was becoming anxious that I'd see the roll and swirl of their backs far away beyond the central channel on the other side of the estuary. Then, as my eyes were straining the distance, they'd suddenly reappear on my side – sudden black explosions – shooting out of the water as though they were playing a game – enjoying the fierce struggle of crossing and recrossing the scour of the tide-race. But even when they were far away from me, the sound of their snorting, the great blow of their breath, carried clearly across the water.

When they were close to me the sound seemed to change – though I probably imagined it – and it seemed more like a whistle; a signal, as though they were calling to each other across the still air.

As I ran after them, seeking over the surface of the water, I remember falling heavily on some rocks. I ripped my shirt across the ribs but it was only later that the cut started to hurt me and it was only later that I realized the palm of my hand was grazed raw and bleeding. And it was while I was standing on these rocks that the porpoises turned and started travelling down the estuary again towards the open sea.

They came in close to the shore only once more. I'd followed them back down the beach until I reached the old jetty again. The tide was much further out and most of the boats were lying keeled over rocking gently in about two feet of water.

They swerved in towards the more distant of the moored boats and seemed to be diving underneath them. And suddenly I knew something. It sounds silly but I knew that although I couldn't see them they were diving close under the boats for the pleasure of scratching their backs. I could hear the slap of little waves and the quiet huff of their breath. And I *knew* what they were doing.

Then, appearing from underneath the nearest boat, they glided into the shallow water. It seemed that they'd deliberately come close to me.

They lay, rolling slightly, as if resting. Only fifteen feet or so separated us. I stepped into the water. The stones and pebbles underfoot were slippery with slime and seawrack. I placed my feet at each step, not wanting to stumble and frighten them. I was breathing through my open mouth. There was a tin-can, I remember, shining, and its label washed almost free trailing with the motion of the tide.

I was within six feet of them when they turned and planed down into deeper water. Slowly; not at all frightened. I stood still, the water round my waist. The larger one surfaced about twenty yards ahead of me and I saw the swirling gleam of his back and heard his whistle.

I moved deeper searching over the empty water, waiting, but the grey surface was quite undisturbed. The only movement was the turbulence of the central tide-water, brief riffling whirlpools, topped with foam, spinning and spinning until they flattened into the water's flow.

The sandbank, as I watched and waited, was dotted with scurrying terns and oyster-catchers but nothing rose to break the water round its edge.

I waited, straining to hear the familiar call, but the only sounds were the slap of tiny waves against the hulls of the yachts and the wheeling gulls screaming in the air.

There came no whistle, no warm huff of breath. Nothing rose to shine above the water. Only the grey surface curving in towards the sandbar at the estuary mouth – a sandbar marked by a distant line of white, troubled water and, beyond, the vastness of the open sea.

And vaguely, yet more insistent than the screaming gulls, I could hear somewhere behind me, distantly, people shouting and a car-horn honking. And then I felt hands grasping my arms and voices talking. Voices talking. Gentling voices. Voices that talk to a frightened horse. And the voices said,

"There we are. You're all right now."

"You'll be all right, boy."

"Steady now."

I felt cold water slop against my shirt as I stumbled.

"Have you got him?" said a voice. And then another voice said, "Nothing to worry about, boy. We've got you safe."

And the hands, the hands and the voices guided me back to the beach.

A story starts for me when I find myself repeatedly seeing in my mind's eye a detail from the past or when I find a phrase or sentence stuck in my mind. The pictures or words – more usually pictures – are important to me; I don't know why but I know them to be significant.

"A Bag of Cherries" started with the picture of the sun perfect with rays like a child's drawing; other stories have started from such pictures as a jam-jar full of dandelions or the iron railings surrounding a playground.

My use of the word "start" is, however, misleading because I do not then try to construct a story around the picture. I sit and wait and the picture always turns out to be something central in a story which my mind has already constructed and organized. The picture I see so vividly and obsessively – the sun or the dandelions – is a signal my mind is transmitting that a story needs to be worked on.

I can describe how the story arrives but I can't really explain why – nor would I dare to try as I regard the whole thing as basically magical. To explain *how* the story arrives I'll have to use a rather simple comparison.

I'll compare my mind with a box which contains an inflated balloon. A picture is painted on the balloon. All the time, more and more helium is filling the balloon. It is struggling to get free but the lid of the box squashes it back in. I am watching carefully all the time. When a bit of the balloon pops up, I see details of the picture. When the box squashes that part of the balloon back in, another part bulges out. And I catch more of the picture. Gradually, I come to know what's painted on half the balloon and I can guess at the general shape and form of the whole picture. When that point is reached, the lid stops holding the balloon in and it rises free. Then I can start writing.

This whole process usually takes two or three weeks, though sometimes it has taken months. I feel an actual, physical pressure inside my head as the balloon bulges about and mounting excitement as details pile up to form a sort of outline.

This image of the balloon in a box is, in one way, inaccurate. It gives the impression that my process of writing is an entirely passive one; that I merely copy down what is "dictated" or "given". But my mind does not, of course, "dictate" words; it shows me pictures. I have to use my own conscious abilities, my craft, to describe the pictures I see; I have to "translate" the story from pictures to words.

198

Nearly everything I write is written a minimum of ten times; some parts of stories get written more than twenty times. In the summer of 1969 I spent more than eight weeks, often working six and eight hours a day, on twenty pages of my story "The Lady Who Sold Furniture." I have to work like this to "translate" as best I can the vividness and emotional power of my pictures. And the final product is always disappointing; it cannot even come close to the shine of the pictures in my head.

I said earlier that I regarded my writing process as magical. I'm not trying to be fey or whimsical in saying this. I'm perfectly aware of all the psychological explanations of what is called "creativity" – that writers write because they hate their fathers/mothers, love their fathers/mothers, resented being bottle-fed or toilet-trained, are lonely or wish for approval that parents never gave – but over and above all this I know that a special power sometimes flows through me. I might call it my Muse if I were being very eighteenth-century. Notice that I am not saying, "I am powerful" but rather, "Power sometimes uses me." There is a difference.

To be used by this Power is a great honour and is, at the same time, rather disreputable. I feel a kinship with witch-doctors, circus performers, water-diviners, layers-on-of-hands, salesmen of patent medicines, auctioneers and hellfire preachers. I suppose we all serve a kind of rhetoric which is the expression of that Power.

Am I being childish or perverse in desiring magic over science? Psychologists dissect writers and artists as though they were dealing with a species of harmless lunatic. Their probing doesn't seem to take into account the finished product – the story, the poem, the novel or painting. It seems to equate the novel or play with abnormality.

"Of course, Mr. Shakespeare, if you'd been properly toilet-trained you wouldn't be troubled now with this obsessive play-writing".

In other words, some psychologists seem to think of plays, stories, and poems primarily as the symptoms of sickness or abnormality.

I think they miss the boat.

There is one question I haven't answered – what inflates the balloon in the first place? (This is not the same as asking *why* a story comes. That is unanswerable.) The answer is simple – my reactions to being alive. Anger, pleasure, the urge to record things before they are lost, the urge to celebrate, the desire to chart where I've been.

A Bag of Cherries is one of a series of stories I have been writing for some years about youths and children and the process of growing up. (Others in this group are "Biscuits", "Early Morning Rabbits", "The Children Green and Golden", "The Tide Line", "A Thing They Wear", "Keys and Watercress" and "Pretty Boy".)

"A Bag of Cherries" explores the sadness of "the generation gap" – a new cliché for an old experience. Adam probably complained that his sons were not true chips off the old rib and they probably complained that he was always mumbling about snakes and apples. But the sadness has always been real.

David's father is a minister. David's feelings for him are complicated. He quite obviously loves him deeply (the memory of the outing and the bag of cherries) yet it is obvious too that the father's priestliness is something that drives them apart. It is significant that in the memory of the outing the father is not wearing the black suit and white collar of his calling; there is the suggestion that their happiness on that day results from the father's release from the priestly role. The father, like David, wipes his hands on his trousers. He also helps David carry home the treasure – "the shining cartridge cases".

David's fantasy at the beginning of the story suggests that one of the things that divides them is attitudes to love and sex, the Protestant churches always having favoured St. Paul, whose opinion of ladies and their machinations was not, as P. G. Wodehouse would say, of the highest. The girl in David's fantasy is not a girl his mother would consider "nice". David imagines himself as an "artist" – a rejection of the middle-class life style summed up in the account of the mother's letter.

Yet for all the division between them, David is inextricably a part of his parents. The second paragraph, for example, associates him intimately with his mother.

The treasured memory of the outing with the father is contrasted with the reality of the conversation between father and son which concludes the story. The conversation winds down to inconsequence and silence.

The question everyone asks about such stories: are they autobiographical? Is David, who appears in both stories, really John Metcalf? I would *like* to answer that by saying: does it matter? But if I do, you will conclude that you *are* reading autobiography.

I think it is more intelligent to treat the stories as composed things, as fictions. To insist on anything else is really to say, "If these stories are autobiographical they are more 'real' than 'made-up' stories and therefore better." Which is to deny and misunderstand the point of all art forms.

It's interesting to consider what "real" or "autobiographical" means in this argument. I would describe *all* autobiographies as fictions or inventions. They are the highly selected and arranged events of a lifetime so recorded as to simplify and flatter the subject. Pure fiction.

Perhaps we invent everyone we know? Perhaps we simplify them and shape them to fit our needs? Perhaps we invent ourselves?

Let's imagine a straight line which starts at *a* and ends at *m*. Let that line represent ten years and *a* to *m* represent thirteen events occurring during those years. The events are "real" yet if a writer rearranges the events, combines some, removes others, to eventually produce a series *f*, *ga*, *l*, *c* – is this not invention? The writer had to have the sensitivity and artistry to see the possibility of a form or pattern and so rearrange events as to produce an artifact. To search for "autobiography" is to be anti-literature; it is to avoid confrontation with the reality of the imagined world; it is to ignore the form, shape and purpose of the composed work in front of you.

The emotional impulse of nearly all my stories is autobiographical; the events are not necessarily so at all. Various people have told me that the story "The Estuary" seems very real to them yet it is almost entirely non-autobiographical.

It is a fact that my father was a minister and this fact appears in various stories yet I do not think that I am letting an accident of auto-biography dominate my work. I don't feel that this autobiographical fact *limits* the story. Instead of religion and its effects coming between a father and son, the wedge that let the sadness in might have been politics, educa-tion, career, race – anything strongly held on either side. Had my father been a leper, *that* accident of autobiography might well have been limit-ing. A writer uses what is usable.

I wrote "The Estuary" out of some teaching experiences in England. I was working in a Catholic secondary-modern school in a slum area – not because I'm Catholic but because the Education Authority couldn't get anyone else to go there. I was unaware of the school's reputation.

My classes were filled with Pakistani boys who spoke no English, all the local hoodlums not yet graduated to Borstal, girls who confided that they only came because of the cooking lessons, and half-wits. One boy used to wear a German World War II helmet all day and burst into tears and maniac fits if asked to remove it. The principal, at the first sign of trouble, used to lock himself in his office, murmuring, "We are all tainted with Original Sin."

This school bred in me the kind of feelings that David has for the library. Feelings that countless thousands have for the mindless, boring jobs which destroy them. I hope "The Estuary" does more than explore the wounding of a single, sensitive little ego. The CLICK click CLICK of the date-stamp stamps all our lives away. David's anger and distress is

not purely narcissistic; it is also social. His vision, if that isn't too pretentious, is expressed in a series of what I intended as almost cinematic
images, shots held for a long time.

A huddled figure on a municipal bench. The hands of the girl in the
bus queue. The rheumatic fingers of the bus-conductor. The feet of the
pigeons – *red like sores. Like the hands of the girl in the bus queue.* At
the end of the story: *And the hands, the hands and the voices guided me
back to the beach.*

I think it's a good job I don't work for the National Film Board!

The vision to which David escapes is a pastoral one. This theme, I
realize, occurs again and again in my stories. It is only the natural world
which *makes sense.* We are a part of the land and its animals –the quality
of our relationship is the touchstone of our state of grace.

William Blake wrote more memorably of this relationship in his poem
"Auguries of Innocence".

> *A robin redbreast in a cage*
> *Puts all Heaven in a rage.*
> *A dove-house fill'd with doves and pigeons*
> *Shudders Hell thro' all its regions.*
> *A dog starv'd at his master's gate*
> *Predicts the ruin of the State.*
> *A horse misus'd upon the road*
> *Calls to Heaven for human blood.*
> *Each outcry of the hunted hare*
> *A fibre from the brain does tear.*
> *A skylark wounded in the wing,*
> *A Cherubim does cease to sing.*
>
> . . . .
>
> *The wild deer, wandering here and there,*
> *Keeps the Human soul from care.*

(The Pickering MS.)

The sea-creatures give David a "salt gift"; a vision of beauty and
freedom which will help to keep his soul from care. It is a knowledge he
can hide behind his "frank and honest eyes".

Alden Nowlan asks at the end of his commentary that you do not
understand him too quickly. I'd like to ask exactly the same thing in a
more obvious way. I would ask you not to approach my stories as things
to be understood but rather as things to be lived through and experienced.
I spent a long time at the beginning of this commentary explaining how

202

stories arrive for me to make quite clear that they do not originate with *ideas*. Please don't try to quarry ideas from me.

The bald and explicit statements I've made about my stories are not the equivalents, the "meanings"; a paraphrase of a poem bears a distant relationship to the original. The life, the reality of my stories is elsewhere – *Miss Nevins' withered dress, the attic where his past was stored with other lumber, each footstep caught and ringing* –in pictures, images, turns of phrase, in the echoes and reverberations the stories set up in your head.

JOHN METCALF

BIBLIOGRAPHY

New Canadian Writing 1969. Toronto: Clarke, Irwin and Co. Ltd., 1969. [This volume contains five stories by Metcalf, four by D. O. Spettigue, and three by C. J. Newman.]

The Lady Who Sold Furniture. Toronto: Clarke, Irwin and Co. Ltd., 1970. [Stories]

Ray Smith

Ray Smith was born in 1941 and is from Mabou, Cape Breton. He lived most of his early years in Halifax, where he graduated from Dalhousie University. Having served in the RCAF and worked as a systems analyst, he began writing on Mayday, 1964. He has concentrated on short stories.

He now lives in Montreal and is working on a novel. He is married; enjoys thrillers, good food, coffee, hockey and his collection of Canadian paintings.

His work is distinguished by its style: mannered, inventive, highly crafted. It is mainly on this basis that it has been judged, whether with praise or condemnation.

Colours

Colours, colourist, *The Colourist.*
Colour: many app. but n.b. esp. *sb.* II 5. 'A particle
        of metallic gold.' and *vb.* 2. b.
        To misrepresent. (*S.O.E.D.* – used throughout.)
Indirection.
Episodes, episodic. *vide intra*; II.
The Search.

I. Pillsbury
    sombre, rich; *q.v.*
    London (memory of, not locale.)
    HIS NICHE.

"Port is the well-spring of anecdote, I always say. A few glasses in the
afternoon . . ."

Pillsbury told anecdotes. The first concerned a little girl rather like
Alice who dearly loved her pet civet; the second, almost neat enough to be
fiction, was of a chance meeting with a dwarf on a train; the third, while
amusing, was incomprehensible.

"In those days, though, you could expect that sort of thing . . ."

"Yes."

Pillsbury lived, dwelt in two rooms, alone with his port, his fireplace
and his researches. He enjoyed a small fame. On that wet autumn afternoon the shadows stood stacked in the corners like magazines or memories. On one wall hung a penny farthing bicycle.

"Oh, they're a lot of old fogies." Pillsbury was a fellow of some Royal
Society; it was of the other Fellows that he now spoke. "The banquets are
beastly affairs. Half of them senile and one carries a whacking great ear-
trumpet which keeps getting in the soup."

Pillsbury heaved and pivoted on one elbow to gaze at Gerard, for his
neck would not turn much.

"After all, I'm only seventy-six meself, don't you see?"

Gerard nodded and sipped his port.

"Ahh," sighed Pillsbury, "those were the days . . ."

The landlady brought in a tea-tray. Pillsbury pointed to the low table
before him and grunted. She put down the tray and shuffled out again,
leaving behind her (or stirring up) an odour of mold which the tea steam
did not entirely dissipate.

"I always have my tea," Pillsbury explained, "even out here. There's something to be said for tradition . . ."

Gerard sipped and nibbled and listened for half an hour to what could be said for tradition. "I have a piece in EHR. Can't remember the number but I'm sure the library could dig it up for you . . ."

Tea time and Gerard's visit drew to a close. In desperation he alluded to his purpose in coming.

"Ah yes . . . yes, an enquiry of some sort didn't you say?"

Gerard had written a letter asking for the interview.

"Well, well. Hum, hem, harmpf . . . I'd like to help, but I'm afraid you've got the wrong man."

'Wrong man?'

" 'fraid so. I've never been to Tibet, I fancy you're thinking of old Philbrick the occultist . . ."

II. Patchouli the Passionate
    gaudy, sordid
    Set piece: stage, carnival, etc.
    preference of cold cream to Kant.

That night Gerard sat in the dressing room of Patchouli the Passionate at the Club Marrakech and thought about one of the big questions. Gerard disliked thinking about the big questions; he liked particular things, like that jar of cold cream. Surely if one considered a particular jar of cold cream one could . . .

Episodes: That was it, that was how Gerard lived.

Episodes. Take an episode and understand it one way or another. Take It. Belief exists only in action.

Episode: interlocutory parts between two choric songs; an incidental narrative or digression in a poem, story, etc., separable from, but arising naturally out of, the main subject; *transf.* Incidental passage in a person's life, in a history, etc.; *Mus.* In ordinary fugues, a certain number of bars allowed to intervene from time to time before the subject is resumed.

Gerard yawned.

Why should the subject be resumed? If the episode arises naturally out of the main subject, then the main subject is . . . in (let us say), is in the episode. Or, say, let us examine the pearls one by one and surely we shall know of the string? Pearls are more interesting than string.

As for the choric songs, Gerard had sat through ten minutes of Patchouli's belly-dancing and there were a lot of people around and Gerard had enjoyed that. After all, one man can't make a crowd scene,

206

rhythmic or otherwise. So, after Patchouli had read Gerard's note and agreed to the interview Gerard pushed the chorus (laughter, sweat, smoke, gaping mouths) into the wings and, led by a man with six fingers, came and sat in her dressing room.

Soon the big question (Appearance and Reality or the General and the Particular) drifted from his mind, he yawned and Patchouli came in.

"Hi-ya, Sweetie," she said. "Like the act?"

Gerard explained that while he had only seen a bit of it and was no judge of belly-dancing he had thought it rather good.

"Well, you're wrong; I was lousy. I'm not an exotic at all, I'm a stripper. My agent bungled the bookings."

No, she wouldn't have a cigarette. Instead she ran a glass of water and swallowed a tablet for relief from indigestion.

"It's a rough life," said Patchouli the Passionate.

They talked a while about it being a rough life. Patchouli, her body hidden behind a screen, changed her costume. "I mean, hell, I don't have the costumes to be an exotic."

Gerard noticed that her make-up did not coincide with her features. True, she had two (no more, no less) make-up eyebrows, two make-up lips (upper and lower), two sets of false eyelashes and so on; but while her own upper lip was rather level across the top, the make-up upper lip arched high in the center and down to points at the corners; and while her own eyebrows, even plucked, curved out and down attractively and naturally, the make-up brows flared up and out at a vicious angle, etc. Gerard's mind was so little interested in the big questions that he quite failed to see the two faces of Patchouli as a metaphor, which failure, had he known of it, would have made him happy.

"I mean, how am I supposed to be an exotic in a G-string, you know what I mean?"

He said he thought he did.

Patchouli issued from behind the screen and sat down to replace some sequins on her first G-string.

"Now, this matter I came to see you about . . ."

Patchouli wasn't sure she knew what was the matter, for which reason Gerard had to find a way of referring to her casual prostitution without insulting her.

"Yeah, I seen something of a few colonels in my day. Which one in particular?"

Gerard named one and she said yes she had seen something of him. "But that was two years ago. I haven't seen him for two years. I think he got transferred away somewhere."

207

Or died, said Gerard to himself. People were always dying.

"What do you remember about him?" He would hide his particular question in a chorus of others.

She said the colonel was something-or-other and Gerard figured out after a time that she meant he was impotent.

"Did he have any scars or tattoos? Any distinguishing features?"

"He had big ears. I suppose you noticed that . . ."

No, he hadn't noticed that the colonel had big ears.

"Well, he had big ears."

Patchouli yawned. Gerard sighed. Patchouli picked at a frayed tassel. Gerard eased into another cigarette.

"Do you remember off-hand if he had long toe-nails?"

"Long toe-nails?"

"Long toe-nails."

"Hummmm . . ."

The man with six-fingers rapped upon the door and told Patchouli she had three minutes. 'No rest for the wicked,' she sighed. Gerard gave her a wry smile as she double checked the hooks and snaps of her costume, as she reinforced her make-up. At last he had to cough.

"Oh yeah, you wanted to know if the Colonel had . . ."

"Long . . ."

"Yeah, long toe-nails. Well . . ."

Six-fingers rapped again and called one minute. When Patchouli stood up her joints cracked. She yawned and stretched and walked to the door. Gerard followed with his head down. In the dim hallway they paused. People, noted Gerard, rarely sweep right into the corners.

"Well, I'll tell you, I don't know if he had long toe-nails or not. I'm sorry."

She seemed truly sorry. Gerard tried to reassure her. "Well, ha-ha, at least I know he had big ears."

Patchouli considered this. "You know, I'm not sure now that he *was* the one with the big ears. It's been two years now since . . ."

She had to rush off to her fanfare and her audience. Gerard walked silent, alone in the other direction, yawning.

III. The Painter

The next morning Gerard climbed two flights of stairs to the studio of a young painter who had a beard. The painter was painting and yelled for Gerard to come in:

"Come in!"

208

Gerard came in.

The painter stood facing the door with his back to the large windows with the blue north light falling in. Gerard could not see what the painter was painting because the canvas faced away from him. Other canvases and boards stood facing the wall so that Gerard could not see what the painter had painted on them either. The painter stopped painting and offered Gerard a cup of coffee.

"I work pretty steadily," said the painter, "but I always like a break. Only the fanatics can ignore visitors and hunger and such. They're lucky that way. They do so much that some of it has to be good. For the rest of us . . ." – he made a gesture at the turpentine and linseed oil and the tubes of paint – "it's a living."

They talked a while about painting being a living. The conversation consisted of fourteen syllables and lasted some minutes. They both seemed glad they got on well together.

"Well . . ." said Gerard at last. The painter offered him another cup of coffee and accepted a cigarette in return.

"Do you ever use female models?"

The painter yawned and picked a particle of sleep from the inside corner of his right eye.

"Not much lately. I've been doing landscapes. A few years ago I was doing figures more . . ."

Gerard asked if he remembered a model named Charlene.

"Charlene?"

"That's not her real name; her real name was Virginia but after a while she decided it was inaccurate so . . ."

"Charlene . . ."

"Um."

"But really Virginia?"

"Originally Virginia . . . Yes."

"I'm not sure. Did she have thick ankles? I used a lot of thick-ankled models a few years ago."

"It is possible."

"Um."

With the coffee cup in his hand the painter went around by the window and stared at the painting he had been painting. "Charlene," he said. "Humm." Then, "Look, do you like games?"

Gerard said he liked games (which made the painter happy) so the painter explained a game and Gerard said he'd like to play it.

"It helps me to forget things and then I can usually remember. I play games a lot."

The painter put on a sport coat and they went down the two flights of stairs and to a square near the painter's studio. Around the square were half a dozen bus stops. The painter went and stood in the queue for the 59A bus and after a few people had fallen in behind him, Gerard strolled over. Apparently quite on impulse he stopped beside the painter and shuffled his feet until the painter had finished talking about the weather with a little old lady with a spray of artificial violets on her lapel.

"Uhh . . . say, you don't happen to have a . . . pork chop, I suppose?"

The painter considered this a moment.

"Pork chop? . . . Humm . . ." – he felt in various pockets – "Why yes, I believe I . . . yes . . . yes, I do. Here you are."

From the inside pocket of his sport coat the painter took a pork chop wrapped in cellophane. He gave it to Gerard who put it in the inside pocket of his sport coat.

"Thank you," said Gerard.

" 's all right, man. Anytime."

Gerard strolled on to the queue for the 38 and engaged a mother with child in a conversation about the weather. Presently the painter, abstractedly scratching his beard came . . . "Say, man, do you . . ." Etc.

Gerard quickly learned several good lines and tones to use and they played the game three times around the square. Then the painter sat on a park bench and when his bus had come and gone, Gerard joined him.

"Fine game," he said.

"You play like a pro, really. Better than anyone else I've seen."

"You're not bad yourself."

After a while this conversation died and a while after that Gerard had to cough.

"Uh . . . oh yeah," said the painter, "you wanted to know about this broad named Charlene . . . but really Virginia?"

"Yes."

"Who had thick ankles?"

"Possibly."

"That's right, you did say possibly. You qualified it like that."

"Yes."

"Well, I've remembered."

"Have you? Great."

"Yeah, the game did it all right. Yeah, I can say without fear of contradiction that I have never used a model named Charlene or Virginia or both with possibly thick ankles. I'd swear to that."

"Would you sign a statutory declaration?" Gerard asked cautiously.

"Umm . . . I'm not sure. I mean I'm sure about the broad named Charlene, etc., but I'm not sure I'd sign a statutory declaration, not sure at all . . ."

Gerard wanted to ask for an explanation but he knew the painter would explain. After a minute the painter did explain.

"See, a painter is a few steps ahead of the law because he travels light and fast and the law is big – like an elephant – and goes slowly. This has to be, because the painter is alone and can take chances on unknown ground and narrow trails while the elephant has to be careful or he will trample things under foot and wreak havoc and so on. So painters and the law should avoid each other if possible; they don't get along. It's sad but it's the way it is."

"Yes."

"So when there's a choice, you know, you usually choose . . ."

Gerard waved his hand and said that it was all right, the painter would not have to sign a statutory declaration. They parted on good terms and Gerard promised to come back some day to play the game. He did not come back and he never saw any of the paintings the painter had painted. But he did know that the painter would swear at least verbally to never having used a model named Charlene and/or Virginia with or without thick ankles. The painter's memory might have been faulty or the girl might have used a different name. But it was reasonably certain and that was something. It sure made you think.

IV. Asp
   a tableau . . . a crack appears
   Pastels: a jungle.
   Focusing.

The highest building in the city was topped by a penthouse. The penthouse was decorated with taste. The drawing room of the tastefully decorated penthouse was coloured mauve and white and was softly lit. In this room, in the bay of a window overlooking the city stood a table of great value and on it stood chess pieces of inestimable value. The players sat facing each other on either side of the bay. They would have made a pretty picture for Lorraine because of the light, but Lorraine was not there; the formalized composition did not allow for more than two people. They were Gerard and an expensive woman of the world called Aspidistra, by friends, Asp.

Asp had been rescued from the gutter at the age of fifteen by an aged, gouty and bumbling ambassador. He was a gentle man, a gentleman. For want of anything better he taught her chess through the long winter evenings. Her game showed promise. Nervously, his hand shaking, his eyes averted, moving, accompanied by unfinished phrases, he gave her, wrapped in decorative paper, several books on the game: Capablanca's Primer, Znosko-Borovsky's little book of openings, several by Euwe and *My System* by Nimzovich. She pretended to study them, but in fact slipped out the back way to more interesting games. The ambassador never found her out for her game continued to improve. She possessed a cruel and penetrating tactical sense and never made the same mistake twice.

"Tinkle tinkle," laughed Asp. "Tinkle tinkle rasp." Her 9 . . . N-K5 had opened up numerous variations. Gerard, who had studied the above mentioned books and others, knew that theoretically the move was unsound. He cast about for its refutation.

"If you were rich, Gerard, I think I could love you."

"I am not rich, Asp. So do not speak of it."

"Glum, glum, Gerard. Tinkle tinkle."

The chess set of inestimable value had been sculpted for Asp by a sculptor who had loved her from afar and wished to do so from much closer. It was of ivory with trimmings of gold leaf and had taken two years to complete. He took it to three independent judges who assured him it was of inestimable value (Gerard had checked this) then appeared at Asp's door in the evening (the doorman had seen him enter the building at 7:23: "I was waiting for the duke of J - - - to take 'is constitutional at 7:25 . . .") with the table of great value and upon it the exquisite box of mahogany open to show each piece resting in its individual velvet lined place.

"Why how lovely," Asp claimed to have cried. "Would you like a game?"

"Umm-umm-umm . . ."

People who spend their lives making chess sets of inestimable value do not have time to learn the game. The sculptor suffered so brutal a defeat that Asp laughed, "Rasp," and spurned him.

"He was *so* desolated; it was a shattering experience for him. But then, artists . . ." and right out of the air she made an epigram.

The desolated sculptor took the quickest way out of the tastefully decorated (olive green and blue at that time) penthouse and other problems (poverty, rotting teeth, etc.): the bay window overlooking the city. In an investigation out of curiosity and not connected with his everyday investigations (like this one with Asp) Gerard had ascertained that the sculptor had hit a borzoi twenty stories directly below (there had been no wind so a few simple trigonometric calculations had proved this) Asp's window at 8:17 on the evening of the day the set had been valued as inestimable by the three independent judges. As to whether or not it had been Asp's window (and not one of those directly below), she did have the set and the table and the sculptor's love for her had been no secret. The world had Asp's word on it (and why should she lie?) that the fall had not been an accident or a murder attempt, but a suicide attempt. The word 'attempt' is used here because the sculptor had survived, a featureless blob of gibbering, chess-playing jelly. The borzoi, on the other hand, died instantly.

The refutation of Asp's 9 . . . N-K5 seemed to be in capturing the piece: exchanges are favoured by the positional player who wishes a controlled game which simplifies quietly to one of half a dozen or so basic endgames.

Gerard took the piece.

"Chomp!" cried Asp in delight. "Tinkle rasp."

Nothing disturbed the pastel light. In fact, the reach of a hand to move a piece was illusion; nothing moved for fear of destroying the composition. Sound was light, mauve furniture was light, the white rug was light, the white walls and the mauve walls; the brandy in the brandy glasses but a glint.

Gerard groaned. Leading from the capture of Asp's knight was a line for her which he had judged suicidal. He saw now that it was instead brilliantly sacrificial. Unless Asp blundered her victory would be undeniable after ten moves or so. He would not resign until she grew bored.

"Gerard, you are a darling, you really are."

"Why so?"

Asp lifted the stopper from the decanter and poured into each glass (or: certain lights altered). Asp detested explanations.

"A . . . friend, a very good friend who is in the army says life is much like war: years of training for a few moments of passionate action."

"That seems possible."

"Have you ever felt passionate, Gerard?"

He had, but said not. She teased him about this a while, answered his moves without ostentation and soon changed the subject to flowers which she also detested.

". . . and daffodils. God!"

"I once ate a daffodil," said Gerard without looking up. "I ate a lot of funny things when I was a kid. I suppose everyone eats funny things when they're kids, even the Queen of Sheba or Columbus or . . . Z - - - the violinist."

"As a matter of fact, Z - - - once told me that in his native country at the age of seven he ate an orchestration of Mozart's Symphony No. 40 because . . ."

Because: Gerard was not interested in motives. No. 40 in G Minor, K. 550, he said to himself. As soon as decently possible he laid his king upon its side and left.

Asp, fragile light above the chess table, pondered the game a while. Then she began to brood. Some time after that tears filled her eyes and the wonderful pieces of inestimable value upon their table of great value shattered in the tears. She did not know why she was crying. She was crying because the composition was broken and would not anymore have made a pretty picture for Lorraine. But then. Lorraine preferred outdoor scenes and was long dead.

V. Mr. Rufulus
    the crisp and the decaying . . . putrescence . . . horror . . .
    'Ultima Thule' – called by some 'the White Island.'

The girl at the information desk told Gerard where to find the elevator and what the room number was. He paused at the gift shop and considered a magazine but decided against it. When a man is slipping into death he is not interested in magazines . . . No, that's not necessarily true. He might. Why shouldn't he? But he didn't buy one for he didn't know the man's taste in magazines. On the other hand, perhaps the dying man would just like a magazine, any one at all. By this time Gerard was half a dozen floors above the gift shop and did not bother going back.

The hall was as clean as a new cigarette and for its size contained as much death. The duty nurse pointed out the direction and Gerard walked until he saw the room number. The door was closed and a sign saying "Staff Only" hung from the knob. Gerard considered this a while then took a seat in the little alcove next down the hall.

On a little table beside his chair, Gerard found a pictorial magazine. Because he liked pictures he leafed through it, looking at the pictures but not thinking about them much.

Then he came upon a black and white photograph of a man sitting in an alcove in a hospital reading a magazine. The man's head was bent down so you could not recognize his face. Gerard recognized the hat and the trenchcoat, however. They were his own, or very good copies. On one finger Gerard wore a ring; the man in the picture also wore a ring, though it showed indistinctly due to the modish graininess of the print. Gerard was, it seemed, living inside a rather stale joke. Fortunately he had a rather stale sense of humour.

214

Here I am looking at myself looking at . . . obviously, myself looking at, etc. That old one. Now, if I look at the camera, will he also look up?

Gerard looked up and saw no camera. Of course, he realized, if I look up I can't see if the picture man is also looking up.

On the other hand, what if I turn the page? Will he also turn the page? That is, will he continue to do all the things I do or will the page go blank until somebody else sits here to look at it? Is it a picture of me, essentially, or of the alcove?

At last he realized that he need only move an arm or leg and see if the photo-man did it too. The muscles in Gerard's leg had just tensed for the action when he chuckled: no, I shall not do it. This is either miracle or mundane coincidence. If I let it alone, I can always believe it was a miracle.

So he closed the magazine and called to a nurse who had just come out of Mr. Rufulus's room.

"I'd like if I could to see Mr. Rufulus."

The nurse asked, in a friendly enough way, if Gerard was a friend or relative and Gerard explained that he was neither but had made arrangements to see Mr. Rufulus today on a very important matter.

"Well, Mr. Rufulus is very ill . . ."

"Yes," replied Gerard in lower tones. "I understand he will probably not live the night. But if at all possible . . ."

"I'll ask the doctor . . ."

Gerard felt compelled to tell the truth; he had to play by the rules.

"I just wish to ask Mr. Rufulus a question, in person. The answer he gives is of great importance to me, but I must admit it is of no importance to him. If I were allowed it would be a great favour to me. Is Mr. Rufulus conscious?"

"At times. He is very sick."

"Yes."

She went away. Gerard now realized she was quite pretty. He hoped she was also happy.

Some time later a doctor came and, in an English accent, asked the same questions the nurse had, adding the same objections more forcefully. He also picked up the point – which the nurse had missed – that Gerard required to ask the question in person.

"Well, it's difficult to explain. I am making certain enquiries and their validity is – without questioning your integrity, Doctor – called into question when not received directly. Just as you might doubt a patient with a twitching left arm who, in all sincerity, says another doctor told him the twitch was caused by myopia . . ."

The doctor screwed his face into one of those expressions of irony for which the English are so famous. Gerard glanced up, then back at his hands, then coughed.

"Yes, I see," said the Doctor with a glance at his watch. "I shall do what I can."

"Thank you doctor."

Gerard settled down for a long wait. It would be a near thing. Near things were best. Finding out that a certain newspaper had been published on a certain day was too easy; discovering whether or not a certain native in the congo had eaten a mango from a certain tree on August the ninth twenty-one years ago was clearly impossible. Mr. Rufulus was going to be a near thing and that made Gerard quiver (as much as he ever did) with the challenge.

At last the doctor returned (while Gerard was yawning) and asked the same questions again. Gerard answered politely and honestly. The doctor put his head in the door of Mr. Rufulus's room and whispered to someone. He nodded to the unseen speaker then to Gerard.

"Thank you Doctor," Gerard whispered. He was in the presence of death, he could almost feel the soft swish of the blade as it moved in hungry practice.

"Don't thank me. Thank the patient for staying alive."

Gerard considered a pun on patients and patience but decided against it.

A lamp with an intensity control had been turned low. A nurse stood aside to whisper with the doctor. Gerard heard, "Yes, Doctor," and such and understood that he had very little time with Mr. Rufulus. The doctor went out and the nurse closed the door softly. The room smelt of various things.

Holding his hat by the brim, Gerard tip-toed to the bed and sat down. Mr. Rufulus consisted of a thin old face on a pillow. His eyes were closed and his breath came in quick little gasps with long spaces of silence between. Tubes entered orifices.

"Mr. Rufulus?"

All searches are the same. Utter success and utter failure are both perfection and perfection is denied man. The tubes gurgled.

"Mr. Rufulus."

"He is very weak," the nurse whispered. "Even if he can hear you he probably won't be able to answer."

Gerard waited until she had gone to the other side of the room before putting his question.

"Mr. Rufulus, my name is Gerard. I wrote you two days ago because I wanted to ask you a question. Now, I know you are very tired, but I would like very much if you would answer my question if you could. Can you talk at all? Can you say yes or no?"

The eyelids raised a moment and the lips, dry as dry apples, quivered.

"That's all right, Mr. Rufulus, I won't tire you, don't talk if you don't feel like it. Now, I'm going to ask you a question and if the answer is yes, open your right eye; if the answer is no, open your left. If you are undecided, open both and if you refuse to answer, keep them closed. Do you understand? If you understand, open your right eye, then close it and open your left."

After a few moments the right eye flickered. Then it flickered, then held, then closed. Then the left flickered, held and closed.

"Very good, Mr. Rufulus. Now here is the question: in your long and honourable life, sir" – the nurse was fiddling with a complex instrument covered with dials and knobs and attached to Mr. Rufulus's orifices' tubes – "did you like parsnips?"

At first, nothing happened.

"The right eye opens for yes, and the left . . ."

The lips began to quiver. They moved up and down with involuntary movement at a great rate like a vibrating guitar string.

"Did you hear me, Mr. Rufulus?" Gerard whispered. He spoke with urgency and his hand went forward as if to clutch the bed clothes or the tubes. The nurse was not watching.

"Mr. Rufulus, can you hear me?"

Mr. Rufulus had apparently heard. His head lifted from the pillow and his eyes opened and turned on Gerard. They opened wide in horror and the toothless mouth opened wide. Still no definite yes or no.

"Just this one thing, Mr. Rufulus. I realize it is of no importance to you but . . ."

Mr. Rufulus's head jerked up another inch and at last the mouth managed a sound:

"ArrhrrhrrH."

Then the head fell back. The eyes stared into space and the horror was still in them.

"Mr. Rufulus! Mr. Rufulus!" cried the nurse.

Gerard got out of the chair and out of her way before she found it necessary to hit him. As she called Mr. Rufulus's name and probed for a pulse, Gerard slipped into the corridor. He would never know now, not directly, at least. It was not the sort of thing a man's correspondence would make clear. The widow might remember Mr. Rufulus liking parsnips but that was of little value. Mr. Rufulus might have been forced during the first month of marriage to say he did and never have had a chance to tell the truth all these years. More serious deceptions exist in every marriage.

The doctor gave Gerard a scowl and ran past. It was too bad. People, searchers all, have no sympathy with the searches of others. The pattern Gerard was seeking might look quite different from the Doctor's. But the pattern was there, it was there and it was the truth and all you needed was to look hard enough and long enough and you could find it.

Gerard walked slowly out of the hospital. The sun was due in a few hours and Gerard was tired. He wanted sleep because at noon he was to meet a woman named Culver who might or might not have had a great-grandfather with the middle name of Jonathan. Or was it Nasturtium? Or Bicycle? Ah well, the details did not matter. In the end there was only the search and, with luck, the pattern. It sure made you think. Gerard yawned.

AUTHOR'S COMMENTARY

1. INTRODUCTION

A writer can usually say what his work is, but he cannot so often or so easily or so accurately say what it is about.

"All right, "Colours" is a short story, *so you say*. But what is is *about*?"

"Ohhh . . . this and that . . . people . . . truth and beauty . . ."

Let me suggest that a story is about what the writer was concerned with when he wrote it. This seems simple enough. You might say:

"When he wrote 'Colours', Smith was concerned with searching. This is clear from the plot, what there is of it, and especially from the last two paragraphs. We all live in search of something – happiness, contentment, love, etc. He writes about a man who goes about asking questions. To us these questions seem idiotic. People like Gerard should be locked away. But Smith is using extreme exaggeration to show us that we may not always understand the searches of others, the reasons behind their lives. Just as the business man may not understand the movie star's search for frame: 'Veronica V. wants publicity,' he says, 'because it helps her at the box office. The more famous she is, the more money she gets.' He cannot see Veronica except in terms of his own search, he cannot see that while she enjoys the pleasures that money can give her, she loves fame more. It is this failure of understanding, failure of sympathy that Smith was concerned with; so this is what the story is about."

Well, Smith answers, that's all very true, but it is not the whole truth. Otherwise I would have written the last two paragraphs and not bothered with the rest of the story.

2. MAIN TITLE

The writer says what the story is about *in the whole story*. He does this in a variety of sneaky ways and for a variety of sneaky reasons. But he always presents all the evidence. He begins with the title: *War and Peace; The Tragedy of King Lear; Gone with the Wind*. This last is the sneakiest, being a metaphor and not explaining what exactly is gone.

I have given my story an eight-line title; each part has an additional title. This should seem odd right off: a 1,000 page novel has a three-word title – *War and Peace* – while an eight to ten page story has an immense title. From this you can conclude that I am going out of my way to be sneaky; that I am interested in the technique of titles; that the story is to some extent about titles; that an examination of the titles will help in understanding the story.

"*S.O.E.D.*" stands for Shorter Oxford English Dictionary. You should be able to read the story without it, but it will help you with certain curious or key words. "Colour" and its variations are a good example of this. "A particle of metallic gold" is a metaphor for the breaking of the story into five separate parts, each of which is meant to be pure, glittering, valuable. Some would add precious.

"To misrepresent" is a bit of cuteness: the story is very obviously fictional, fiction also means a lie, while a writer will claim that fiction is truer than fact.

"Indirection" refers to the method of the story. An essay, like this one, should proceed in a logical and direct way through an argument or explanation. A story moves by its own rules and reasons which are often not clear, even to the writer, until after the story is done.

"Episodes", as noted, is discussed in Part II. Gerard compares his life to a pearl necklace, and his life is the story. A necklace is valuable because of the value of each pearl. When a woman wears a necklace we do not see the string though we know it must be there. So I have tried to write a story composed of five "pearls" (like five particles of gold). The reader cannot see the string or plot, but he should be able to deduce it as a line through from the way the incidents hang together.

3. PILLSBURY

The titles to each part operate in the same way as the main title. "Q.v." means "which see"; that is, look up "sombre" and "rich" in the *S.O.E.D.* Neither is quite so applicable as "colour". They describe the mood I was trying to catch. "Rich" is often used to describe the colour of port.

"London (memory of, not locale)" is about atmosphere. The English climate is so cold, damp and miserable that Englishmen and their writers have a natural interest in cosiness. If you have read some Sherlock Holmes stories you were probably struck by the cosiness of the rooms at 221B Baker Street. Whenever Holmes readers feel cosy while the wind moans outside the window or the fog gathers about the streetlamps, part of that cosiness is due to the memory, however unconscious, of Holmes and Watson in their overstuffed chairs, the fire casting a warm glow, the pipe smoke drifting between them. It was the memory of this London sort of cosiness I was trying to catch.

Pillsbury, an Englishman, has found a London kind of niche, presumably in Canada. He is a bit of an eccentric with his antique bicycle, he is an amateur scholar (not a professional in a university), and he keeps up the old traditions of tea and port.

Cosiness, the peace of finding a niche (his rooms, his research, his small fame), certain English traits – Part I is about these things.

"a little girl rather like Alice" – in Wonderland.

"EHR" – *English Historical Review.* Scholarly journals are usually referred to by their initials.

"In desperation he alluded . . ." – Gerard is rather indirect himself.

"Tibet" – Holmes spent some time there.

4. PATCHOULI

A set piece is a scene that has been done before and will be done again. Most painters will do a "Mother and Child" or "Madonna and Child." Writers have to do party scenes, waking-up scenes, lovers' goodbye scenes in train stations.

Parts II, IV and V are set pieces: the theatre dressing room, the game of chess, the death-bed. You could make a moderate case that the Pillsbury scene is one too. A set piece gives the writer an extra dimension to work with because the reader can be presumed to have read similar ones. Every dressing room scene you have read (or seen in a movie) will add something to this one.

Dressing rooms are often used by artists to deal with the big question of "What is real and what is illusion?" Actors have faces but they disguise them with make-up. They can almost become Hamlet or Lady Macbeth. Patchouli's make-up is so extreme that it has no relation to her face. (A friend of mine, a painter, once met a stripper with make-up like this.) She does sexy dances on stage, takes stomach pills in the dressing room. Which is the real Patchouli (surely that's not her legal name?), which the illusory one?

"Patchouli" is a penetrating Indian perfume.

"Kant" – We all ask ourselves the big questions from time to time; philosophers make it their business. Emmanuel Kant (1724-1804) was a German Philosopher reputed to be good with the big questions.

"Marrakech" – If you don't know where it is, consult an atlas, one of my favourite books.

"an exotic" – trade term for belly dancer.

5. THE PAINTER

I suppose this section is about casualness, a sort of indirection. The dialogue is casual, Gerard and the painter are casual with each other, the painter speaks casually of his work. It is also about repetition: the repetition of certain words, especially in the first two paragraphs. This comes up again in the next part. The porkchop game is also repetitive.

There are no extra titles because I am an artist like the painter. Most of what I am is being a writer. I think we all would find it difficult to describe ourselves or our professions in a few words. Besides, the whole story is a commentary on me, on artistry, on the short story. I could have put "repetition" in the title but did not want to draw attention to it.

"blue north light" – Light from south or sun windows is yellow. North and south light both affect the tone of paint colour, but painters traditionally consider north light more neutral for some reason.

"the fanatics" – Would the sculptor in Part IV be one?

"It's a living." – An artist is trying to make pictures or stories of truth and beauty. This is his day's work. He doesn't succeed all the time and so needs immense arrogance to keep on. But to make himself bearable to others he will often pretend he is modest or casual about it.

"thick ankles" – Painters will often become interested in features we do not necessarily consider beautiful.

"a square" – Friends of mine used to play this game in Dominion Square in Montreal.

6. ASP

An asp is a poisonous snake found in Egypt and Libya, famous because Cleopatra committed suicide by embracing one. See the *S.O.E.D.* for "tableau".

This scene is a formal and elegant one. The style is supposed to be appropriate to the setting and mood. There is symmetry in the seating of the characters. But by the end certain things have cracked. The symmetry is broken by Gerard's exit; Asp's veneer of poise is cracked when we see her crying; her chess set, room, world appear shattered through her tears; and something in Gerard's so-far polite character is broken for us, we see him a bit differently, a bit selfish or cruel.

The jungle is the world that goes on far below Asp's peaceful penthouse; it is the morbid and violent fate of the sculptor; it is what we glimpse behind Asp's veneer.

Pastel is the colouring of the apartment and the soft colouring of the technique. I was trying to work a number of subtle shifts in tone, mood, character, sentence structure. If I succeeded, you should be able to feel them, but should have difficulty in saying just how it was done.

"Lorraine" – Claude Gellée, known as Le Lorraine because that is where he came from, was an 18th century painter remarkable for his delicate handling of light.

"Tinkle tinkle rasp" – Asp's laugh is part pastel, part jungle.

"9 . . . N-K5" – Ask a chess player. Also ask him if the move and its implications are appropriate.

" . . . and daffodils. God!" – The writer takes an indirect snipe at Wordsworth's poem, "Daffodils."

"K.550" – Mozart's manuscripts were placed in chronological order by Köchel. His initial precedes the number he gave.

7. MR. RUFULUS

Besides what the *S.O.E.D.* tells you about Ultima Thule (see "Thule") it means the death of Mr. Rufulus and the end of the story. It is also the end of whatever suspense the reader has felt over the hidden significance of Gerard's questions: there is none. The reader who believes a story should have a plot must now decide either to throw this one in the garbage or to look for some other point to it. There is no law that a story must have a plot. Most do because a plot holds the reader's attention: "I want to see how it comes out." This reader, looking for a satisfactory resolution to the suspense, is liable to be frustrated with "Colours". Plot is also seen as a line through of actions, causes leading to effects. Clearly, "Colours" does not have this.

"Crispness" is the hospital atmosphere, the sheets, the nurse's uniform. It is also Gerard's obsession for accuracy and precision which has been evident throughout. Notice his phrasing to Mr. Rufulus about the eyelids or the last few lines of Part III.

I am unable to figure out the meaning or reason for the incident with the photograph. It has to do with illusion and reality, with accuracy and evidence, with Gerard's loneliness. Sometimes I feel it works, sometimes I feel I should cut it out. Maybe I will one of these days.

"Thule" is also a town in a most appropriate place.

"Mr. Rufulus's orifice tubes" – This is only the most obvious example of the sort of word play I and some readers find amusing. Others find it annoying, outrageous, disgusting. Depends on your taste.

8. CONCLUSION

The crispness of Part V is also my own striving for precision and accuracy, for the exact word, phrase, setting. Increased concern for *le mot juste* does not necessarily improve the work. Dostoyevsky never used one word when ten would do, Hemingway never one when none would do. In

"Colours" I have tried to write for clear and easy reading: you should always know where the characters are, who is saying what, you should never have to read a sentence over twice to get the sense of it. But if you are willing to linger a bit over the somewhat obtrusive precision work you may get great pleasure out of Asp's exact chess move or checking to see if the chess books mentioned are real and if so, how good they are.

You can say that *Hamlet* is about a guy trying to avenge his father; that *Macbeth* is about a guy trying to usurp the throne of Scotland; that "Colours" is about a guy who goes around asking weird questions. I can't speak for Shakespeare, but I have tried to show that my story is about many other things. I have mentioned most of the important ones: titles, plots, England, a dictionary, make-up, casualness, set pieces, soft lights, accuracy, etc. I have not mentioned that it is also about the use of the semi-colon (so is this essay); the use of "he" (first paragraph, Part V); the naming of characters (I figured you'd see that); contrasts (Pillsbury's room and life – Patchouli's); and so on and so on.

A story is many more things to a writer than to any one reader. Even a careful reader would not have seen all the things I have mentioned; but he might have seen things I haven't mentioned, even things I can't see or can't recall putting in. Another might enjoy reading it through quickly, noticing only a few things in passing. You should not have to use the *S.O.E.D.,* know where Thule is or have seen paintings by Lorraine to enjoy the story, though I make it clear they will help. You definitely don't have to play chess.

"I don't know art but I know what I like" is valid to a point. But the more you know about art the more the liking, the more pleasurable the quality of the liking.

RAY SMITH

BIBLIOGRAPHY

Cape Breton is the Thought Control Centre of Canada. Toronto: House of Anansi, 1969. [Stories]